Santa Monica Pub

I SMP 00 27

D0056528

SANTA MONICA PUBLIC LIBRARY

AUG - - 2017

SANTA MONICA PUBLIC LIBRARY

THE BERTIE PROJECT

Center Point
Large Print

Also by Alexander McCall Smith and available from Center Point Large Print:

Bertie Plays the Blues
Sunshine on Scotland Street
Bertie's Guide to Life and Mothers

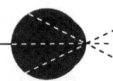

This Large Print Book carries the Seal of Approval of N.A.V.H.

THE BERTIE PROJECT

A 44 Scotland Street Novel

Alexander McCall Smith

Illustrations by Iain McIntosh

CENTER POINT LARGE PRINT
THORNDIKE, MAINE

This Center Point Large Print edition is published in
the year 2017 by arrangement with Anchor Books,
an imprint of The Knopf Doubleday Publishing Group,
a division of Penguin Random House LLC.

Copyright © 2016 by Alexander McCall Smith.
Illustrations copyright © 2016 by Iain McIntosh.
All rights reserved.

This book is excerpted from a series that originally
appeared in *The Scotsman* newspaper.

This is a work of fiction.
Names, characters, places, and incidents either are
the product of the author's imagination or are used
fictitiously. Any resemblance to actual persons, living or
dead, events, or locales is entirely coincidental.
The text of this Large Print edition is unabridged.
In other aspects, this book may vary
from the original edition.
Printed in the United States of America
on permanent paper.
Set in 16-point Times New Roman type.

ISBN: 978-1-68324-428-8

Library of Congress Cataloging-in-Publication Data

Names: McCall Smith, Alexander, 1948– author.
Title: The Bertie project : a 44 Scotland Street novel / Alexander McCall Smith ;
illustrations by Iain McIntosh.
Description: Center Point Large Print edition. | Thorndike, Maine : Center Point
Large Print, 2017.
Identifiers: LCCN 2017013432 | ISBN 9781683244288 (hardcover : alk. paper)
Subjects: LCSH: Mothers and sons—Fiction. | Large type books. | Domestic
fiction. | GSAFD: Mystery fiction.
Classification: LCC PR6063.C326 B48 2017 | DDC 823/.914—dc23
LC record available at https://lccn.loc.gov/2017013432

In memory of Dr. Herbert Gold,
a wise and kind doctor.

THE BERTIE PROJECT

1

Beer and Knees

On any Friday evening, the Cumberland Bar, just round the corner from Drummond Place and Scotland Street, might be expected to be busy, the meeting place of assorted mercantile tribes, of office workers from further down the hill, of young accountants, of estate agents and lawyers, and, conspicuous by their less formal attire, of some of the more bohemian, the more artistic inhabitants of this eastern corner of Edinburgh's Georgian New Town. At least two of this last group were present early that evening—Angus Lordie, portrait painter and owner of the dog, Cyril, and his friend, Matthew, proprietor of a small art gallery on Dundas Street, husband of Elspeth, and father of the robust and increasingly rumbustious triplets, Tobermory, Rognvald, and Fergus. Cyril, the only dog in Scotland to have a gold tooth, and the only dog anywhere to have been trained to lift his leg at the mention of the controversial conceptual art award, the Turner Prize, was also there, lying contentedly beneath the table at which Matthew and Angus sat. Underneath this table was to be seen an empty metal bowl, licked clean of the dark stout

9

poured into it only ten minutes earlier, and the consumption of which had induced Cyril's state of somnolent contentment.

"Your dog," observed Matthew, "really is a most peculiar creature. I've never quite worked him out, you know. He keeps looking at me in a distinctly disconcerting way."

Angus glanced down at Cyril. Although one of the dog's eyes was closed, he saw that the other, half-open, was focused on Matthew's feet.

"It's as if he had something against me," Matthew continued. "Some canine grudge perhaps."

"Oh, I don't think Cyril dislikes you. Quite the opposite, in fact." Angus smiled at Matthew. "It's just that he's always had this thing about your ankles."

"He nipped me," said Matthew accusingly. "Remember?"

"Yes. That was when he couldn't control himself any further. He yielded to temptation." Angus paused, ready to defend his dog. "We all have our temptations, don't we? Some hidden desire, something we're perhaps a bit ashamed of. Nobody's immune to that." He paused again, before concluding, "Chocolate . . ."

Matthew stared at Angus. He blushed. He had yielded to temptation only that afternoon, eating an entire bar of expensive Belgian chocolate bought by his assistant, Pat, as a birthday present for Elspeth. The chocolate had been entrusted to him, beautifully wrapped, for delivery to Elspeth, and he had sat and gazed at it, struggling with temptation, until at last he had succumbed. He had then eaten it in a single sitting when Pat went to post some letters, afterwards concealing the wrapping in the drawer of his desk. He had told himself that he would replace it in good time and that Elspeth would never know. But it was, he later decided, an entirely shameful thing to do—no different from the act of a postman who steals a parcel, or a charity collector who pockets donations. Was it possible that Angus had guessed what he had done? That seemed so unlikely, and yet why else would he suddenly bring chocolate into the conversation?

He dismissed his scruples; it was hardly anything to get into a *fankle* over, hardly an issue at all . . . chocolate was a fungible, after all; something that could be replaced by more of the same. A *fankle*—the Scots word seemed just right for its purpose, as so many Scots words did; a *fankle* was a mess, a state of confusion, sometimes leading to a *stramash*—another useful Scots word—and it was something one sought to avoid if at all possible.

Angus raised his glass to his lips. Having broached the topic of temptation, he was keen to abandon the subject. He himself experienced the occasional temptation—nothing serious, of course, and barely anti-social—but he was not sure that he would actually own up to such thoughts. Better, though, to think about something else altogether, which was, of course, a recommended way of tackling temptation in the first place.

But it was Matthew who moved the conversation on. "Oh well," he said. "Be that as it may, have you seen the plans for that new building?"

Angus had, and sighed. "You'd think . . ." he began, and then stopped. There was not much one could add, he felt, to the charges of gross Philistinism that had already been levelled at the developers.

"Exactly," said Matthew, "you'd think, wouldn't you? However, I just don't have the energy to protest. I know I should; I know we should all rise up as one and flood the council with objections, but do they care? Does anyone actually imagine they give any weight to the likes of us, Angus? *Les citoyens*?"

Angus thought for a moment, and then answered, "No."

"So perhaps we should just give the matter a Gallic shrug . . ."

Angus looked puzzled. "A Gallic shrug?"

"The French are always shrugging," explained Matthew. "You ask their view on things and they give a sort of insouciant shrug, as if to say

12

that these things happen and they, at least, are completely unsurprised."

Angus knew what Matthew meant. He remembered a visit that he and Domenica had been paid by a French anthropologist a few months previously. The topic of French politics had cropped up in the conversation—there was a long and crippling strike in France, with the government digging in against virtually everybody—and the French visitor had simply shrugged. *Pouf*! he had said, adding, for clarification, *Bif*!

"Perhaps a shrug is not such a bad response," Angus said. "What's the alternative? Getting all steamed up? Hot under the collar? You end up being angry—outraged even—but does that actually do any good?"

Matthew himself was about to shrug, but stopped in time. One could not pronounce on shrugs with a shrug. "I suppose that a shrug indicates acceptance," he said.

"Which is what we should all cultivate," added Angus. "Those who accept things are calmer, more resolved . . . and, I imagine, live much longer than those who rail against them."

"Probably," said Matthew.

"I can't abide moaning," said Angus, taking a sip of his beer. "Moaning gets us nowhere. It confirms the moaner in his state of discontent, and it irritates those who have to listen to the complaints." He paused, and looked enquiringly at Matthew. "Have I told you about my knee?" he asked.

Matthew shook his head. "You're having knee trouble?"

"A bit," said Angus. He looked at his beer glass, half full, with an expression of regret. "I can only have one beer; you know—because of my knee."

Matthew frowned. "Because of your knee?"

Angus told him. "You see what happened," he began, "is this . . ."

2
News of Bruce

"I first noticed it," said Angus, "when I was driving up to St. Fillans. We have friends there, you see. Actually, she's some sort of cousin of Domenica's, and he used to manage a branch of the Bank of Scotland in the days when banks had proper managers in their branches—somebody you could actually speak to."

Matthew rolled his eyes. "Yes," he said. "Remember our wonderful, solid, *Presbyterian* banks, Angus?" He paused. "Who wrecked our banks? Who actually *did* it? And I don't mean who lost the money by gambling on toxic mortgages and things like that, but who actually decreed that we shouldn't be able to speak to anybody if we phoned the branch? Or who said that banks needn't answer letters their customers wrote to them? Who ended the idea that banks actually supported people through rough times? Who ended all that?"

"People down in the City of London," said Angus. "Avaricious, arrogant people. I have a list of them somewhere. I cut it out of the newspaper. But, as I was saying . . ."

"Of course—as you were saying."

"We were driving up to St. Fillans, going by way of Comrie. You know that back road that goes from Braco—up over the hills?"

Matthew thought for a second before he remembered. As a sixteen-year-old boy he had gone to cadet camp during the summer and they had been driven in an ancient green army truck along that winding road, half looking forward to, half dreading the experience ahead: the tepid, frequently cold, showers, the rough camaraderie of the Nissen huts, the bullying (both subtle and unsubtle), the shouting and the crudity of males living in close proximity to one another for a week or more. "Past Cultybraggan Camp?" he said.

"Almost," said Angus. And he, too, remembered what that had been like in his own day. For a moment there was an additional bond between them, a bond that surpassed the ordinary ties of friendship, a bond based on a shared tribal experience. He continued, "It was on that road, just as it begins to drop down sharply towards Comrie—that's when I felt this pain in my knee. I thought I'd pulled something."

"You often don't notice it when you actually pull the muscle," said Matthew. "Then later on the pain starts."

"It was quite intense," said Angus. "It was a sharp, insistent pain. Quite bad."

"And?"

"Well, it got steadily worse after we got to St. Fillans. That night I found it difficult to bend my knee at all. It was hard to get into bed—I had to sit on the edge of the mattress and then swing the useless leg up. It was far from easy."

Matthew shook his head in sympathy. "Poor you."

"We were due to come back to Edinburgh the following afternoon, but we cut our trip short and drove back the next morning. Domenica drove, in fact, as I couldn't move my leg. It was that painful."

Matthew waited. He was thinking of Cultybraggan Camp and the generations of young men who had passed through it, for some of whom, of course, it had been the prelude to real conflict, to war with real explosives rather

16

than the fireworks their instructors used to simulate explosions.

Angus continued his story. "I saw my doctor in Edinburgh and he prescribed a pretty strong anti-inflammatory. Cyril had something similar from the vet when he caught his front paw in a drain cover. It did the trick for me. I also had a blood test."

"And?" prompted Matthew.

Angus looked morose, and Matthew wondered whether he was about to hear bad news; Angus did not look unwell, but then seriously ill people could often look perfectly healthy.

"Gout," muttered Angus.

Matthew was relieved. "Oh well," he said. "At least . . ."

He did not finish.

"It's no joke," said Angus. "People make light of it, you know. They know that gout often goes for the big toe, and they find that amusing, for some reason. But it can flare up in other joints."

Matthew started to grin, but checked himself.

"Of course, the diagnosis is not definite," said Angus. "Apparently the only way in which you can really confirm gout is to stick a needle into the joint and see if there's any sign of uric acid crystals."

Matthew, being squeamish, made a face.

"It's crystals that cause it," Angus continued.

"They form if your uric acid level is too high. They're shaped like needles—hence the pain."

"And how do they treat it?" asked Matthew.

Angus's face fell again. "There are pills you can take," he said. "They neutralise the uric acid. But you can also treat it by avoiding the foods that cause it."

"Well, there you are," said Matthew.

"Which means cutting out everything I like the most," Angus said. "Seafood, steak, red wine and . . ." He pointed to his glass of beer. "This stuff too."

Matthew sympathised. "Oh, bad luck."

"I was given a leaflet published by the British Gout Society," said Angus. "It tells you about all the foods you have to avoid—or, if you must, eat in moderation."

Matthew could not help but imagine meetings of the British Gout Society. "The British Gout Society," he mused. "Do you think they have an annual dance, like other societies?" he went on. "Can you imagine how much fun that would be?"

Angus looked at him reproachfully. "I don't find that at all funny," he said. "And anybody can get it, you know. Not just men who drink port in clubs . . ."

Matthew assumed a serious expression. "Of course. Sorry." The problem, he thought, was that so much humour involved human misfortune of one sort or another, and now that same human misfortune was out of bounds—interdicted by self-appointed guardians of sensitivity. There was somebody to be offended by everything, he thought, which left little room for laughter.

"I wasn't making light of it, Angus. It's just that the name of the society . . ."

Angus waved a hand. "No, I know that. And I'm not hyper-sensitive. But I don't think people should make light of gout. People don't laugh at other conditions."

Matthew knew Angus was right, and decided that another change of subject was called for.

"Bruce," he said. "I saw him the other day, you know. He's back in circulation—with a new Australian girlfriend."

"Poor girl," said Angus.

Matthew shook his head. "If sympathy is called for," he said, "it should be directed towards Bruce. He's the one I feel sorry for."

"I find that hard to believe," said Angus. "Poor girl. Does she have any idea what he's like?"

"I suspect she does," replied Matthew. "If I had to describe her eyes, I think I'd use the expression *wide open*."

"Ah," said Angus. "Doe-eyed?"

Matthew shook his head. "No," he said. "Far from it."

3

Bruce in Danger?

When Angus returned to Scotland Street, he found Domenica in her study. She was reading, engrossed in the latest issue of *The Review of Contemporary Cultural Anthropology*, the arrival of which, at quarterly intervals, was a high point in her calendar.

He let Cyril off his lead. "Anything interesting?" he asked.

Marking her page with a scrap of paper, she put the journal down on her desk. "A rather interesting piece on shifting identities," she said. "Or perhaps it's not so interesting—I haven't quite made up my mind yet. And something on parting ceremonies in Java."

Angus contemplated shifting identities. He was not quite sure what they were—could identity really be shifted, or was it something that you acquired in your early years and kept for life? Could he, by some act of self-revision, become somebody other than the person he had always been? Of course people could change—they grew out of their earlier selves and sometimes became completely unrecognisable, looking the same, perhaps, but having a wholly different view of life. He suspected, though, that this was not the sort of shifting identity that the *Review* had in mind. These shifts, he imagined, were those created by changes in the identity of whole groups of people, perhaps even of nations, caused by . . . by what? What led to a change in identity so significant that the people who experienced it became different people altogether? Conquest, migration, religious conversion, the subjection of the poor and vulnerable by the strong and solvent?

And parting ceremonies?

"Formal acts of farewell," explained Domenica. "We have them too. Retirement parties. Graduations. Waving goodbye to those embarking on a journey."

Angus looked thoughtful. "Do we still do that?"

"Do what?"

"Wave goodbye to people."

Domenica frowned. "When we get the chance to do so. Mind you, I don't suppose that's all that often. You can't wave farewell to people at airports. You don't see them go. They disappear through a doorway and that's that—in much the same way as they do at Warriston Crematorium."

Angus remembered his father talking about waving farewell to people boarding planes at Turnhouse Airport. "He said they used to let you go out onto the tarmac and wave to the plane as it took off. You could even pose for a photograph in front of the plane."

Domenica smiled. "That seems so quaint now. So trusting. Now we've come to expect that everybody we see wants to kill us."

"And ships too," continued Angus. "Didn't people stand on the quayside and catch paper streamers thrown down from the passengers on the deck of liners?"

"They did," said Domenica. "They held on to the streamers as the liner pulled away—until they broke." She paused. "The streamers represented the links between those embarking on the journey and those staying behind. It was rather touching, don't you think?"

Angus nodded. *"The Parting Glass,"* he said. "Do you know the words?"

Domenica did not, and so he told her. *And since it falls unto my lot / That I should rise and you should not* . . . "That song," he said, "makes me choke up. That and *Auld Lang Syne.*"

"And don't forget *Soave sia il vento*," added Domenica. "That great song of parting. *Soave sia il vento*—may the breeze that carries you on your journey be a gentle one . . ."

They looked at one another, and became briefly silent. Then Domenica said, "Perhaps we've no stomach for parting any more. Perhaps it's denied, just as we tend now to deny death. We pretend it's not happening. Pretend that we're not actually saying goodbye."

"This conversation," said Angus, "is becoming maudlin. Let me tell you, instead, about what happened at the pub."

Domenica smiled. She had been tempted on more than one occasion to conduct an anthropological study of the Cumberland Bar. "Matthew was there?"

"Yes."

"And he said?"

"He saw Bruce the other day."

Domenica raised an eyebrow. "The young man with the . . ."

"With the hairstyle. Yes. And with the attitude."

"You told me once that Matthew didn't like him."

Angus paused before saying, "I don't think he does. They're meant to be friends, and I suppose they treat one another as friends, but I get the impression that Matthew simply tolerates him. He has no great enthusiasm for him."

Domenica did not think this unusual. "Which I suspect," she said, "is how many people think about at least some of their friends. They're landed with them. They continue with the relationship, such as it is, simply because they can't bring themselves to break it off."

"Perhaps," said Angus. "But the point is this: apparently Bruce has found a new girlfriend."

"Not surprising. He's very good-looking, isn't he?"

Angus's lip curled. "Not my type," he said.

Domenica laughed. "Like all men, Angus," she said, "you suffer from the male inhibition about commenting on the looks of other males. It's a very strong taboo, isn't it? The most that men will say is something like, 'He's thought to be good-looking' or 'I gather women find him handsome.' They won't say they do."

Angus remained silent, and Domenica continued, "Whereas we women—not being afflicted with this inhibition—are very happy to comment on female beauty. We find no difficulty in saying to another woman, 'You're looking very pretty today.' Can you imagine many men saying that to another man?"

"They wouldn't use the word pretty," suggested Angus. "Or . . ."

"My point," interjected Domenica.

"Or they just don't see it."

But Domenica disagreed. "Oh, they see it all right. Men are quite capable of judging male beauty in exactly the same way as women are."

"Well, they may be able to detect it," conceded Angus. "But perhaps they don't like to say anything because they actually resent it."

"You mean they're envious of it? I think you may be right. But anyway, what about Bruce's new girlfriend?"

"Australian," said Angus. "Six foot tall. Blonde."

"He'll like that, no doubt."

"Apparently she was a waitress on an airline."

Domenica looked puzzled. "A waitress on an airline?"

"You know," said Angus. "The people who bring you your meals and serve coffee and so on."

Domenica's look of puzzlement changed to a broad smile. "No, Angus; stewardess, you mean. Or flight attendant, now. Not waitress."

"Same thing," said Angus casually. "Anyway, she was a wait . . . a stewardess for Qantas and then she decided to come and work in Scotland as a personal trainer. She's very sporty, apparently."

"I suppose six-foot Australian stewardesses are highly likely to be sporty," said Domenica.

"Yes, but she's keen on extreme sports," said Angus. "You know, jumping off structures and so on. Can you believe it? Matthew thinks that Bruce is going to end up being killed."

Domenica's eyes widened. "Oh, surely not."

"Her last boyfriend was," said Angus.

"But to lose two . . ."

"As Oscar Wilde would say . . ."

"To lose two vehicles sounds like carlessness."

They both laughed. Then Angus asked, "What's for dinner, Domenica?"

Domenica was about to reply when she remembered something. "I saw wee Bertie today—on the stair. We had a long conversation."

"Poor Bertie. I don't suppose there's any chance of his mother going away again?"

Domenica shook her head. "Alas," she said. "Not the slightest chance, I fear."

"If only *she* would take up extreme sports."

"Charity, Angus," admonished Domenica. But then she added, "Yes, if only."

4

An Inquisition Begins

In the flat immediately below Angus and Domenica's, Bertie Pollock (7), the son of Stuart and Irene Pollock, and brother of Ulysses (1), was sitting on the floor attempting to complete a jigsaw puzzle. The picture in the puzzle was a distant view of Stirling Castle, with the curious tower of the Wallace Monument in the background. Unfortunately for Bertie, several pieces of the jigsaw were missing, including half of the Wallace Monument and several important parts of the castle's defences.

Irene was browsing through various magazines that had arrived during her recent prolonged absence in the Middle East, where, owing to a misunderstanding with a Bedouin sheikh and his staff, she had been sequestered for months in a remote desert harem. Now back in Edinburgh, remarkably unaffected by her experience—durance it might have been, but hardly vile—she was busy catching up with things that had happened while she was away.

"I'm not going to be able to finish this puzzle, Mummy," said Bertie from his position on the floor. "There are ten really important pieces missing. I've counted them."

"Ten?" said Irene. "You should take more care of these things, you really should. If we all lost our jigsaw pieces, then nobody would be able to complete a puzzle, would they, *Bertissimo*?"

Bertie smarted under the injustice of the accusation. "But it wasn't me," he protested. "It was Ulysses. He ate them. I saw him spit some of them out, all chewed up. I saw it, Mummy. And that piece over there—the top of the Wallace Monument—he swallowed it. I saw him do it."

Irene glanced at Stuart, who was sitting on the other side of the room tapping an e-mail into his laptop computer.

"Oh, really," said Irene, becoming severe. "You shouldn't have let your brother swallow things, Bertie. We're old enough to prevent such things, aren't we? Seven is old enough to take on responsibilities like that."

"But I wasn't looking after him," said Bertie. "Daddy was."

Stuart looked up from his computer, but said nothing.

"Stuart," said Irene, her voice quiet enough, but now carrying a note of menace. "Bertie says that Ulysses ate the Wallace Monument. Surely you must have noticed."

Stuart looked evasive. "He's always putting things in his mouth. It's difficult sometimes . . . I don't know why he does it."

Irene put down her magazine. "It's perfectly normal, Stuart. Oral gratification." She spoke patiently, as if explaining something simple to one who might nonetheless not quite grasp it. "And during that stage we must be especially vigilant."

It was a reproof—Stuart was in no doubt about it—but he had learned not to argue with Irene. What was the point? Resistance, he felt, often just made matters worse.

"Granny stuck a dummy in his mouth," said Bertie. "That stopped his girning. It also stopped him swallowing things."

Irene bristled. "A dummy?"

Stuart glanced at Bertie, as if to warn him—but it was too late.

"Do I understand correctly," she said, glaring at Stuart, "that your mother put a *dummy* in Ulysses's mouth?"

It was Bertie who answered. Eager to protect his father, he brought up something he had heard at school from Pansy, whose mother was American. "You know what they call those things in America? They call them soothers." He felt increasingly concerned for his father; Irene was now glaring at Stuart. "I read that the German word for dummy is *Schnuller*, Mummy. Did you know that? That's because . . ."

This did not distract his mother. "Stuart," she said, ominously.

Bertie persisted. "And he really loved it. Babies like dummies, Mummy. Pansy's little sister used one until she was five."

Irene ignored this. "Stuart," she said. "I thought I had made our policy crystal clear. No dummies."

Stuart fixed his gaze on his computer screen.

"Stuart," hissed Irene. "We need to talk. In the kitchen."

Sensing the danger his father was in, Bertie suggested his parents could talk where they were. And then he added, "It was my fault, Mummy. I told her he wanted one."

But Irene was already on her feet, signalling to Stuart. Bertie sighed, and returned to his puzzle. The Wallace Monument looked odd enough, he thought, even when complete; without its crown spire and top section it looked even odder—rather like an overgrown grain elevator. He wondered whether he could draw a substitute piece, or perhaps cut a photograph out of a brochure and repair the puzzle that way.

Ulysses was all right as a brother, he thought, but he had no respect for other people's property. This worried Bertie, as he was a prodigious reader and had recently read something about psychopaths. The article had said nothing about baby psychopaths, but presumably they existed, as adult psychopaths must have been babies at some stage. If Ulysses was a psychopath, as seemed likely to him, then Bertie felt he was in for a difficult few years, having to protect his property against the depredations of a younger psychopathic sibling. Perhaps he could be kept locked in his room, thought Bertie. He could be let out for meals and for short expeditions to Valvona & Crolla, chained to his pushchair if necessary, but for the most part he would have to be kept confined. He would be kind to him, of course, and pass on his older toys, but it seemed to him that community safety should come first.

Behind the closed door of the kitchen, Irene confronted Stuart in a lowered, but chilling tone.

"Your mother, Stuart . . ." she began.

He swallowed. His mother had provided a lifeline. ". . . was very helpful," he interjected. "She came to our rescue. How could I have looked after Bertie and Ulysses and gone to work? She saved the day."

"I'm not denying she helped," said Irene. "But you could have found somebody local. There are plenty of local girls looking for this sort of job."

The way that Irene said *local girls* irritated Stuart. There was an ocean of condescension, he felt, in those two words.

"Local girls," he began. "By that I take it you mean proletarian."

"Oh, don't be ridiculous, Stuart. You know my political views. I identify with the proletariat."

Stuart's eyes widened. Irene had been brought up in Moray Place. Whatever that was, by no stretch of the imagination was it proletarian. "From somewhere like Muirhouse?" Stuart persisted. "Is that what you meant?"

Irene's voice turned into a hiss. "Don't try to obscure the issue, Stuart. The point is that your mother clearly has all the wrong ideas about child-rearing—just as I expected."

"She raised me," said Stuart.

"Let's not go there," said Irene.

"And she was a very good mother," continued Stuart.

"Dummies!" exploded Irene. "Dummies are a way of shutting the child up, of distracting her from engagement with the world. You may as well plug the child into the television set." She paused. "I take it she didn't allow the boys to watch television?"

Stuart was silent.

5

Irene on Popular Culture

"Well, Stuart?" challenged Irene. "Did she or did she not?" Stuart looked out of the window. On the other side of the street, the impassive windows of Scotland Street, beautiful in the regularity of classical Georgian architecture, offered no help to one in a corner, as he was. The sky, though, did; it was high and clear, a pale blue patch of hope above the roofs of the tenements; it reminded him that what he suffered down below was just that—suffering down below.

Irene repeated her challenge. "Did Bertie and Ulysses watch television in my absence? It's a simple question, Stuart—one to which an unadorned yes or no will be sufficient answer."

Stuart worked for the Scottish Government, and this involved close contact with politicians. He knew that there were ways of avoiding a yes or no question—some politicians were masterly at executing such side-steps, but as he withered under Irene's forensic gaze he found it difficult to remember how they did it. But from somewhere deep in his mind the appropriate answer surfaced.

"They were given a great deal of intellectual

stimulation," he said. "My mother was . . ."

Irene cut him short. "I'm asking a very simple question, Stuart, and I assume by your refusal to respond that the answer must be yes, they did."

"I didn't say that," said Stuart. "Did you hear me say yes? You did not."

Irene's nostrils flared. "There are more ways than one of saying yes. Non-verbal communication, Stuart—you should be aware of that."

Stuart tried another tack. "There's a great deal of evidence that forbidding children to do things simply makes the forbidden thing more attractive to them."

If he had imagined that this might mollify his wife, he was wrong. "Oh yes?" she crowed. "And where exactly is this evidence? Chapter and verse, Stuart."

"You quote evidence to me without giving the source. You're always doing it."

Irene inched forward. "Oh, I am, am I? And are you now presuming to teach me about infant psychology, Stuart? Are you suddenly the big expert in a subject you've never studied? Or does being a statistician make you a psychologist too? Perhaps I'm missing something here."

Stuart sighed. "I don't want to argue with you," he said.

"Good. Well, let's look at the damage. What did they watch?"

"I wasn't always there."

This did not satisfy Irene. "Well, did Bertie tell you?"

"He might have."

"He *might* have . . . What exactly does that mean?"

Stuart realised that it was a lost cause. "I think that they watched some discs she had of pre-recorded television shows. There was something called *Andy Pandy*. It's a classic, I believe. Very old-fashioned."

It was the wrong term to use.

"Old-fashioned?" Irene burst out. "It's out of the Ark, Stuart. Look at the gender roles. Looby Loo is subservient—Andy is the initiator of the little schemes. It's atrocious, Stuart."

Stuart gazed out of the window. He had always thought *Andy Pandy* rather appealing—in an innocent sort of way.

He decided on full disclosure. If Irene were to find out later that he had not told the whole truth, the situation could become far worse. "They also watched a film, I think. I believe. Something historical."

The steely tone returned. "Oh yes? And what was that? I know I'm only their mother, but I feel I have a right to know what films my children are watching."

"Something to do with Scottish history."

Irene's eyes narrowed. "What exactly?"

Stuart had no further room to wriggle. "*Braveheart*, I believe."

For a moment Irene said nothing. Then, when she spoke, her voice was thin, each chiselled word falling from her lips like a sliver of ice.

"Your mother allowed them to watch *Braveheart*? That . . . that *travesty*? That meretricious two hours of *nonsense?* That catalogue of tribal violence? We'll have Bertie painting a saltire on his face next."

He sought in vain to defend the film. "I don't know if it's that bad," he said. "The essential story is there. William Wallace . . ."

He remembered that Ulysses had eaten the Wallace Monument and that he had been blamed for that too. And he thought: what would Braveheart himself have done had he been obliged to deal with a hectoring wife like Irene? He would have chopped her head off, probably, with his claymore or whatever it was that the Scots wielded with such enthusiasm before they all became new men. That would have stopped Mrs. Braveheart's nagging.

Irene interrupted his reverie. "Any other films?"

"*The Cruel Sea*. We all watched that together— my mother has always loved that film. She liked Jack Hawkins, you see . . ."

"Jack Hawkins!"

Stuart threw caution to the winds. "And *The*

Jungle Book. Bertie loved that. He liked Shere Khan."

This was too much for Irene. Now raising her voice almost to a scream, she gave Stuart her views on *The Jungle Book*. "Do you realise, Stuart, that *The Jungle Book* is by Rudyard Kipling. Kipling! The arch-imperialist! Why not throw John Buchan into the mix while you're about it? You might as well let Bertie watch *The 39 Steps*."

"Well, actually . . ." They *had* watched *The 39 Steps* and enjoyed it immensely, even if Ulysses had been sick three or four times during the film.

"Not only is *The Jungle Book* by Kipling, but it's also by way of Walt Disney." Irene paused to let the name sink in. "Walt Disney, Stuart!"

Stuart thought that children rather enjoyed Disney films, but did not think it wise to point this out. In a last desperate move, he threw in *Mary Poppins*. "Bertie loved Julie Andrews as Mary Poppins," he said.

Irene looked at him with scorn. "Flying nursemaids? Sweeps with very bad attempts at English accents?"

"It sounds as if you've watched it yourself," said Stuart.

There was a silence, and Stuart realised he had overstepped the mark.

"Only joking," he said. "I imagine you read about it in the *Guardian*."

Irene shook her head. "I'm very disappointed in you, Stuart," she said. "When you consider how much time we've invested in the Bertie Project. When you think of the efforts I've put in to protect him from the baneful effects of popular culture—an uphill battle that has to be fought every inch of the way, Stuart, and then that mother of yours goes and destroys the whole thing with a flood—a positive flood—of cinematic rubbish. I despair, I really do."

Stuart transferred his gaze from the window to the floor. "I suggest we just forget about the whole thing," he said. "You're back now—that's all that counts."

Irene pursed her lips. "We'll see. These ideas, you know, are insidious. This dross is addictive. It's like sugar—give children a taste of sugar and they clamour for more."

Stuart nodded, miserably. "If you say so," he muttered.

"I do," said Irene.

6

A Letter from Portugal

The ire that Irene felt over Nicola's spell of looking after Bertie and Ulysses hardly needed to be communicated verbally. Ever since coming home, Irene had conveyed her message unambiguously through a combination of glassy stares and a stiff, antagonistic body posture. Finally, after she had suggested Nicola should leave for Portugal within forty-eight hours of her own return from the Middle East, all pretence of civility had been abandoned and open battle lines were drawn up.

Had Irene been less unpleasant, Nicola might well have left Edinburgh, but her daughter-in-law's attitude was so confrontational—not to say shockingly ungrateful—that she decided she would not give her the satisfaction of outright victory. It also occurred to Nicola that although she had never interfered in her son's marriage, now she might do just that. Stuart was weak, but he might have just enough backbone to be persuaded to stand up to this dreadful virago whom he had married.

Having abandoned a plan to live in Moray Place, Nicola had then managed to secure the tenancy of a Northumberland Street flat belonging to a distant cousin of hers. This cousin, Dorothy MacNab, was spending a year in London to be near her married daughter in Chiswick. The daughter already had two children and needed help with her eight-month-old son when she went back to work as an optometrist. Dorothy also had a son, Siggi, who had until recently played rugby for Scotland and was famous for bursts of speed unseen on the rugby pitch since the days of David Johnston.

Stuart did not comment on his mother's decision to stay longer in Edinburgh; he foresaw trouble, but was unwilling to interfere. He felt immensely grateful to Nicola for her uncomplaining help while Irene was in the desert. He also rather liked the idea of having his mother in Edinburgh for a longer period; it was true that she had a slight tendency to direct him—what she called "jollying him along"—but if a mother did not encourage her son, then she would not be doing her job. That, he felt, was what mothers did— they encouraged their sons. And they also turned a blind eye to their sons' shortcomings, which meant that although Stuart knew that he did not stand up for himself enough in the face of Irene's onslaughts, Nicola was tactful enough to make only indirect and very gentle allusion to this failure.

It was shortly after she moved into the flat in Northumberland Street that Nicola received a letter from her husband, the Portuguese wine-grower, Abril Tavares de Lumiares. In it, Abril began by saying that there were some things that it was easier to say in writing than to another's face. This prepared her for a shock— indeed it enabled her to guess immediately what was to follow. The ground prepared, the letter went on to express the view that their marriage

39

was not going anywhere. Nicola struggled with that phrase: were marriages expected to go somewhere? Surely the whole point of a marriage was to provide the emotional security implicit in stasis, in not moving into unsettling waters; marriage was about contentment in the place where one was. Or so Nicola had always thought.

"I have been aware of this for some time," he wrote, "and while I wanted to talk to you about it, I have always felt incapable of raising the issue directly. You know how fond I am of you, but somehow I feel that the road we have travelled together has come to a dead end. Raising my eyes to look beyond this point on that road, I see green fields and uplands that I fear we shall never reach together."

She grimaced. The Portuguese could be flowery in the way they expressed themselves: *green fields* and *uplands*. What exactly did that mean?

"And so," Abril continued, "I feel that we should go our separate ways, each taking the path that God has set out for him or her . . ." And why bring God into this? Nicola asked herself. If God had any views on the subject he would surely say: *Be very careful of green fields and uplands*.

"God has in fact spoken to me," wrote Abril, "and he has suggested that I should marry Maria." For a moment Nicola imagined that Abril had completely lost his reason, but then she realised that he did not mean marriage to the

Blessed Virgin, but to Maria, the housekeeper.

"This is not Maria's idea . . ." Of course it is, thought Nicola. It's the one thing that Maria has wanted for years. Now at last she is getting her way.

"As to financial matters, you will be hearing from the lawyers with an offer that I am sure you will consider very generous. You need have no concerns on that score. You will be looked after handsomely.

"So, my dear Nicola, we set off into our futures. May yours be one that is filled with the spring flowers of delight and discovery—the future that I have been unworthy of giving you but that I am confident you will find yourself. And I shall cherish memories of our time together and reflect how fortunate I have been to have had you in my life. Your loving friend, Abril Tavares de Lumiares."

Nicola re-read the letter. She rose to her feet. She tore up the sheet of letter-paper into small fragments and let them fall to the floor. She closed her eyes. Suddenly, and with brutal swiftness, her feelings for him changed. She loathed him. She had never loved him—never. She had thought that she did, but how could love, if it had been that, give way so rapidly and completely to loathing?

She went into the kitchen and opened her fridge. She took out a bottle of gin and made herself a martini, dry, with a twist of lemon. She raised the glass to her lips.

She looked out of the window onto the street below. There was a poem that she remembered— or half-remembered—about a man hearing bad news in a doctor's surgery in London, in Devonshire Street. She had forgotten who wrote it—Betjeman, perhaps—but she recalled the line: *No hope. And the X-ray photographs under his arm / Confirm the message.* The man looks at the people in the street. In his eyes they become *merciless, hurrying Londoners* indifferent to his fate. She looked now at the few people she saw in Northumberland Street down below. They were not in a hurry. They walked slowly. And she thought that they looked merciful; of course they did.

She began to weep, but stopped herself. No, she would not cry. She was free. She had her task ahead of her: to bring that freedom to those from whom it was currently withheld. And she knew exactly who they were: her son, Stuart, and her grandson, Bertie. She would not allow herself the luxury of tears until their hearth, from which freedom was excluded, knew it once more.

7

Coulter's Candy

Just round the corner from Nicola's rented flat was Big Lou's Coffee and Conversation Bar, the haunt of Matthew and Angus, and of many others who lived or worked in Dundas Street. Neither Matthew nor Angus had been in that morning: Angus was busy with a portrait sitting and Matthew was viewing paintings at Bonhams auction house. Big Lou felt their absence; although she maintained a stream of banter with her two regular customers, it was at heart friendly and was something she looked forward to each day. She tried to remember what they had said the previous day about their plans for the week ahead; she thought that Angus had mentioned what he was proposing to do, but she could not remember what it was.

The absence of her regular customers was all the more noticeable because for some reason there was nobody else in the café. There had been the usual early morning rush, when those on their way to work called in for coffee and the Aberdeen buttery rolls that Big Lou had taken to serving, but by nine thirty the last of those customers had departed for the office and the café was quite empty. There were things for Big Lou to do, of course: the large Italian coffee machine, the *Magnifica*, always benefited from cleaning, and the counter, possibly the cleanest café counter in Scotland, could be given another scrubbing with the special green cloths reserved for that task. If you came from a farm in Angus, as Big Lou did, then the training you received in keeping the milking parlour clean never left you, and would show in the cleanliness of your kitchen or, as in this case, your café.

As she performed her tasks, Big Lou thought of young Finlay, the small boy whom she had recently fostered, and whom she now planned to adopt. She had raised the possibility of adoption with the council's fostering department, and they had been cautiously encouraging. She should think further about it, they said, as the process was a lengthy one that some people found distressing. She would have to submit, they explained, to the most rigorous screening process, as children could not be given to the first person who came along and offered a home. "Some people find it intrusive," said the social worker. "You can't have a thin skin. We have to find out a lot about you."

She had wondered about this. What more did they need to know about her? They had taken character references when she had first been considered as a foster parent; they knew who she was and where she came from. She had told them how much money she had in her bank account and how much the café made each year. She had explained to them that she owned the flat outright, as she did the café, thanks to the legacy she had received from the patient she had looked after in the Granite Nursing Home in Aberdeen. What more could they possibly want to know about her? They could ask Finlay, perhaps, and he would confirm that he was happy and wanted to stay.

"We need to be sure of your motivation," said the social worker.

"Aye," said Big Lou. "You need to know that I'm serious about it—I ken that. And you already know that, don't you? I've looked after that wee boy for some time now and I want to look after him for the rest of his childhood. Surely that's obvious."

"It's not that simple," said the social worker.

"Why?" asked Big Lou.

The social worker had frowned. "You may not be sure of your own motivation. You may think you want something, but do you?"

"You mean I dinnae ken my own mind?" retorted Big Lou. "Is that what you're saying?"

"I wouldn't put it that way, Lou."

"No, you wouldn't, would you? You'd find some fancy words for it."

It had not been an entirely satisfactory

conversation, and it had left her vaguely anxious that bureaucracy could somehow prevent her from the obvious next step. She had grown to love Finlay, and for her that had been a revelation. Of course she had loved people before this: she had loved her parents and other members of her family; she had loved one or two of the boyfriends in whom she had placed trust and hope. None of those boyfriends had proved worthy of that love, it transpired, but of course that might change. Yet what she felt for Finlay was very different from what she had experienced previously; there was a tenderness in her feeling for him, a cherishing that was quite unlike anything else she had known before. And she realised that what she was feeling was the love that a parent feels for a child—something that she had not had the opportunity to feel before.

She had been uncertain at first as to whether that love was reciprocated, insofar as a child can return these things. There was little time for anything to be said. Finlay was now seven and had all the physical energy and enthusiasm that makes small dynamos of seven-year-old boys.

And yet, in the midst of all this activity, there were quiet moments, and it was during these that Finlay made the little gestures that told her that she need not worry about his feelings for her—that he loved her, in his way, as intensely as she loved him. Sometimes, as she was reading him his bedtime story, he would climb out of his bed to sit on her lap, nestling his head against her and taking her hand in his. His little hand felt warm and dry, and it squeezed hers gently, almost making Lou stumble over the words of the story, so moved was she.

"You won't go away," he whispered one evening. "You won't go away, will you, Lou?"

"Of course I won't," she said. "I'll never go away."

He looked up at her. "And you won't die, will you, Lou?"

"Ach, away with you. Why would I die? I don't think there's anything wrong with me."

She felt the pressure of his hand. "I'm glad about that," he said.

And when, as occasionally happened, a nightmare had awoken him, she would lie down on the bed beside him, his head cradled in her arm, and sing him back to sleep. He loved *Coulter's Candy*, which had been sung to her as a child. *Ally bally, ally bally bee, Sitting on your mammy's knee, Greetin' fur a wee bawbee, Tae buy some Coulter's Candy . . .*

The words made Lou sad. *Living's awfie hard the noo, Faither's signing on the broo . . .*

She thought of what his life would have been in the past and how different Scotland now was. It was not perfect—far from it—as few, if any, countries can be said to be perfect. But, she wondered, who changed it? Who made it better— what effort, what sacrifice had gone into that? People like Keir Hardie, who had seen what was wrong and had striven, against all the odds, in the cause of justice. And she thought about that as she lay there in the darkness with the young child beside her breathing in and out now with the regularity that comes when sleep creeps up on you and leads you away to another place.

8

The Case for Matron

At half past ten Matthew's assistant, Pat, came in to Big Lou's café. She was carrying a sheaf of papers and explained that she had to check the proofs of a catalogue for an exhibition.

"James Cowie," said Pat. "You'll know all about him."

Big Lou nodded. "Hospitalfield," she said. "That's where he taught. It's not far from our farm."

"Do you like his work?" asked Pat, as Lou prepared her coffee.

"Oh, he could draw," said Lou. "Those pictures of young people—his students, I think."

"They're lovely," agreed Pat.

Pat retreated to a table to correct her proofs, and Lou returned to her cleaning.

"We're gey quiet the day," Lou said from behind the counter.

"That happens," said Pat from the other side of the room. "The other day we had one person come into the gallery all day. Just one. And I think she was just killing time."

The door opened. A man had made his way down the steps unnoticed, and now he was on the threshold, looking about the café as if uncertain whether to enter.

"You can come in," Lou said. "We're open."

The man smiled. "I wasn't sure. I remember this place as a bookshop a few years ago."

"Well, that's what it was," said Big Lou.

The man looked about him, taking in the new arrangements. "I bought Douglas Young's *Braid of Thistles* here. It was a lovely book with . . ."

"With illustrations by George Bain. Celtic art."

The man looked surprised—and pleased. "I wouldn't think that anybody would know it," he said.

"Well, I do," said Lou. "I bought his entire stock when I took this over. I took all the books down the hill to my flat. There were six copies of that book—they must have bought a job lot. I've still got them."

The man's face lit up. "Would you sell me one? I'd like to give it to somebody."

"If you want," said Big Lou. "They're just sitting on my shelf."

"Or even two," said the man. "I could take two off you."

"All right.

"Two pounds each."

The man protested. "That's far too little. Ten pounds would be more like it."

Big Lou shook her head. "I said two."

He did not argue, but looked at her with a new admiration.

Pat had been distracted from her proofs and was staring at the man. He half-turned and smiled at her; she looked away, embarrassed by being caught staring.

"Could you do me a latte?" said the man. "Skimmed milk, if possible."

"Skimmed milk, it is," said Lou. "Your weight or your heart?"

"Both," said the man. "I happen to be a doctor, and I'm always telling people to cut out fats. I thought I should practise what I preach—at least occasionally."

Big Lou glanced at the newcomer. He was, she thought, a few years younger than she was— about mid-thirties, and he had a reassuring, gentle face. It was a good face for a doctor to have, she thought.

"So you're a doctor," she said. "Not a poet."

He laughed. "I like poetry," he said.

50

"MacDiarmid came down here," said Lou. "He fell down those steps."

"Whisky?" asked the man.

"I don't think so. The whisky made no difference to him. I think it was the stairs themselves." She took a large plastic bottle of milk out of the fridge. "So where do you work?" she asked as she poured the skimmed milk into a heating jug.

"The Infirmary," he said. He hesitated, and then added, "My name's Hugh."

"I'm Big Lou," said Big Lou. "And that's Pat over there."

Hugh turned round and nodded to Pat.

"May I ask what sort of doctor you are?" said Big Lou.

"Vascular surgery," said Hugh. "Circulation problems. I get the smokers and the diabetics."

"I've never had any time for tobacco," said Lou. "You may as well stick your head up the lum."

Hugh laughed. "You're right. In fact, if anybody were ever thinking of taking up smoking, I'd say: *come and see my ward*. If ever there was an advertisement for the dangers of smoking, it's that."

Big Lou turned a wheel at the side of the coffeemaker to produce a satisfying hiss of steam that was directed into the jug of milk. "Oh yes?"

"I have to amputate legs," said Hugh. "Smoking can lead to vascular disease, you see. I have a man in at the moment who lost one leg two years ago and now he's losing the other. He didn't stop smoking in the interim . . . couldn't, rather."

"It's a grippy drug," said Lou.

"You can say that again, Big . . . er . . ."

"Big Lou," said Lou. "That's what everyone calls me."

She passed the cup of coffee to him.

As he took it, he said, "Do you mind my asking where you're from?"

Big Lou told him. He seemed interested; he had an uncle who farmed near Forfar. He gave the name, and she knew it. The farmer's wife was a cousin of her mother's half-brother's cousin.

"There you are," said Hugh. "We're all related, aren't we?"

He began to drink his coffee at the counter rather than going to a table. They talked. Big Lou told him about her experience working in the Granite Nursing Home. He listened attentively.

He asked for another cup of coffee, and as Big Lou prepared it, Hugh mentioned that he was engaged in research. "It's got nothing to do with vascular surgery," he said. "Or, maybe it's indirectly concerned with it. It's really to do with how we run our hospitals."

"That could do with some improvement," said Big Lou.

Hugh nodded. "I'm afraid you're right. I fear we've lost sight of a very basic principle."

"Which is?"

"A ship requires a captain," said Hugh. "All human institutions need leadership."

"Aye," said Big Lou. "You can't sail a ship by committee."

"Or by manager," said Hugh. "Tell me—at the Granite Nursing Home up in Aberdeen—was there a matron?"

"Yes," said Lou. "Matron Russell. She was from Elgin. She ran things very well. We were all a bit feart of her."

"Of course you were," said Hugh. "And of course she ran things well; Matron always did."

"So . . ."

"But we've abolished Matron," said Hugh. "Hospitals don't have matrons any more—certainly not matrons of the traditional sort."

"We should bring Matron back," Big Lou remarked.

"Of course we should," agreed Hugh.

Pat looked up from her table. Matron?

9
I Want to Eat You Up!

Bruce Anderson was in love, and it was for the first time, at least it was the first time he had been in love with somebody else. Up to this point in his life—and Bruce was now twenty-seven—the person he had most admired was himself, which of course is nothing unusual in a narcissist. This infatuation with self had been shown in an unduly high regard for mirrors, or any reflective surfaces, in front of which he could never resist preening; in prolonged sessions in the gym, in which he assiduously cultivated even the most obscure muscle groups; and in the application each morning of a carefully calculated amount of clove-scented hair gel into his well-groomed *en brosse* hairstyle.

Of course others had been in love with *him,* and this had been going on ever since Bruce had reached the age of fourteen. That was when his dark good looks had first begun to interest the girls at Morrison's Academy, the school he had attended in Crieff. He had soon come to take this interest for granted, and had allowed a series of teenage hearts to be broken over the years that followed. Female adulation seemed to him to be only natural—something that he neither encouraged nor discouraged; it was just there, following him around like an attendant micro-climate. It was to be taken advantage of, of course, which meant that Bruce inspired intense envy in most of his schoolfellows, whose success with girls was either less assured or, in some cases, non-existent.

Bruce wore his success lightly. "Yes, I suppose girls do like me," he said. "They can't help themselves. It's just the way they are." And then he would turn to the boy who had broached the subject with him, and say, "Never mind, girls are over-rated, you know. You'll find out it's not much to get excited about." And then he added, "When your time comes, whenever that may be."

That, of course, hardly made matters easier, and by the time that Bruce left school at eighteen he was thoroughly unpopular with the other boys. He did not notice this, though, as it seemed to Bruce that there was nothing wrong with him—how could there be? That fatal question is one that all narcissists ask and all answer in exactly the same way.

During the years that followed, Bruce had enjoyed a series of affairs, including an engagement. That came to nothing, when his wealthy fiancée realised in time that Bruce's interest might have been financial rather than romantic—not that the break-up bothered Bruce, who was soon involved with somebody else, the latest in a progression of young women who simply did not see that any relationship with Narcissus must involve three, rather than two parties: the two principals and the reflection in that fatal pool.

But then, for some reason connected with the changes that can occur in a young man's personality in his twenties—a well-known issue in developmental psychology—Bruce's narcissism diminished, and this meant that he developed a greater capacity to see others not just as adjuncts to himself, but as people in their own right, with emotions and interests that needed recognition and tending. The change was dramatic—where there had been selfishness there was concern for others; where young women had been judged simply by their attractiveness, there developed an interest in what they thought. And it was against the background of this maturing and enlargement of personality that Bruce met Clare Hodding, a young Australian who had decided to spend six months working in Scotland and who happened to wander into the Cumberland Bar with her friend Penny one Tuesday evening, to find Bruce there with a friend from his days as a surveyor. The chemistry, and indeed the electricity, were both immediate, and that evening as he sat over the dinner table in the Café St. Honoré with Clare—Penny and Bruce's friend having gone to a club in the Cowgate—Bruce realised that his interest in the young woman on the other side of the table was of an intensity and a nature that he had never before experienced.

They saw one another the following day, and that evening Clare made him dinner in the flat she was sharing with another young woman, a New Zealand nurse. Bruce took her flowers, the first time he had done this, and was surprised by her reaction. Rather than find a vase and enthuse, Clare tossed them onto a table.

"You need to put them in water," said Bruce.

Clare looked carelessly at the flowers. "They're nice colours," she said.

"They totally need water," said Bruce.

"Whatever," said Clare, but did nothing.

Later that evening, Bruce raised the question of the flowers' welfare. "They'll be dead by tomorrow morning."

Clare frowned. "Oh yes, those flowers. Well, they don't last long, do they?"

"You could make them last longer if you put them in a vase."

"I don't think we've got a vase. This flat's hopeless. We haven't even got one of those thingies—you know, for crushing garlic."

"Or a jug. You could use a jug, you know."

"Yes, I suppose so. We might have a jug—I don't know."

Bruce had not expected this indifference to his gesture, but it did not affect his enthusiasm. He was overawed by Clare's sheer physical presence—by her stature—she was almost as tall as he was; by her classic profile—the line of her brow and her nose might have distinguished a sculpture by Praxiteles; and by the air of pent-up energy that accompanied even her slightest movement. He knew that the open-air life-style pursued in Australia could produce a healthy, outdoor appearance, but he had never seen it in quite so striking a form. It fascinated him, and he felt himself being drawn towards Clare in an inexorable helpless way. And he surrendered.

They lay together on the sofa of the darkened sitting room once her flatmate had considerately retired to her room.

"Tell me about yourself," said Bruce as he ran his fingers dreamily through her hair. "I feel I don't really know you."

"Well, you don't," said Clare.

"Tell me then."

"What? The whole story?"

"Yup. The whole story. From the beginning, or close enough."

"Where I was born? That sort of thing?"

"Yes. That sort of thing."

She was silent for a while. "Why do you want to know?"

"Because . . . well, because I think I've fallen in love with you."

"My God!" exclaimed Clare. "Do you realise what you've just said?"

"Oh, I know what I've said."

Clare touched Bruce's lips with the tip of a finger. "You're so amazingly cute," she said.

Only a few months earlier, Bruce would have replied, "I know." But not this time.

"I want to eat you up!" said Clare, opening her mouth and then closing it with a snap. "But since you asked me to tell you my story, I will."

10

At Presbyterian Ladies'

Clare was a compelling storyteller, even if she skated over her early years.

"Not much to say about the first eighteen years," she said. "Never is, I think."

"Oh, I don't know," said Bruce. "You read a biography and they usually spend quite a lot of time going on about childhood." As he spoke, Bruce realised that he could not remember ever having read a biography, but he felt that did not detract from his point.

Clare looked at him. Their heads were close together on a large sofa cushion. She moved her head slightly so that she could touch the tip of his nose with her tongue, which she now did.

"So what was the last biography *you* read?"

He drew back slightly, but she pursued him and licked the tip of his nose again.

"And I'm telling the story, Brucey!" she continued. "So you just listen. OK?"

He nodded. It was not an unpleasant sensation having the tip of his nose licked and he tried to remember whether anybody had ever done that to him before, except the family dog in Crieff, when he was a boy. That dog, Gavin, had licked everybody's face—nose, lips, chin—whenever he had the chance.

Clare continued. "Anyway, as I was saying, not much to say about that—other than that I grew up in Western Australia. Been there, Brucey?"

"Nope."

"We'll go some time, you and me. Maybe. If you're good."

"Brucey's a very good boy," said Bruce. "Always is."

She licked the tip of his nose again.

"We lived near Margaret River. My dad used to work in mining, but he gave that up when one of their properties turned out well. He bought a vineyard—they make really good wine in Western Australia, you know. I had some in the fridge, but Anna's boyfriend drank it yesterday. He drank *my* wine. A real cheek." Anna was Clare's flatmate, and her boyfriend, Freddie, who worked for Scottish Widows, helped himself to the contents of the fridge at will.

"Men," said Bruce.

"You can say that again. So there we were. I went to a local school to begin with and then had to go into Perth for senior school. I went to Presbyterian Ladies' College. It was in Peppermint Grove, which is a really nice part of Perth. We had Black Watch tartan for our uniform and we had a well-known pipe band."

"*Très* Scottish," said Bruce.

"Yes," said Clare. "My old man was Scottish, you see. He was born in Oz as well, but his father came from some dump called Glasgow. Only joking! My brother, Barry, went to Scotch College, which is this boarding school for boys in Perth. We used to have dances and debates with them all the time. You know the sort of thing. When Scotch College had a dance for the seniors, they used to bus girls in from Presbyterian Ladies'. It was like taking cattle to market—just like that, I swear."

"I went to a heterosexual school," said Bruce. "Only joking. But we had heaps of girls. Heaps of them. All over the place."

"So there I was at Presbyterian Ladies' and I stayed there until I had just turned eighteen and then I had to decide whether I should go over to Sydney or Melbourne to uni, or stay in Perth. I almost went to Melbourne, not to Melbourne Uni but to a place called Victoria Uni. They do a Bachelor of Physical Education course there and that's what I wanted to do. They have these sports labs and things like that. But then I decided I didn't want to live in Melbourne because it's so big. It goes on and on, you know. It's a great place for coffee bars and stuff like that, but Perth's got these great beaches, you see, and for some of the things I wanted to do, Perth would be much better."

She looked at Bruce. "You paying attention, Brucey?"

"Sure. Carry on. So you stayed in Perth. What then?"

"I applied to the Uni of Western Australia—or I suppose they call it the University of Western Australia. It's got a pretty cool campus on the river there. Pretty old, but pretty cool. Lots of girls from Presbyterian Ladies' went there. Quite a few of my friends did, including a girl I knew called Helen MacFarlane. She was quite a good friend of mine at school—her folks came from way up the coast there, some godforsaken place, and she never went home very much. It was really boring, apparently. Anyway, she went to the UWA with me and you know what she said? I'll tell you. She said, 'I can't wait to get to uni with all those guys being there.' That's what she said. She was boy-mad. She had pictures of guys all over her locker at school—once you opened it. We weren't allowed to put guys on the outside, just the inside, and usually we just had a few guys, one or two, real hunks, that sort of thing. Well, she had guys all over. Every inch of space was some guy flexing his muscles. Honestly, let's say you came from Mars and you saw that locker you'd think to yourself *These strange creatures haven't invented the shirt yet. Or underpants!* You didn't know where to look. Honestly."

"Cool," said Bruce. "She sounds great."

Clare affected to ignore his comment.

"You know," she continued, "when Helen got to uni, you never saw her. She went to a few lectures and things, I suppose, but most of the time . . . Well, it was guys. She had about five boyfriends in the first year, and that was her only year. She failed every exam—every single exam, and some of the subjects she was doing were designed not to be failed. Sociology, for instance. If you're really into guys, then you should study sociology, that's a well-known fact. You don't have to know anything. Media Studies is another one—maybe even more so. Or Film Studies. I swear, if you do Film Studies at uni all you have to do is watch movies. Then you write an essay saying why you liked the movie, and that's it. I knew somebody—this guy from a place called Nannup, which is in the sticks outside Perth—he knew nothing. Zero. Zilch. He enrolled for Film Studies and he spent all day on Cottesloe Beach and at night he watched movies. He did really well."

"Cool," said Bruce.

"He got bitten by a shark, though. Not a big bite, but he had a whole bunch of stitches. He showed me. And then . . ."

"And then?" said Bruce.

"He graduated."

11

Quandong Berries

"Where were we?" asked Clare, lying back on the sofa, staring now at the ceiling of her Newington flat, Bruce beside her, his hand resting on her shoulder. She had just noticed water stains on the ceiling; from where she was, they looked rather like the outline on a map of continents and seas. There must have been a flood, she thought, and the plaster had simply been left to dry out rather than be replaced. Scotland, she thought, was so damp, with its lochs and its rain and its mists; there was water everywhere, even on the ceiling.

"You were going off to uni," said Bruce. "With Helen."

Clare laughed. "Her! OK, right, I went to UWA and I started studying physical education. I'd always been good at it and the gym teacher at school—she looked like a man, but was really nice, and we all liked her—she encouraged me to do PE at uni. She said if you want an outdoor job—and I did, I couldn't stand the thought of being in an office—then you should be a PE teacher like me. I thought about it a bit and went to visit the department and they said they would love to get an application from me. So I applied and they wrote back and said I was in as long as my exam results were good enough."

"And they were?"

"Just. So I started at uni and I lived in a hall of residence that was not far from the main campus. It was a bit of a dump and there were not enough bathrooms, but it was all right and we had a good time, I suppose. I made a lot of new friends and I enjoyed my course. We did psychology of sport, which was really interesting. And there was physiology, which was great, as it told you what happened when you breathed, and stuff like that."

Bruce raised an eyebrow. "I know what happens when you *don't* breathe," he said.

Clare looked at him scornfully. "Yeah, we all know that. The interesting thing is where the oxygen goes. People think it goes into the lungs, but it actually goes into the blood. Lots of people don't know that there's oxygen in their blood. And how you regulate your temperature. People don't know how long you can survive in cold water, for example."

"About twenty minutes in Scotland," said Bruce. "I learned that when I was at school. We went for a sailing weekend at Port Edgar and they told us about survival times in the Firth of Forth in winter. Not long. And your muscles stop working quite quickly, and then you're toast."

"Yeah," said Clare. "We learned all that stuff—and more."

"So how long did you do that for?" asked Bruce.

Clare hesitated before she gave her answer. "I didn't finish the course," she said. "I did a year and a half. Then I dropped out."

Bruce looked surprised. "But you said you enjoyed it."

"Yes, I enjoyed it but . . ."

He waited. He noticed that she closed her eyes briefly, as if trying to shut out a painful memory.

"There was a row," she said at last. "It wasn't my fault."

"What happened?"

Clare sighed. "It was halfway through my second year. We had to do teaching practice. We had to go to a school for a month and understudy the PE teacher or, as in my case, actually be the PE teacher if the regular one was on holiday. I was allocated to a school where the PE teacher was on maternity leave. I was in charge of the department for the whole time I was there."

Bruce nodded. "So they threw you in the deep end?"

"Yes, exactly," said Clare. "And one of the things I had to do was to take a group of the kids for an adventure weekend in the bush. They had to do a ten-mile hike, then camp for the night and try to find some bush tucker if they could. We had rations, but not quite enough. They had been given lessons in getting bush tucker from roots and stuff and so they were meant to do that. They had to show the stuff to me and get it checked out in the book I had before they ate it."

"I've heard you can live on that," said Bruce. "The aboriginal people can get by for ages on it, can't they?"

"They're really good at survival in the bush," said Clare. "They've handed down the knowledge from way, way back." She paused. "Anyway, they took us out on a Saturday morning and dropped us off at the start point, which was a sheep station in the middle of nowhere. The kids had to make their way to some hills they could see in the distance. They couldn't get lost. That was where we were going to camp that night."

"How old were they? Were they small kids?"

"No. They were sixteen."

"So, how did it go?"

Again Clare hesitated before replying. "It went well enough to begin with. They all reached the campsite no problem. Then we looked for bush tucker . . ."

Bruce felt the suspense. He wondered whether the problem had been mushrooms. He had always been deeply suspicious of wild mushrooms and would never eat them himself.

"They found quite a lot of things," Clare went on. "One of the kids even found a comb of wild honey—there were no bees around, and so nobody got stung. That was a great find. There were also witchetty grubs. Have you ever seen those things? You probably don't get them in Scotland."

"Never seen them," said Bruce. "You eat them?"

"Yes, they're sort of fat white grubs, a bit like caterpillars. You can eat them raw or you can cook them. They taste a bit like almonds."

Bruce made a face.

"I know," said Clare. "People don't like the idea of eating things like that, but if you're in the bush and you're hungry, you have to. You soon stop minding, I can tell you."

"And what else?"

"Well, that's where the problem came in. One of the kids came up with some quandong berries. These are bright red thingies that are full of vitamin C. They taste all right, too—a sort of bush tucker dessert."

"Weren't they ripe?" asked Bruce.

Clare shook her head. "No, they were ripe . . . The problem was that they weren't quandong berries at all. They were something else."

12

Poor darling. Poor you

As she continued, a note of defiance crept into Clare's story.

"I didn't say what the kids claimed," she said. "They said later that I told them that the berries were quandong. I didn't. Definitely. You remember what you say, don't you, Brucey?"

Bruce did not hesitate. "Yeah, sure I remember. Every word. It's all recorded in here." He tapped his head.

"What I said was that I *thought* they were quandong berries but I'd have to look them up in my book. There's a difference, you know."

Bruce nodded. "Of course there's a difference." He had a sense of where the story was heading and was keen to hear more. "So, what happened?"

Clare said that she was glad he saw the distinction; many people, she said, had failed to grasp it. "So I went off to get my book," she went on, "which was in my backpack. I found it and I looked up quandong. I studied the picture, and I thought that although the berries the kids had picked looked very similar, I decided I would check them against the colour photograph in the book. But then I noticed that one of the students had left a fire unattended. He had made it for his billy, and the water was boiling. So I decided that I would take the billy off the fire and put the embers out—just to be safe. I did that, and it took a bit of time—these fires can get going and you have to use quite a bit of sand to put them out altogether.

"Then I went back to where the kids were sitting. As I arrived, one of them said, 'We just finished them, Miss.' I asked them what they were talking about, and they said they had shared out the berries amongst themselves but had kept a few for me. I took these, and I examined them against the picture in my book. There were differences."

Bruce groaned. "Too late?"

"I didn't know what to do, so I told them off for eating the berries before I said they were safe. One of the boys became pretty lippy. 'You told us they were okay, Miss. It's your fault if we're going to die now. My folks are going to be really mad at you, Miss.' That sort of thing."

"Oh no," groaned Bruce. "So all the kids died?" He paused, and then added, "Not that I'm saying it was your fault."

"They didn't die," said Clare. "In fact, they were fine for about half an hour. Then they began to complain about pain in their stomachs. One or two started to bring things up and made a big fuss about that—far more than was necessary, I thought. Then a couple of them started to writhe about a bit, and that's when I realised we were in trouble."

Bruce winced. "And you were right out in the bush . . ."

"Yes, we weren't close to help. I had to do some quick thinking."

"And you decided what?"

"I had a portable radio with me—it belonged to the school. I used it and I got in touch with a farmer who said that he'd alert the police. They sent a helicopter and started to take the kids back to a hospital. They had to do four trips."

Clare became silent, as if brooding on the outcome. Bruce asked her if everybody had survived, and she said they had. "They had diarrhoea for a couple of days," she said. "But apart from that, none of them were really harmed—not that you'd think that from the school's reaction."

"They were unreasonable?" asked Bruce.

"Seriously unreasonable. They believed the kids, of course, rather than me. The Principal called me in and told me that I had been grossly irresponsible and that they were going to file a report with the uni to that effect. Then they ended my teaching practice and told me to go back to the uni."

"Were they supportive?" asked Bruce. "The uni people?"

Clare answered bitterly. "Them? Well, they were all right about it, but they insisted that I would have to undergo safety instruction if I were to be allowed to be in charge of kids again. I'd had enough. I didn't need to be lectured about safety."

Bruce touched her neck gently. "Poor darling," he said. "Poor you."

"Thank you. So I told the uni where to go and I left. I went back to my dad and gave him the story and he was really mad. He went up to the uni and told them to sort out the school. They said they couldn't do that, and I swear he tried to sock the head of department in the jaw. And the Vice-Chancellor, I think. I was really proud of him. Then we went home and I had a rethink about my future."

"And that's when you joined Qantas?"

"Yes. Well, I didn't join straight away. I went to a sort of career counsellor and told her about what had happened. She said that it sounded as if I had been unfairly treated by the school, and that I should go and see a lawyer. But I didn't want to do that. I'd had enough at that stage. And that's when I saw an ad in the paper for cabin crew trainees. I went off to a place they have and signed up. There was a medical, of course, and they said that I was just the sort of person they needed because I'm a bit stronger than a lot of girls . . ."

"Girls are so weak," interrupted Bruce. "Only joking!"

Clare ignored this. "The training was really interesting," she continued. "There was more psychology—how to deal with difficult passengers and so on, and a lot about safety procedures. You know; what to do when your plane goes down? You make sure you know where the exit is. That's the important thing, because there's often smoke, you see. We learned all that sort of thing. Also, how to push the trolley down the aisle without hitting people's elbows. Oh, and how to open the toilet door if a passenger's trapped inside."

Bruce laughed. "Didn't somebody have to spend a whole flight in the toilet because the vacuum system had gone wrong and trapped them on the seat?"

"Not on Qantas," said Clare firmly.

Bruce looked disappointed. "Pity. Good story." He paused. "How long did you work for the airline?"

"Three years," said Clare. "I really enjoyed it, and I would have stayed had it not been for what happened."

Bruce gave her a sideways glance. Was Clare one of those people who attracted misfortune? He wondered about that, reflecting that he might need to be cautious; but caution, of course, although it operates in at least some of our affairs, does not necessarily operate when the affair in question is an affair.

13

A Sighting in the Museum

The entrance hall of the Royal Museum of Scotland was thronged with visitors, including a number of groups of children, all chattering excitedly, all being marshalled for a walk round the exhibits by tense-looking teachers and their helpers. That morning the Steiner School had sent Bertie's class for a visit, and so it was that Bertie, Tofu, Olive, Pansy, Hiawatha, Larch and several others were being led up the staircase to the atrium.

"Now, boys and girls," said the teacher, Miss Campbell, "we are about to embark on a little voyage of discovery. We are about to take a walk round Scotland's past—amongst lots of other things. Isn't that interesting?"

"Not really," muttered Tofu. "All the stuff here is old, really tired stuff."

"Did you say something, Tofu?" asked Miss Campbell.

"Not me, Miss Campbell," said Tofu.

74

"Because I can't imagine," the teacher said, "that you would be so silly as to say that museums are full of things that are old and tired."

Tofu was adept at speaking without moving his lips, and now he said, *sotto voce*, "Just like you."

Bertie felt he had to respond. "Tofu," he whispered, "you shouldn't say that teachers are old and tired—even if they are. That's really unkind."

Olive, standing not far away, gasped. "Miss Campbell," she blurted out. "Did you hear that? Bertie said that teachers are old and tired. I heard him."

Bertie defended himself. "I didn't," he wailed. "I didn't say that, Olive." And to Miss Campbell he said, "I promise you, Miss Campbell. I promise you I didn't say you were old and tired."

"I'm sure you didn't, Bertie," said Miss Campbell, glancing discouragingly at Olive. "And anyway, we haven't come here to argue about who said what; we've come here to explore this fascinating world we live in."

That settled, the group continued its progress up the stairs and into the nineteenth-century hall of the museum, a great white cathedral of light. High above them a vast glass roof was a window onto a whole slice of the sky, allowing the morning light to fill the hall below with brilliance. Behind the walkways that clung to the walls of this hall, the museum's galleries stretched invitingly: science, the natural world, clothing; whales, rockets, pots and pans; medicine, heat, electricity. Awed by the sheer size of the hall, the children listened to their teacher's plan: they would visit natural history first, then science, before seeing the display of Scottish history.

In the science section, Miss Campbell pointed out a small glass inhaler, the product of Stevenson's scientific instruments firm.

"This was for chloroform," she announced. "You see that bit there? That was put over the patient's mouth so that they could breathe in the chloroform."

The children peered through the glass.

"And does anybody know what chloroform was?" asked Miss Campbell.

Bertie looked about him. He knew, but was aware, too, that one had to be careful about displaying knowledge in the presence of people like Tofu and Larch, who, as far as he could tell, knew very little and resented anything that revealed their comparative ignorance.

Miss Campbell was looking in his direction. "I'm sure you know, Bertie," she said. "In fact, I think you have the look of one who knows what chloroform was all about."

"He didn't say he knew," muttered Tofu.

"No, he didn't," agreed Larch. "Bertie doesn't know everything, do you, Bertie?"

The look that Larch shot in his direction persuaded Bertie that he had been right not to disclose his knowledge. But now Miss Campbell was waiting for his answer and he could not tell a lie.

"I sort of know," he said, hoping that this ambiguous answer might deflect hostility. But Larch was staring at him, almost sneeringly, and he knew his strategy had not worked. He sighed. "It puts people to sleep."

"Exactly," said Miss Campbell. "Well done, Bertie! And do we know who invented it—right here in Edinburgh? Do we know his name?"

This was the signal for Tofu's suggestion of a well-known Scottish politician, generally known to put people to sleep while talking to them.

"No, Tofu," said Miss Campbell. "Not him." She turned to Bertie. "Well, Bertie?"

"It was Mr. Simpson," said Bertie.

"Well done again, Bertie," said Miss Campbell. "Yes, it was James Young Simpson. He had dinner parties in Queen Street where he showed his friends how it worked. They all sat round the table and breathed in chloroform. It put them to sleep."

Larch nodded. "My mum and dad have dinner parties like that," he said. "They sit at the table and sniff . . ."

Miss Campbell cut him off. "That's enough, Larch."

"That's different," said Tofu. "They not sniffing chloroform, they're . . ."

Miss Campbell raised her voice. "I said that was quite enough, Tofu."

Olive now chimed in. "My father says that Larch's parents are a disgrace, Miss Campbell. He says that he knows all about them."

"Shut your face, Olive Oyl," snapped Larch.

"Hush!" said Miss Campbell. "I will not have language like that, Larch! You apologise to Olive."

"What for?" asked Larch.

"For telling her to shut her face," intervened Pansy. "Look, Miss Campbell—look how upset Olive is."

Larch made a grudging apology, received in stony silence by Olive.

"Dr. Simpson was a very brave man," said Miss Campbell, eager to revert to history. "It's called self-experimentation, and that means that rather than experimenting on other people, he used himself. That's very brave. And of course it meant that people could have operations without feeling any pain. That made a big difference, as I'm sure you can imagine." She paused. "And now, boys and girls, I think we can make our way to the Scottish history section, where we shall see how people lived a long time ago when Scotland was a very different place from what it is today."

They moved off, following the teacher in pairs. And it was while they were making their way down the stairs that led to the Scottish galleries, that Olive suddenly stopped, stared across the hall, and gave Bertie a nudge.

"Isn't that your dad, Bertie?" she said.

Bertie looked in the direction in which Olive was now pointing.

"I don't think my dad's here," he said. "He goes to the office during the day."

Olive persisted. "But it is him, Bertie. Look, he's over there."

Bertie looked again. Olive had been pointing in the direction of the museum café, with its open expanse of tables and chairs. The café, a popular drop-in place, was busy, and Bertie had difficulty in making out the man whom Olive was talking about. But then he did, and it was his father—he could tell that now.

"And who's the woman he's with, Bertie?" asked Olive. "That's not your mummy, is it? No, I don't think it is, Bertie. So who is it?"

14

The Intimacy of Tents

Stuart was late home that evening, but was just in time to read Bertie his bedtime story, which currently was Robert Louis Stevenson's *Kidnapped*, substituted by Stuart for Irene's proposal of *The Young Gandhi*, an entirely worthy, but rather slow book on the early life of the Mahatma. There would be time enough, Stuart thought, for Bertie to learn about Gandhi; for the moment he would find more pleasure in the travails of David Balfour and his experiences in the Hebrides and the Highlands.

Ulysses, of course, was already asleep; in spite of his gastric issues—he tended to be sick whenever Irene picked him up—when it came to matters of day-to-day routine he had proved to be a very easy baby, sleeping through the night from the age of four months onwards, and awaking promptly at seven each morning. This regularity had been of great assistance to Irene, who was never at her best in the early morning and who greatly appreciated the extra hour or two of sleep that this routine afforded her. Stuart, by contrast, was a light sleeper, and there were few nights during which he did not wake in the small hours, sometimes lying in the darkness for an hour or more before sleep returned.

Had Ulysses required feeding or changing during the night, he would have been the obvious person to take that on, and would, as it happened, have enjoyed the distraction. He had done that when Bertie was an infant, and had never minded sitting there in the room they used as a nursery, his tiny son in his arms, watching the level of milky baby formula in the bottle slowly dropping as Bertie sucked his way through his untimely early breakfast. There was so much that he wanted to say to this tiny bundle of humanity—his son—and he often did so, talking to him as one might talk to an old friend, confiding much that he felt he could say to nobody else, indifferent to Bertie's uncomprehending gaze. For Stuart, like many men, was lonely. He had long since stopped being able to say much to Irene; his conversation with her had become progressively more one-sided—any response he made to her observations was never really listened to, nor given much weight on the rare occasions that it was.

He was not entirely without friends. He had kept in touch with some contemporaries from James Gillespie's, where he had spent his high school years, and they occasionally met at the Golf Tavern on the edge of the Meadows. But those reunion evenings had proved to be increasingly difficult for him. These friends, all of whom were, like him, married, seemed to be happy in their marriages, or, if they were not, were adept at concealing their unhappiness. They spoke of holiday plans with real enthusiasm: they were going with their families to Spain, or Portugal, or wherever it was, and seemed to be eagerly anticipating the trip. One of them, Tom, who had been perhaps Stuart's closest friend at Gillespie's, and who was now a successful insurance broker, had told him of a planned trip to Iceland later that summer, and had confessed that what really excited him about the trip was not the prospect of the dips in geothermally heated pools or marvelling at geysers, but the prospect of camping for two whole weeks with his wife.

"Frankly," Tom said, "I can't wait."

"I'd love to go to Iceland," said Stuart.

"Yes, but what I'm really looking forward to, Stuart, is two weeks in the tent with Alice. Two weeks!"

Stuart had looked at him with incomprehension, not sure whether he had understood correctly. Was it the case that Tom liked the idea of being under canvas for two weeks—there were, of course, some people who liked tents—or was he looking forward to being in a tent for two weeks with a particular person—his wife? If it were the former, then Stuart would simply marvel at the different things that people liked. There were some people who sought pleasures that no rational person—in Stuart's view—would espouse. There were people to whom bungee-jumping appealed; there were people who liked four spoons of sugar in their tea; there were people who were never happier than when standing on a dance floor listening to music so loud that their eardrums— or what remained of their eardrums—hurt. And there were people who liked sleeping in uncomfortable, constricting sleeping bags—not infrequently made out of some sort of nylon—under a canvas roof that could not be trusted to keep the rain out entirely; who liked communal ablution blocks shared with total strangers, with showers that dribbled lukewarm water; who liked the feeling of being not-quite-clean, a target for midges and mosquitoes, and other unidentifiable agents of itchiness. There were people who liked all that, and Tom may have been one of them.

Or—and this was slightly embarrassing—it was possible that Tom liked the idea of being in a tent with Alice for that length of time. Stuart could imagine that there would be people with whom being in a tent would be an adventure: a newly found lover, for example, with whom such intimacy was novel; he could understand the attraction of that; but Tom and Alice had been married for years, and presumably lived in close proximity anyway in their Newington flat. Was a Newington flat perhaps too unromantic to inspire excitement? That was possible, he supposed, but he had found his friend's confession an awkward one, and had changed the subject by starting to talk about Iceland's geological instability—a topic that, as it happened, was one on which Tom had views.

"They've been very clever, those Icelanders," his friend said. "Few of their houses are anywhere where they could really be damaged if anything blows up. Humanity in general has a habit of

83

building its house in the wrong place, don't you think?"

Stuart had not given Tom's observation the thought it deserved; his mind had gone back to tents, and he was asking himself how he would feel about spending two weeks under canvas with Irene, whether in Iceland or in a more geologically stable part of the world. And he had come to the conclusion that he would not enjoy it; that two weeks in such circumstances would be a sentence to be served with as much forbearance as he could muster. This realisation then prompted another, and even more disturbing question: if he could not face spending two weeks in a tent with Irene, then was there *anybody* with whom he would like to do just that?

There was.

15

Spitfires, Courage, Statistics

Bertie looked up at his father from beneath the blankets. Perched on the side of his son's bed, Stuart had a tattered edition of *Kidnapped* in his hands and was reading the book aloud, pausing here and there for dramatic emphasis. Bertie's eyes widened with excitement at Stevenson's tale; to think that such events took place just outside Edinburgh, and such a short time ago too. Whatever prodigiousness he might show in the scope of his reading, Bertie was much the same as other young children in having little awareness of time and chronology; for him, the past might be a long time ago, but was not so distant as to have been outwith the experience of most adults. It had never occurred to him that his father might not have been around to witness the Second World War, and he had expressed surprise on learning that Stuart had not participated in the Battle of Britain.

"I suppose you were too old to fly a Spitfire, Daddy," he remarked.

For a moment, Stuart imagined himself, a youthful airman, engaged in aerial ballet with his opponents. Would he have had the courage to fly in the face of those bleak odds? He thought not. He looked at Bertie with regret; sooner or later the admiring son realises the father is not the omnipotent hero, and that day would inevitably come for Bertie. All he could hope was that Bertie's judgment would be gentle. "Actually, Bertie, I wasn't even born then—believe it or not."

When it came to his grandmother, Stuart's mother, Nicola, Bertie had once asked her whether she remembered the 1745 Jacobite Rebellion. "Ranald Braveheart Macpherson says that his grandfather fought with Bonnie Prince Charlie," said Bertie. "Do you remember all that, Granny?"

"I may be old, Bertie," replied Nicola evenly, struggling to suppress her laughter, "but not quite that ancient."

So it was that Bertie felt that the events described in *Kidnapped* were within recent memory, and that the dangers faced by David Balfour had not entirely disappeared. This meant that Stuart had been needed to comfort him after they had read of the disturbing visit that the hero had paid to his Uncle Ebenezer in the House of Shaws. That visit had almost ended the David Balfour story somewhat prematurely, as the uncle had sent his nephew in darkness up a stair-case that ended in an abyss. And there had been nervousness, too, when David had accompanied the same uncle to a pier where he was hit on the head and bundled into a boat bound for the West Indies and certain servitude.

"You must remember that the world was more dangerous in those days, Bertie," Stuart reassured him. "Staircases are generally safer these days. And the risk of being sold into slavery is much reduced." Stuart thought: was this true? Was the world really safer, or did we simply delude ourselves that human nature, with its lengthy and gory track record of cruelty, had in some way changed in its very essentials?

He looked down at Bertie, and wondered what the world would be like when this little boy was forty. Would he even make it that far, or would some cataclysm, natural or man-made, intervene to cut short his life? In our human cleverness, we had dodged any number of bullets, courtesy of antibiotics and statistical good fortune, but Stuart felt that sooner or later microbes would defeat our pharmacopoeia, for all its cunning. Stuart was a statistician, and he understood risk. That meant he knew that our luck would run out, and we would lose this gentle earth that had nurtured us and which we had so thoughtlessly abused. That process had started, and was accelerating. His own generation would not be called to account, but Bertie's would, and by then it would be too late.

"He was a jolly wicked uncle, wasn't he?" said Bertie.

"He was indeed, Bertie," Stuart replied. "And perhaps that's where we shall leave it for tonight. But do remember, everything will be all right for David Balfour—so don't worry too much."

"I want things to work out well for people," said Bertie.

Stuart caught his breath. Of course you do, dear Bertie, he said to himself. Because you—unlike us—are made of unalloyed goodness, and that is what goodness dictates. At some stage, of course, you're going to discover that good does not always triumph and that evil can very easily win the battle; I hope, though, that when that truth dawns you will be old enough and strong enough to make the deliberate effort not to believe it. Because only if we pretend that it is not true can we steel ourselves to fight against it—like those young men in the Spitfires who did not stop to consider the impossible, daunting odds and went up nonetheless.

Stuart snapped *Kidnapped* shut and leant forward to plant a kiss on Bertie's brow. He smelt the slightly soapy smell of a little boy who had recently bathed; he felt the tickle of Bertie's hair upon his lips; he heard the breathing of his young son.

"Goodnight, my darling boy," whispered Stuart.

From a place already halfway to sleep, Bertie muttered his goodnight. And then, as if remembering something that he had forgotten to ask Stuart earlier, he muttered, "Why were you in the museum today, Daddy?"

Stuart froze, and then very slowly straightened up. Speaking very slowly, his voice lowered, he said, "Why do you ask that, Bertie? Did you see me?"

"Yes," said Bertie. "I saw you in the café. I would have liked to say hello but Miss Campbell was taking us to look at something."

"So you saw me," repeated Stuart. "I was . . . I was speaking to somebody."

"I saw her," said Bertie. "Does she work in your office?"

It would have been easy for Stuart to say yes, but suddenly he stopped himself. He had never lied to Bertie, and he would not do so now, whatever the exigencies of the situation might be. "Not in my office," he said evenly. "Another office—not mine."

Bertie's gaze was still upon him. "Olive said . . ." His voice trailed off.

"Yes," said Stuart. "What did Olive say?" He had never liked Olive.

"She said that maybe that lady was your girlfriend."

Stuart bit his lip. "I wouldn't believe everything that Olive says."

"I don't," said Bertie, and then added, "I just believe some of it—not everything."

16

Rhododendron Issues

The garden of the house near Nine Mile Burn had proved more of a challenge to Matthew than he had anticipated. When he and Elspeth had moved in a month or two earlier with their three boys, Tobermory, Rognvald and Fergus—and, of course, with their Danish au pair, Anna, and the au pair's au pair, the equally Danish Birgitte— they had imagined that the garden would require no more than the occasional mowing and perfunctory tidy-up. That was to underestimate grossly the enthusiasm of nature, and the effect of the copious rain that Scotland had received in the early months of that summer. Almost from the very day on which they moved in, Matthew had noticed the exuberant growth of shrubs hc had barely seen when he first inspected the several acres attached to the house. He witnessed the advance of the rhododendrons so that they encroached on the drive; he saw the lawn become a denser green as the grass shot up; he saw patches of fireweed spread as if a paintbrush had carelessly daubed purple across the kitchen garden with all the subtlety of a graffiti artist. It was as if Nature herself were challenging him to assert his ownership of the plot of land for which he had paid so much. You may think you own the land, she said, but you reckon without me. *On ne négocie pas avec Dame Nature*, Matthew muttered.

Surveying the grounds of the house with Elspeth shortly after their arrival, Matthew had wandered into an unexplored area behind the rhododendron bushes that lined the drive. No effort had been made to tame this part of the property, and he noticed that it was heavily colonised by smaller versions of the colourful bushes. These offshoots were smaller than their parent plants, but were clearly thriving and would soon be waist-height.

"These are very pretty," said Elspeth. "I've always loved rhododendrons, haven't you?"

Matthew thought for a moment. Had he a view on rhododendrons? It was possible, he imagined, to go through life without having a view on a large number of things—including rhododendrons—and not to feel that one was in any way evading some central and inescapable issue.

"I haven't really given the matter much thought," he said. "I suppose I've noticed them—yes—but I'm not sure that I've *responded* to them." As he spoke, he thought how much he sounded like a contemporary conceptual artist—such people were always going on about how we respond to things, usually to things that were utterly banal until the conceptual artist came along, marshalled them into a studio (or space, as such artists call their studios, and indeed all rooms and buildings, and flats too; a conceptual artist usually inhabits a space rather than a room or apartment).

This was meant to be art, and we were meant to respond. If we did not respond, of course, that in itself would be considered a response. *To do nothing, is to do something,* wrote one contemporary exponent of this school of art. *Not being is being.* So even if we closed our eyes and said nothing about what we saw, that was every bit as much a response as if we were to make a specific and considered comment. There is no way, thought Matthew, of contesting the agenda of conceptual art: whatever one does, the artist has the last word—even to the extent of defining, in an entirely solipsistic way, the boundaries of art.

"I really like them," said Elspeth. "I like their colourfulness. We have some in Comrie that are a sort of purple—honestly, you've never seen a purple like it."

"They're very colourful," said Matthew. "I'll give you that."

"And it looks as if this whole area here is going to be covered by them," continued Elspeth. "Imagine what fun the boys will have playing in these bushes."

"They're going to love it," said Matthew. He spoke absently; he had remembered reading something in an old copy of *Scottish Field* about how rhododendrons were a problem in Scotland.

"I think I read something about them," he said. "I'd forgotten, but it's coming back to me." He paused. "Yes, it was all about non-native species. Rhododendrons come from . . ."

"The Himalayas," said Elspeth. "Yes, I know all about that. They were brought over by plant collectors in the nineteenth century." She bent down and picked a leaf off one of the bushes. It was dark green, and had a waxy look to it. She held it in her hand and twirled it about on its stem. "And rhododendrons liked Scotland. The conditions are much the same as in the Himalayas."

"I wonder," said Matthew, "what makes a species non-native."

"That's quite complicated," said Elspeth, dropping the leaf to the ground. "Obviously they have to come from somewhere else, but I don't think it's that simple."

"Because everything comes from somewhere else at some stage?"

"Exactly. I think you have to look at things like distribution and how it fits in the ecological landscape."

"How it relates to other plants about it?" suggested Matthew.

Elspeth reflected for a moment. "Yes. And to insects too. If a plant doesn't have local bugs that like to sit on it or eat it or whatever, then it may be from somewhere else."

Matthew pointed to the house behind them. "We need to get back," he said, glancing at his watch. "Remember, we've got the Duke coming for dinner."

They had bought the house from the Duke of Johannesburg, who had been letting it out for some years but who had eventually decided to put it on the market. He himself lived not far away, in Single-Malt House, and had been a kind and considerate neighbour since they had moved in, offering them the names of local tradesmen, sending them a consignment of green vegetables from his own kitchen garden, and generally taking a kindly interest in their settling into their new home.

They, in turn, had come to appreciate his company. They had learned that he was not a genuine duke, not *sensu stricto*, even if he had a claim of sorts; yet this did not affect their attitude towards him. Indeed, if anything, it endeared him to them further; there was something vaguely raffish about the Duke, and the dubiety of his dynastic credentials simply added to this in a rather attractive way. He was a bit like one of those ubiquitous Russian princes who prop up the bars of Moscow—relics of an order that was as irrelevant as it was ancient, but, for the most part, now simply colourful. The Duke had recently experienced a bit of trouble with one of the Lord Lyon's entourage, Marchmont Herald, but seemed to have emerged from this unscathed and had accepted their invitation with warmth and alacrity.

"What a relief!" he said down the telephone. "I thought you were never going to ask me. What are we having, by the way?"

17

Distressed Oatmeal

There was every reason for the Duke of Johannesburg to look forward to a meal with Matthew and Elspeth—even a kitchen supper, which was what Elspeth had mentioned when she spoke to him on the phone. Since she had moved into the house near Nine Mile Burn, Elspeth's reputation as a cook had spread widely, not only in Midlothian, but into East Lothian and Lanarkshire as well. Like many reputations, it had been inflated in the telling: a relatively simple meal cooked for a neighbour had quickly become a banquet; a plate of cheese scones, donated to the local church for its bring-and-buy sale, had been the object of lyrical praise in the church newsletter; even her marmalade, the result of an enthusiastic encounter with a sack of Seville oranges, was talked about in hushed tones by people who had never tasted it, nor seen it, but who knew somebody who had done both. Fairly quickly people had concluded that if there was one invitation to secure at all costs, it was to a dinner cooked by Elspeth and served by Matthew in their still-to-be-decorated dining room.

"Frightfully shabby dining room," it was remarked, "but so chic!"

Shabbiness, in fact, was a highly sought-after quality in that part of the country. The problem was the influx of rather too many young couples from Edinburgh with money but no under-standing of rural life. These people, mostly working in the city's financial institutions, brought with them a demand for expensive fitted kitchens, hardwood conservatories, and gardens laid out by garden designers. Even if they did not initially understand that people who had lived in the country all their lives had none of these, they soon learned that a vaguely threadbare life, lived in rooms that were too large, too cold, and in need of paint, was much more fashionable than one lived in relative opulence. This resulted in complete reversals, all in pursuit of authenticity. Newly installed kitchens were replaced with old pine cupboards that did not close very well; compressed ash surfaces were replaced with rescued chopping blocks from ancient butcheries; and elegant Italian terra-cotta gave way to stone slabs worn down by generations of feet.

Matthew, of course, twigged immediately, and successfully fought off Elspeth's suggestions that they might redecorate the house, install modern central heating, and generally bring the house into the twentieth, if not the twenty-first century.

"No," he said. "It would be a big mistake.

What's the point of living in the country if you're going to bring all your baggage from town? People will laugh at us. Far better to keep the place as it is."

Matthew himself fitted perfectly into his new surroundings. Elspeth had thrown out a lot of his clothes since their marriage, passing on tweed jackets, corduroy trousers and old jerseys to a charity shop in Morningside Road, but she had not managed to get rid of everything and Matthew was still in possession of several distressed-oatmeal sweaters as well as a couple of pairs of trousers in a colour that had been identified as mitigated-beige. Sharper-eyed neighbours had noticed this, and there had been positive comments on the shabbiness of his wardrobe and its suitability for the country.

"He ticks all the right boxes," said one hostess. "Nothing crushed strawberry about him."

Elspeth's reputation as a cook was not entirely undeserved, even if it had been somewhat exaggerated. She had been taught to cook by her mother, Flora Harmony, who had in fact been a domestic science teacher, as they were called before the invention of home economics. Flora, who had been Flora McGillvray from Falkirk before she met and married Jim Harmony, had studied at what had been the Edinburgh College of Domestic Science at Atholl Crescent, known affectionately as the Dough School. It was not surprising then that Elspeth should have developed an interest in cooking, and had even succeeded in getting into the final rounds of a televised national young chef competition. Nor was it surprising that she should have started, at the age of eight, a recipe book of her own, *Mummy's Recipes*, in which she wrote, in copperplate, recipes learned from her mother or painstakingly cut out from the pages of the *Weekend Scotsman* and pasted in under such titles as *Really Good Cheese Straws* or *Mrs. Thompson's (Old Bag) Lamb Ragout* or *Betty's Aunty's Thick Strawberry Jam*.

That book had accompanied Elspeth into her marriage and, although dog-eared and greasy from frequent consultation in the kitchen, was still being added to. Now it occupied pride of place on the kitchen shelf in the Nine Mile Burn House, where it stood alongside various publications left behind by the Duke: an ancient Mrs. Beeton's *Household Management*, a much newer copy of *Even Men Can Cook*, and the Scottish Gas Board's *What To Do When You Smell Gas*.

"Do something from *Mummy's Recipes*," Matthew had suggested. "I should imagine that the Duke likes comfort food."

"I'll do the first course from *Mummy's Recipes*," she said. "But the second course is going to be something suitable for *sous-vide*."

Matthew licked his lips. "You can't go wrong with that."

"Well, actually you can," said Elspeth. "Remember that risotto you tried to make in the *sous-vide* machine?"

Matthew defended himself. "That was not my fault. It was Birgitte's recipe. She gave it to me."

Elspeth sighed. "She thinks she knows everything," she said. "She was lecturing me about how to get red wine stains off a carpet the other day. She spoke to me as if I were six."

Matthew made a face. "What are we going to do about her?" He hesitated. "Shall we ask her to leave?"

Elspeth had been hoping he was going to say this. "We could buy her a ticket back to Copenhagen."

"But she said she didn't want to go. Remember? She said that she liked Scotland so much she was going to stay indefinitely." He paused, before continuing, "What if she met a Scotsman? What if he asked her to marry him?"

Elspeth looked doubtful. "Would she be interested in a Scotsman?"

"What do you mean?"

"Well, you may have noticed that she and Anna get on very well. They tend to spend rather a lot of time in Anna's room."

Matthew frowned. "But they're talking Danish," he said. "I've heard them."

Elspeth shrugged. "Maybe," she said.

She looked at Matthew. She loved him. She even loved his distressed-oatmeal sweaters and mitigated-beige trousers. She loved his innocence.

18

The Rescue of Hollandaise Sauce

Matthew saw the Duke's car as it turned off the main road onto the track leading to their house. Standing out on the untended lawn, he watched as the car disappeared behind the bulk of the rhododendrons to emerge a minute or two later on the other side. Seeing the Duke, not at the wheel, but seated in the back, he remembered that his guest had once muttered something about having a driver.

"I hope I'm not late," said the Duke, as he stepped out of the car. "My watch has got a loose spring somewhere in the works and it's a terrible business keeping it regular."

Matthew reassured him. "You're absolutely punctual. On the nose."

The Duke seemed pleased. "Good. I can't be doing with this business of arriving ten minutes late or whatever. What's the point? Tell people the time you expect them to arrive and that's it.

If you want them to come ten minutes later, then adjust accordingly. Tell them."

"My thoughts exactly," said Matthew.

The Duke bent down to say something to his driver and then turned to Matthew. "I don't believe you've met my driver. This is Padruig."

Matthew shook hands with the driver through the open window of the car.

"Padruig's actually a stockman," the Duke explained. "He does some driving for me from time to time, but his real job is to look after my neighbour's cows."

Matthew smiled at Padruig. "The cows I see when I drive in to Edinburgh? Those cows?"

Padruig, a powerfully built man with sandy-coloured hair, nodded, almost regretfully, Matthew thought. When he spoke, it was with the unmistakeable lilt of the Western Isles.

"The cows are in the field," he said. "They are in the long grass. They are eating the grass."

Matthew was immediately captivated; it was as if poetry were being recited. *The cows are in the field. They are in the long grass . . .*

"After all this rain," said Matthew, "the grass will be long, won't it?"

Padruig nodded. "The rain has been falling," he said.

Again, it was poetry.

"Like tears," Matthew found himself saying. "The rain is like tears."

The Duke tapped the top of the car. "Padruig has to be on his way," he said. "What time should he come back, Matthew?"

It was Padruig who answered. "I shall come back whenever you are ready. I shall not be away. I shall be here."

"Ten o'clock, then," said the Duke, glancing at Matthew for confirmation.

They both watched as Padruig reversed the car and drove slowly back down the drive towards the rhododendrons.

"A fine man," said the Duke. "He likes to drive, and it suits me to get the occasional lift. In return I let him have use of the car whenever he needs it. He goes up to Pitlochry from time to time—I think he has a girlfriend there. Suits everybody."

"It's a lovely car," said Matthew. "What make is it?"

The Duke shook his head. "No idea. There's no name on it, which is strange, but I've looked. Padruig looked too—he said that he thought it might be a Jaguar, but then he decided it wasn't. The mechanic at the garage couldn't tell me either. He said he'd never seen a car like it, and perhaps it was homemade, but it must be very difficult to make a car." He paused. "I bought it from a chap I met at Haymarket Station. Paid quite a bit for it."

Matthew saw the Duke's car turning onto the main road and heading back towards town. In the distance, the evening sun caught the side of the car, and it flashed back a signal to them, a glint of light.

Matthew turned to the Duke. "He has a nice way of speaking," he said.

"Padruig?"

"Yes. I like the West Highland accent."

The Duke nodded. "He's a Gaelic speaker, of course. He goes off from time to time to speak Gaelic. My neighbour says that sometimes he's away for a few days, and when he comes back he simply says he's been speaking Gaelic."

"Odd . . ."

The Duke nodded. "Yes, and did you notice the words? He seems to speak poetry."

"That's just what I thought," said Matthew. He gestured towards the front door. "Shall we?"

The Duke smiled. "That's what I came for," he said. "Dinner."

They went into the kitchen, where Elspeth was preparing the meal. The Duke kissed her on both cheeks, sniffed at the air, and then said, "Oh my goodness, what a treat."

Elspeth had been using a whisk in a bowl. She laid down the whisk. "Disaster," she said. "My hollandaise sauce . . ."

The Duke peered into the bowl. "Curdled," he said.

Elspeth sighed. "I know. I'll have to start again."

"No," said the Duke. "That won't be necessary." He removed his jacket. "Get another bowl."

Matthew watched bemused as the Duke took control.

"White wine?" asked the Duke.

"If that's what you want," said Matthew. "But I can give you a whisky, if you prefer."

The Duke laughed. "No, not for me—for the sauce. A spot of white wine in the bowl."

Matthew found an opened bottle in the fridge, and passed it to the Duke, who poured a small amount into the clean bowl.

"Now," said the Duke. "This is what you do. First you pour some white wine into your fresh bowl—like that—then you spoon in the curdled sauce—gently, *comme ça*. Mix it into the wine and then add another spoonful. See?"

Elspeth peered into the bowl. "You've uncurdled it," she said.

"Amazing, isn't it?" said the Duke, beaming with satisfaction. "It's rather like unmixing whisky after you've put the water in. Or uncooking porridge and ending up with oats and water. The miracle at Cana of Galilee, and all that . . ."

"Who taught you?" asked Elspeth, relieving him of the whisk.

"Mother," said the Duke. "My mother was a remarkable woman, rest her soul. I learned more from her than from anybody else."

"We need our mothers," observed Matthew.

Both the Duke and Elspeth stared at Matthew, surprised at the statement, and waiting for more to emerge. But Matthew had nothing to add, as he thought that what he had just said was in itself quite sufficient and needed no further adumbration.

19

Birgitte Offends

They sat at table, the empty plates of the first course before them. The dining room faced west and was benefiting from the last of the evening sun—a glow, half red, half yellow, in the cloudless sky. Beyond a line of Scots pine affording a foreground, the hills of Lanarkshire were a line of blue, merged into blue, as if a wash of watercolour had been daubed across the sky.

The Duke looked down at his plate, now scraped quite clean; the hollandaise he rescued had accompanied a salmon roulade. "Perfect," he said.

"Claire Macdonald," said Elspeth. "One of her books."

"The woman who runs that place up on Skye?" asked the Duke. "Kin-something or other?"

"Kinloch Lodge," supplied Matthew. "It's up

near Sleat. We went there, didn't we, Elspeth?"

Elspeth nodded. "I wrote down one of her recipes in my book . . ."

"*Mummy's Recipes*," said Matthew.

The Duke thought this a good title for a recipe book. "Mind you," he said, "my own late father, the first Duke—*soi-disant*, of course—always said *Never eat at a restaurant called Momma's*."

Matthew laughed. "Sage advice."

"Nor play cards with a man called Doc," added the Duke. "But that doesn't prevent you having a recipe book called *Mummy's Recipes*."

Birgitte had been asked to help serve the meal, and she now came in to clear the plates. She looked at the Duke with undisguised curiosity, ignoring Elspeth's discouraging gaze. Once the au pair had retreated to the kitchen, Elspeth whispered to the Duke, "I must apologise—that girl is extremely rude. She's pushy, too, although I've never thought of the Danes as pushy, have you?"

The Duke looked thoughtful. "The Danes are most usually described as melancholy," he said. "Hamlet was the original melancholy Dane—and that appears to have stuck. And yet . . ."

"Yes?" asked Matthew.

". . . And yet if you think of their history—which I happen to know a bit about, as I had a Danish teacher once—they've been as pushy as everybody else. It's just that they don't see themselves in that light. But just look at their history."

Matthew tried to marshal such facts as he knew of Danish history. He decided that he knew nothing.

"They have been as expansionist as anybody else," said the Duke. "They like to think they have a more humane history, but remember where the Vikings came from."

"Ah!" said Matthew. "That's a point."

"Yes, indeed," said the Duke. "And Scandinavian countries have not yet paid us a penny of restitution—not a penny."

The Duke took a sip of his wine. "Denmark had colonies too, you know," he continued. "They had possessions in the West Indies. They had outposts in West Africa and they had a place called Tranquebar in Tamil Nadu, amongst others. And Greenland. They had colonies, all right."

Birgitte came back into the room.

"Tell me," said Elspeth. "Did you know that Denmark had colonies, Birgitte?"

Birgitte stared at her. "Of course not. We are not like you English people. Or the French, for that matter. We have nothing to be ashamed of." She paused. "That's the difference between us and you."

Matthew gasped. "We're *not* English, Birgitte. We're Scottish."

"Same thing," said Birgitte airily.

Elspeth drew in her breath sharply. "I'm afraid you're wrong, Birgitte," she said. "On that, and other things too. Denmark had plenty of colonies. You were as bad as everybody else."

"And don't forget the Vikings," added Matthew.

Birgitte spun round to face Matthew. "The Vikings were misunderstood," she said. "They were very peaceful."

The three seated at the table looked at one another in mute astonishment.

"I'm afraid you're misinformed, my dear," said the Duke. "A Scandinavian co-prosperity sphere—is that what you're saying?"

"Do not call me *my dear*," snapped Birgitte. "It's sexist condescension."

The Duke reeled visibly at the reproof. "I was only trying to . . ."

Birgitte stared at him, and he became silent. To Elspeth she said, "Are you ready for the main course?"

Elspeth nodded. And then, when Birgitte had left the room, she said to the Duke, "I'm so sorry, Duke. That's what we have to put up with."

"Goodness gracious," said the Duke. "I was only being friendly. What a difficult young woman."

"We're going to have to do something," said Elspeth. "It's just a bit complicated. She's very good with the boys, I have to admit. It's just that she's a bit intimidating, if the truth be told."

The conversation turned to the paintings that Matthew and Elspeth had found in the house after they had bought it from the Duke. The question of ownership, which Matthew thought would be a difficult one, had been very quickly resolved by the Duke's generosity. Pleased that everything had been so amicably and easily settled, the Duke recalled another art discovery—the Dublin Caravaggio that had been found in the parlour of the Jesuit house in Leeson Street, hanging in the dining room unattributed, neglected, and badly in need of restoration.

"It was only very recently," said the Duke, "that the senior conservator of the National Gallery of Ireland had a look at it. Until then, everybody thought that it was a copy by Honthorst—interesting enough, of course, but not the real McCoy. Then this chap from the gallery started to take the grime off and he saw that the painting technique was pretty impressive and he started to take an even closer look. It was a Caravaggio all right."

"A stroke of good fortune," said Elspeth.

"Yes, that's what a group of nuns down in the Borders thought," said the Duke. "They thought that they'd check up on the paintings they had in their parlour—a whole lot of pictures in elaborate frames. One of them looked as if it could be a di Cosimo; another had a ring of Lippi about it—according to one of the sisters who had borrowed a book on art history from the local library."

"Exciting," said Elspeth.

"And?" said Matthew.

"Well . . ." began the Duke.

20

Fra Filippo Lippi

"Just imagine," said the Duke of Johannesburg, "this small nunnery in the Borders, not far from Kelso. I happen to know the place a bit myself, as my father had a half-share in a racehorse that was stabled nearby, along with a number of other second- or even, dare I say it, third-rate horses. Ours was called Luminosity, and he never won a race, although he took third place on two occasions in Kelso when other horses fell or were ill. None of the amateur jockeys they used down there wanted to ride him, and so occasionally we had to enter him in a race without a jockey at all, which never did much for his chances.

"This nunnery had been a school years ago—you still bump into people down there who remember it—but the nuns appear to have lost interest in education and closed that side of things down. They had a couple of farms thereafter, including a chicken farm at one stage, and they also bred Highland cattle at one point—ill-tempered beasts, those, particularly when their calves are around. Then they lost interest in farming, too, and I think they did nothing in particular after that, although some of the nuns kept bees. They had a small hostel where they took in wayward girls from Motherwell and tried to sort them out—a thankless task with zero chance of success, but there we are, at least they tried.

"Their buildings were rather beautiful, in fact. They had a lovely little chapel that had been decorated by Phoebe Anna Traquair, not that anybody in particular noticed—it's in none of the books, but it really is very fine. There's a fresco of St. Catherine of Siena and her miraculous water barrel, all done in Traquair style—a real jewel.

"Everything was going rather well at the time that this happened. Their numbers were down a bit—fewer vocations, of course, and lots of other things for young women to do other than become nuns. But they were managing all right with several novices coming from Sri Lanka and a trickle of locals who liked the place and who joined up—if that's what nuns do—in their fifties or even sixties. I suppose being a nun is quite a good thing to be in your retirement: fairly decent accommodation, good enough food, peace and quiet, if that's what you want.

"I've never really thought of going into a monastery myself, but I did know somebody who went into one after a career in the oil industry and found it highly congenial. I gather they don't have to get up quite as early as they used to—none of this up at four for prayer or eating in silence. Hc said they got up at about eight thirty most days and had a three-course breakfast, reading the papers, before they got down to the real work of the day. His monastery was an unusual one—it didn't do farming or brewing cider or any of the things that monasteries traditionally do—they actually played the stock market. I suppose it's a case of moving with the times—work patterns change.

"This nunnery had a rather large parlour—much bigger than the usual nuns' parlour, and it was on the walls of this parlour that their pictures were hung. Now of course these were all more or less what one would expect to find in a nunnery—at least in subject matter. There were lots of pictures of the Virgin Mary with the usual supporting cast—Joseph and so on—and I particularly remember a very large St. Jerome and the Lion, with the lion looking utterly depressed. I think there must have been about fifteen of them.

"Now it came to pass—as they say—that the nun I mentioned who had borrowed the book on art history started to identify one or two of the paintings. The Mother Superior of the time was not particularly interested in art, but perked up when the sister in question said that in her view they were possibly sitting on some important art treasures. The finances of the nunnery were not too bad—they had a fairly comfortable endowment—but there was a big roof bill coming up and there was a lot of painting to be done on the walls. Money was definitely needed.

"The Mother Superior telephoned a friend of mine, as it happens, who was an agent for one of the big London auction houses. She explained that they had a number of old paintings that they might consider selling, and she mentioned the fact that one looked as if it might be by Fra Filippo Lippi.

"At the mention of Lippi, my friend became pretty excited. All sorts of people, I gather, phone up and say they have a Lippi in the attic, and he would normally be fairly sceptical, but in this case people were still talking about the Caravaggio in Dublin, and so he was taking it all very seriously. He went down there, had a look, and broke the news to the Mother Superior. They were all nineteenth-century copies—every one of them. The total value for the whole shooting match, in his view, was about two thousand pounds, if that.

"The Mother Superior was obviously disappointed, but cheered up considerably when, the following week, quite by chance, an antique dealer from Glasgow turned up with a couple of his shady friends. This man knew nothing about paintings, but scoured the country looking for furniture he could buy from people who had no idea what they had. In other words, he took advantage of them.

"The Mother Superior said to him that they had some old paintings in their parlour that they might consider selling if the price were right. She took him along and showed him, saying that she thought some of them might be quite good, particularly one by somebody called Lippi, whose name one of the sisters had seen in a book. She went on to say that this painting could be worth as much as forty thousand pounds if it were given a good scrub.

"The dealer's ears pricked up. He knew enough to realise that the real value of a painting of that importance would be in the millions, but he went along with her suggestion that it could be as much as forty thousand. He offered thirty-eight thousand—maximum—and said that he would take the others for a few thousand pounds each. All in all, he paid seventy thousand for the lot and agreed to go down to the Bank of Scotland in Kelso to get his cheque cleared there and then and paid into the nuns' account. Then he loaded them into his van, barely concealing, I imagine, his delight at the deal, waved goodbye, and drove straight up to Edinburgh to an appointment with my friend the auction agent—the same man who had valued them for the Mother Superior a week or so earlier."

Matthew burst out laughing. "Not a satisfactory meeting for him!"

"No," said the Duke. "But there you are." He paused. "Not only is their roof now in good order, but I gather they also have rather a good cellar."

"The rewards of virtue," said Matthew.

"Well, sort of," mused the Duke.

21

Stuarts and Campbells

That Saturday, Bertie followed the new routine into which he had settled since the return of Irene from her sojourn in the Gulf. This was to be taken round the corner from Scotland Street to his grandmother's flat in Northumberland Street. This happened at half past eight in the morning, as Irene, who was not at her best in the early mornings, or indeed at any other time, liked to have a long lie-in on Saturday. Ulysses would accompany them in his pushchair, but would not be left at Nicola's; he would be taken home for breakfast and entertained by Stuart until Irene emerged.

Irene only grudgingly permitted Bertie to continue to see his grandmother. "Your mother," she said to Stuart, "is hardly what I would call a good influence, but I suppose she is Bertie's grandmother, after all, and we have to give some weight to that."

Stuart stared at her in frank disbelief. "But your own mother . . ." he began, and stopped. He had intended to point out at least some of the more egregious faults of his mother-in-law, but Irene's glance silenced him.

"My mother," she said, "doesn't enter into the equation. She very rarely, if ever, has the opportunity to see her grandchildren."

Just as well, thought Stuart, but did not say it. Irene's mother, Stephanie, who like Nicola had been widowed, had remarried, to an Adlerian psychotherapist, and gone off to live on Osney Island, a small island in the Thames in its meandering passage through Oxford. She had never taken to Stuart and he, in turn, had given up on ever establishing much of a relationship with her. She was close to Irene, though, even if the four hundred miles between Edinburgh and Oxford meant that they spent little time together. What they lacked in physical contact they made up for in long telephone conversations, in which Stephanie, now herself firmly in the Adlerian camp, would talk at length about compensation and overcompensation, about fictive goals, and other subjects of common interest.

Nicola had only met Stephanie once, and the two women had taken an instant dislike to one another. "I can imagine no possible world," said Stephanie, "in which I would find myself drawn to the company of that woman."

And for her part, Nicola simply smiled and looked out of the window whenever Stephanie's name was mentioned.

Bertie, of course, being the boy he was, tried to be positive about his maternal grandmother, but did not receive a great deal of encouragement. Nicola, of course, was different. She doted on Bertie and Ulysses, and made sure that the time they spent in her company was filled with as much fun and excitement as could reasonably be mustered. During Irene's absence, this programme had included trips to pizza restaurants and ice cream parlours—now both out-of-bounds, unmentioned and only dreamed about under the Irene regime.

That morning Nicola had planned a trip to the Scottish National Portrait Gallery café on Queen Street, where she would have a cup of coffee and Bertie would have a large milkshake. That would be followed by a visit to the gallery itself before they walked down the hill to Valvona & Crolla's delicatessen on Elm Row. There they would meet

Stuart at noon, and Bertie would be handed back to his father's care.

Bertie enjoyed the Portrait Gallery. He had acquired a small red Moleskine notebook, in which he had written a list of portraits, and had then filled in notes with such details as he could muster on the lives of the people portrayed. He also liked the frieze in the gallery's Central Hall, where around the room paraded figures from Scotland's past, portrayed against a gilded background. Craning his neck, Bertie would point to those he could identify, and on each visit would concentrate on a particular section, inscribing the names in his red notebook. That morning he focused on the figures between James VI and Mary, Queen of Scots, an unedifying group, but one that fascinated Bertie.

"That's King James, isn't it, Granny?" he said, pointing at the instantly recognisable melancholy figure of the Stuart monarch. "He always looks unhappy, doesn't he?"

Nicola nodded. "He was," she said. "And I suppose you'd be unhappy too if your mother got her head chopped off." She pointed to Mary, Queen of Scots, a few figures away.

Bertie did not answer immediately, and for a moment Nicola entertained a mental picture of Irene, in the dress of the time, being led off to Fotheringay Castle. No, she thought; one should not even *think* such things.

Bertie was looking at Mary. "She looks nice," he said. "And that's her husband there, isn't it, Granny? That's Mr. Darnley."

Nicola looked at the young man partly obscured by the figures of his wife and of Mary of Guise. "Yes," she said. "That's Darnley."

"He was blown up, wasn't he?"

"Yes he was, Bertie. At Kirk o'Fields, where the university is today. He was, I'm afraid to say, blown right up in the air."

Bertie gazed up at Darnley. "Ranald says that he deserved it. Ranald says that Darnley stabbed Rizzio with a Swiss Army penknife right there in Holyroodhouse."

Nicola smiled. "I don't think they had Swiss Army penknives in those days, Bertie. They used hunting knives, I imagine."

"Was James unhappy just because his mummy got her head chopped off by Queen Elisabeth?" asked Bertie. "Was that why?"

Nicola's gaze moved to a figure close by—the humanist, Buchanan, the young James's severe tutor—such joy as there was in that young life would have been nipped in the bud by that grim killjoy.

"There were other reasons, Bertie. He had a very strict teacher."

"Did he hit him? Did he hit James?"

Nicola shook her head. "Probably not. But I'm sure he frightened him. And then . . ." And then what? When did the frustration of love denied first begin to distort the soul? And how could she explain that to Bertie? She could not.

But she did not have to. Bertie had moved on and was gazing up at the figures of Mar and Argyll. "That's the Earl of Mar, isn't it, Granny? He was very brave, wasn't he?"

"He was, Bertie."

Bertie pointed to Argyll. "And the Duke of Argyll," he said. "He was a Campbell, wasn't he?"

Nicola confirmed this.

"You'd think he'd look more ashamed of himself," said Bertie. "You'd think that he'd look more ashamed of being a Campbell."

22

Outside the Playhouse Theatre

Immersed in Scottish history, Nicola came up for air only just in time to realise that if she and Bertie were to meet Stuart as promised they would have to leave the Scottish National Portrait Gallery without delay. Prising Bertie away from a portrait of Professor Higgs contemplating an opaque set of scribbled figures, Nicola led the way out into York Place.

"Daddy will be meeting us at Valvona & Crolla

very soon," she said. "So we mustn't linger, Bertie."

Walking beside her, his hand in hers, Bertie looked down at the pavement. There had been a time when he would have taken care to avoid stepping on the cracks—an elementary precaution observed by any sensible child keen to avoid bears or other, unnamed dangers. Now, however, he realised that he simply did not care, no matter what dire warnings Olive had once given in the playground that his general conduct would have terrible consequences.

"You may think you're above it all, Bertie," she had threatened, wagging her finger at him. "But I've got news for you. God's going to get you one day, Bertie Pollock, and when he does, boy, are you going to regret what you've done. He keeps a note, you know; he writes it all down."

"That's right," said Olive's lieutenant, Pansy. "It's all written down, Bertie. You've had it, you know."

"And what about you?" challenged Bertie. "Do you think God hasn't noticed what you do? All those fibs you tell?"

Pansy had hesitated, and Bertie had thought that his question had struck home. But then Olive had retrieved the situation for the girls.

"This is all about boys," she announced. "They're the ones who have to worry."

"That's right," said Pansy, relieved at the immunity. "This is not about girls."

"Yes," said Olive. "Boys have had it, Bertie. They're finished. There's no point in being a boy any more. Everybody knows that."

"Exactly," said Pansy. "Everybody—except some boys, of course."

That brought peals of laughter from Olive, and the two girls had sauntered off, secure in their understanding that girls had inherited the world and that boys were, for the most part, a spent force.

Now, walking purposefully with Nicola down the urban brae, Bertie transferred his gaze from the ground to his grandmother. He had a question to ask, and he was struggling to find the right words to ask it.

"Do you think that . . ." he began, but then trailed off. The noise of a passing bus drowned his voice.

"What's that, Bertie?" asked Nicola. "Do I think what?"

She had, in fact, been thinking at the time of what she would buy at the delicatessen and was contemplating the purchase of a large Milanese salami and a wedge of ripe Parmesan. She had a friend coming in to see her that evening and they would sit in the kitchen with the salami, the cheese and a glass of Puglian wine, and imagine they were in Italy. Bliss! She had read, as everybody had, that salami was suddenly on the list of things you should not enjoy because they were bad for you, but where did it end? Was Parmesan cheese also to be avoided? And Puglian wine? Surely not. The Italians lived to a ripe old age, particularly in the south, where everybody knew they sat about munching away and drinking their wine and generally enjoying themselves—for eighty or ninety years in most cases until they eventually breathed their last and were taken skywards by hosts of angels and *putti*. Those baroque Neapolitan artists captured all that so vividly in those overwrought paintings of theirs, and presumably the image sustained people, made them more content, and increased their hedonistic Mediterranean lifespan. Whereas in Scotland, we shivered and battled with our consciences, iconoclasts all, and looked askance at people who were enjoying themselves too much. *We'll pay for it* might be a Scottish motto; far more fitting than *Nemo me impune lacessit* . . . wha daur meddle wi' me?

That was what Nicola had been thinking when Bertie began to find the words to express himself.

"It's just that I was wondering," continued Bertie. "I was wondering whether . . . not that I'm actually saying we should do this, but I was just wondering: do you think that . . ."

She squeezed his hand. "Come on, Bertie, out

with it. You can say anything to me, you know that."

Bertie took a deep breath. He was a loyal child, and the expression of a sentiment as disloyal as the one he was about to reveal troubled him. "I was wondering whether I could come and live with you?"

There, he had said it. And the words, simple in themselves, and quietly uttered, nonetheless seemed to reverberate across the sky.

Nicola stopped. She looked down at her grandson. "Live with me, Bertie? In my flat?"

Bertie nodded. He did not dare meet Nicola's eye but stared firmly at the pavement. And he was standing on a crack, directly across it, in such a way that no supernatural force, no matter how temporarily unobservant, could fail to notice.

"Yes," he said. His voice now sounded small and faltering.

Nicola squeezed his hand again. "You mean that you'd like to move out of Scotland Street altogether?"

He nodded.

Nicola was gentle. "But you're happy enough, aren't you? You're happy living with Daddy and Ulysses and . . ." She had to summon up all her reserves to complete the sentence. ". . . And Mummy?"

Bertie shook his head. "No, I'm not, Granny. I'm not happy. I want to come and stay in your house and do these things with you. Go to the Portrait Gallery. Eat pizzas. Watch films."

Nicola swallowed hard. "Oh, Bertie, my darling wee boy." She bent down and put her arms around him. What could she possibly say to this request—a request that came from a small and sorrowful heart?

Another bus went slowly past and then stopped, waiting for traffic to clear. It was only a few feet from them, and as Nicola looked out from her embrace, out beyond Bertie's shoulder on which her hand rested, she found herself staring straight into the eyes of one of the passengers on the bus, a woman of about her own age. The woman was looking back at her, and seemed to know, in an instant, what she was witnessing. Only a pane of glass lay between them, and that is too little to suppress fellow feeling—as when we see a person who weeps on one side of a barrier while we are on another. Human barriers are permeable to tears—and always have been.

23

At Valvona & Crolla

Bertie, though, was filled with regret. Having asked Nicola whether he could come to live with her, from her reaction he realised immediately that this was an impossible request. The roof you were allocated in life was the roof under which you had to continue to stay—at least until you were eighteen, when you could go and live in Glasgow if you were lucky. So, rather than persisting with an impossible demand, as most children of his age would do, Bertie backtracked.

"I don't really want to leave Scotland Street," he said, trying as hard as he could to sound cheerful. "I was just wondering, Granny—that's all."

Nicola said nothing, but hugged him more closely to her. What could she say? There was no freedom wand to wave—there never was.

"Well, be that as it may, Bertie," she said at last, releasing him from her embrace, "we need to get down to Valvona & Crolla and see whether we can find some . . ." she paused, watching his expression, and then added, ". . . some *panforte di Siena*. Would you like that?"

There was only one answer to that. There might be those who, for some inexplicable reason, do not like *panforte di Siena*; it is possible, too, that there are misguided souls who cannot abide truffles lightly sprinkled over scrambled eggs, or marzipan, or an Aberdeen buttery, or haggis— such people exist, of course—but Bertie was not one of them, at least when it came to *panforte di Siena.* So with a renewed spring in his step he accompanied Nicola the last few hundred yards to the inviting doors of Valvona & Crolla, registered providers of cheese to Holyroodhouse and others. And purveyors, too, of almost every sort of delicacy, hard, soft, or liquid, that the Italian peninsula gives to the world.

Mary Contini met them at the door. "So, Bertie," she said, "how's the Italian going?"

Bertie had regular Italian *conversazione* sessions with Irene, and was reasonably fluent in the language—rather better, in fact, than Irene herself, who made regular grammatical errors. The reason for that, of course, was that Irene rarely bothered to check whether what she said was correct, so convinced was she of her vision of the world: if the Italians used a slightly different construction from that which she chose to use, then that said more about the Italians than it did about her.

Bertie replied politely. "*Va bene, grazie.*" He did not enjoy his Italian *conversazione* sessions, but he was too polite to say this. Nor did he enjoy, for that matter, his yoga classes and his psychotherapy, but he had long since come to understand that these were features of the firmament under which he lived, and there was no point in arguing against your personal planets: these were as fixed in the heavens as Edinburgh Castle was on earth. And what made this hard to bear was the knowledge that whenever he proposed that one of his activities be dropped, then he would simply be told that he should be happy to be having something that many children would love to have, if only they had the means. Bertie simply did not believe this; he could not imagine that any child, anywhere, would willingly submit to psychotherapy, talk Italian— unless of course they *were* Italian—or submit to the ministrations of the teacher at *Yoga for Tots* who was constantly seeking to bend Bertie and other members of the yoga class into positions that human anatomy was simply not intended to assume.

Mary knew of Nicola's tastes, and so they were quickly led off to sample a consignment of *salame calabrese* that had arrived the previous day.

"This has wild Italian fennel seeds in it," explained Mary, as she cut off a slice and handed it to Nicola. "Highly recommended."

Bertie tried a piece too; it was a bit too spicy for him, but he was pleased that Nicola appeared to like it. His eyes, of course, had wandered and he had spotted the section on the shelves reserved for sweet products: for *amaretti di Saronna*, *anicini* and *canucci*. Mary Contini, noticing the direction of his gaze, led him by the hand to choose a suitable small box of *panforte*. That done, she suggested that the three of them go into the cafeteria in the back, where Bertie could sample his newly-acquired *panforte*.

Stuart arrived twenty minutes later, after Mary had left them in the café. Bertie rushed up to greet him, hugging his father's legs in a gesture that was as possessive as it was proud. Nicola watched, and swallowed.

"We had an interesting visit to the Portrait Gallery," she remarked to Stuart. "Bertie's compiling a list of portraits in that red book of his."

"I saw a picture of Professor Higgs," said Bertie. "He's looking at some sums on a board, and smiling."

"That's how they always portray physicists," said Stuart. "Look at those famous pictures of Einstein with all those symbols in chalk on the board behind him."

"No sign of Professor Higgs's boson, though," said Nicola, "although it must have been there in the picture."

"It's everywhere," said Bertie. "Even in your nose."

"Oh well," said Nicola, "we shall get by somehow."

Stuart nodded; it seemed to Nicola that he

was slightly distracted. Perhaps he was busy; sometimes his duties as a statistician in the Scottish Government weighed heavily on him, and this might be such a time. Of course there was the additional strain, she told herself, of Irene's return and the readjustment to normal family life after an unusual interlude.

"So, everything all right, Stuart?" asked Nicola.

Stuart nodded. He looked away.

"I saw Daddy in the museum," said Bertie brightly.

Nicola raised an eyebrow. "In Chambers Street? In the museum in Chambers Street?"

Bertie continued. "Yes. He was meeting a lady there."

Stuart glanced discouragingly at Bertie. Nicola noticed.

"Business," he said hurriedly. "One of my colleagues."

At that moment, Nicola knew that he was lying. Mothers know—they just know. Sons may try to lie to their mothers—some sons may lie to their mothers over years and years, but mothers always know. And at that moment, Nicola knew not only that Stuart was lying, but that he was having an affair.

She was delighted; the warmth arising within her was, she thought, not unlike that feeling one experiences when spring arrives and things begin to live again.

24

Silting Up

After twenty minutes of conversation, Stuart looked at his watch and declared that it was time to leave. Nicola glanced at Bertie, who briefly met her eyes, and then looked away. Under the table, she reached for his hand and held it briefly, knowing that there were things she could not say and he could not hear. Whatever Irene's faults—and where would one begin to enumerate them?—she was Bertie's mother, and he should stay with her. And yet, when Stuart had unwittingly revealed that he was having an affair, she felt not the normal regret that a mother would have on learning that all was not well with her son's marriage, but unalloyed joy at the thought that at long last Stuart was making a break for freedom. The initial euphoria that accompanied this realisation, of course, would soon be tempered by concern about what this would mean for Bertie and Ulysses, but there would be time enough for that later on; for the moment, all that mattered was that Stuart was showing some signs of resistance to tyranny— and tyranny, Nicola thought, was not too strong a word for Irene's regime.

"So," said Nicola, as she rose from the table in the Valvona & Crolla cafeteria, "what lies ahead this afternoon?"

Stuart was helping Bertie with his coat. "Bertie is going to . . ."

"Yoga," said Bertie, with a sigh. "Mummy's taking me to yoga in Stockbridge."

"Well, isn't that nice?" said Nicola, summoning all her resources. "And is Ulysses going too?"

Bertie nodded. "He's hopeless at yoga because he doesn't know how to walk yet. So he lies on the ground and Mummy lifts his arms and legs up and down."

Nicola exchanged a glance with Stuart. He looked away quickly, and she thought: *he knows, he knows! Of course he knows how ridiculous that woman is.*

"And what about you, Stuart?" she asked.

He took a few moments to reply, and she noticed the hesitation. "I was thinking of going for a walk," he said. "Later this afternoon."

"How wise," said Nicola. "We should all be walking more. Did you read about the latest advice on this? We should get up from our desks, they say, and walk around the room every fifteen minutes."

"That sounds reasonable enough."

"Because there is nothing worse than sitting at a desk all day without moving," Nicola continued. "Apparently you silt up that way."

Stuart nodded vaguely; he was thinking of people in the office who had silted up. There were quite a few, he decided, and for a moment he imagined their obituaries, *Died of silt* . . . It would be a fate redolent of being swallowed by quicksand—not a common fate, he imagined, but one that presumably did overtake people from time to time. As a statistician he was well aware of the surprising ways in which people left this life, and just how many succumbed to the rarer strokes of fate. There were forty-six thousand people killed by snakebite in India each year—the real figure, Stuart had read, in spite of official claims that it was only two thousand; and as for shark attacks, he had seen a report that the risk of being eaten by a shark was one in 913,200,766. That was not a significant risk, but it did not take into account that many people never swam in the sea at all, whereas some took their surfboards into the very waves where great whites liked to lurk. Their risk, surely, was considerably greater.

Nicola ended his reverie. "Are you going to walk in the Pentlands, perhaps? It's a nice afternoon for it. Remember how we used to go there?"

He did—and she did too, remembering Stuart as a boy, in those grey trousers of his, the serge ones built to withstand the ravages of active boyhood, clambering down towards the Logan Burn with the wind off Scald Law behind them. The memory brought a pang, as such memories often do; the world was more innocent then, or at least Scotland was.

Stuart shook his head. "No, not in the Pentlands."

"We went there once," interjected Bertie. "Remember, Daddy? We went fishing in Glencorse Reservoir and I almost caught a trout."

Stuart smiled. "I remember that very well, Bertie."

"And then we got lost on the way back and that haar came down and . . ."

"And we ended up at that farmhouse," Stuart said. "And there was a wee boy there, about your age—what was his name?"

"He was called Andy," said Bertie. "He was my friend."

"Of course he was," said Stuart.

For a moment, they were silent—all three of them—each with a memory, and then Nicola said, "So where will you have your walk, Stuart?"

Stuart shrugged. "In town. Maybe along the Water of Leith. There's that path you can follow."

She realised that he did not want to be more specific, and she knew the reason why.

"Well," she said, "I might come to Scotland Street later on."

Stuart looked at her sharply.

"No, not to the flat," said Nicola hurriedly. "I was going to visit Domenica. She asked me to pop in and I thought I might do so this afternoon."

Stuart nodded. "I saw her yesterday—she said something about that."

He was glad that his mother and Domenica seemed to have established a friendship. Stuart had always admired Domenica, even if he was slightly in awe of her intellectual ability and her reading, which was so much wider than his own. He struggled to remember what he had read; he had read a fair amount, and he wanted to read more, but he always found himself too tired to read in the evenings when he came back to the flat after a day of juggling with statistics.

They made their way out of the shop. Nicola had shopping to do, and so she kissed Bertie goodbye outside the delicatessen. As she bent down to kiss him, she whispered, "Don't worry, Bertie—life has a way of getting better, you know."

He looked up at her, and nodded. "I'm all right," he said.

She left them, but turned to look over her shoulder as she made her way up Elm Row. She saw Stuart leading Bertie across the road towards Gayfield Square. How strange, she thought, that anybody else, looking at this scene, would see only a man and his young son walking hand in hand and presumably think nothing more of it, whereas the real story was almost Shakespearian in its intensity.

25

The Anthropology of Electricity

Nicola called on Domenica at three thirty that afternoon. She entered the main door of 44 Scotland Street with some trepidation. It was, of course, the address of her son and grandson, and as such was rich in positive associations, but it was, of course, also Irene's address, and that was a different matter altogether. The stone stair that wound its way past the Pollock door and up to Domenica's flat on the top floor was deserted when she came in, but there was always the possibility that Irene could emerge onto the landing—perhaps on her way to yoga with Bertie and Ulysses. If that happened, Nicola would have to manage the encounter as best she could. She would be polite and would ask after Irene's health, perhaps even going so far as to enquire whether she was missing the desert. No, she thought, perhaps not that; one did not ask those recently released whether they missed the place of their durance. So she would confine herself to an anodyne remark about the weather; Irene usually disagreed with everything Nicola said—sometimes quite volubly—but she could hardly dispute an observation on the fineness of the afternoon. Or could she?

Nicola imagined the exchange.

"It's a nice afternoon, isn't it?" she would say.

And Irene would reply, "Hardly. If you think back to what it was like last year at this time, then you'd hardly say it was nice today. It's much colder."

To which Nicola might reply, soothingly, "Well, at least it isn't raining."

Normally that might be conceded, but not by Irene, who would probably say, "But we need rain. Haven't you read about the level of the reservoirs?" She would then add, cuttingly, "Perhaps you don't care about such things."

And at that point it might even deteriorate, with Nicola saying, "Yes, rain is good for the grass, and cows need grass, Irene, as you, more than others, should know . . ."

But she would never say that, tempting though it might be. Nicola had recently read a magazine article entitled *Keeping your channels of communication open,* and the advice of the writer, described, as the writers of such articles often are, as a *prominent psychologist and life-style expert,* had urged readers never to stop talking civilly to those whom they found difficult. It was good advice, and she realised that it applied to her. If she ratcheted up the gap between her and Irene— if indeed one could ratchet up a gap, which she thought one probably could not—then that could compromise her access to her grandchildren. So not only should channels be kept open but metaphors, she thought, should be kept unmixed.

She need not have worried. The common stair of No. 44 Scotland Street was deserted and silent, with not even the sound of a radio or conversation drifting out from under the landing doors. The thick walls of Edinburgh buildings—several feet of stone in most cases— were effective at deadening sound from outside; floors and ceilings, separated by thick layers of ancient clinker, had a similar effect on descending and ascending noise. Only stairwells provided, in the right conditions, a common acoustic space, allowing conversations in the entrance hall or on the first flight of steps to be listened to on the top landing. This led, of course, to a general lowering of voices lest neighbours hear; the *Edinburgh whisper,* a way of speaking still encountered in places, was a direct result of this phenomenon, and was, in the view of some, the explanation for the traditional success of Edinburgh candidates in the upper echelons of the British Civil Service.

The fact that nobody could hear what was said in the *Edinburgh whisper* meant that those using it were thought to be both discreet and endowed with extraordinary wisdom—the latter on the grounds that what we cannot hear is usually believed to be considerably more important than what is plainly audible: a principle equally applicable to beauty—those we cannot see are almost certainly more attractive than those we can see close-up; to food in restaurants—those dishes we see passing us by on their way to other tables are inevitably more delicious than those we have ourselves chosen, *Mahlneid* (food envy) being the German composite noun for such a conviction; and to the romantic lives of others, which are almost always more exciting than our own. The popularity of Tolstoy's *Anna Karenina*, of course, is a great antidote to that last feeling, especially in Scotland, where there is a strong view that all enjoyment will be paid for sooner or later—except in relation to public spending, which is free.

On the top landing, Domenica answered the door to her pressing of the bell and led her into the kitchen. Nicola saw that the pine table in the centre of the room was littered with papers, topped by a copy of a journal, opened and spread out. "I'm obviously disturbing you," she said.

Domenica smiled. "I was ready for tea. I've been reading."

Nicola picked up the journal and glanced at the cover. It was an anthropological review and the issue was dedicated, a heading announced, to the anthropology of electricity.

"The anthropology of electricity?"

Domenica nodded. "Fascinating. That's cultural anthropology. It may concern itself with anything that affects human life."

Nicola read out the title of one of the papers. " 'The Charge against Electricity.'" She replaced the journal on the table and looked up at Domenica. "Really?"

Domenica reached for the journal and paged through it. "That was actually the article I was reading," she said. "It's rather good. It presents both sides." She remembered the old Hebridean saying *Tha dà thaobh air a'Mhaoil—The Minch has two sides.* So many people's Minch these days had only one.

Nicola wondered how there could be two sides to the issue of electricity. "I would have thought that electricity was overwhelmingly desirable." She paused. "Don't you think people without electricity would take that view?"

"Like food and water? As desirable as those?"

Nicola thought for a moment. "Not entirely. Food and water are absolute essentials—along with oxygen. But once you have those . . ."

"Then you yearn for electricity?" Domenica asked.

"Yes, I think you do."

Domenica nodded. "I think you're right," she said. "But I think we need to be aware that the things we want may not be good for

140

us—or may change our lives in ways we may not at first detect, but which are very significant." She crossed the kitchen floor as she spoke and switched on the kettle.

26

We Are Surrounded by New Puritans

Over their cup of tea in Scotland Street it was not the anthropology of electricity that formed the basis of the conversation between Domenica Macdonald and Nicola Tavares de Lumiares (formerly Pollock, and now on the verge of returning to Pollock); rather it was the mundane parish-pump chat that people so relish: the prospects of a popular tennis player at Wimbledon, the relative merits of the Cameo and Dominion cinemas, and the attractions of the sausages made by the local butcher, Mr. Crombie. It was a wide agenda, but at the end of half an hour a great deal of progress had been made in addressing the issues raised: the tennis match was a foregone conclusion, they agreed; the Dominion Cinema was still superior to the Cameo, although both were exceptionally good; and when it came to sausages there was nobody to rival Mr. Crombie in Edinburgh, or possibly the whole of Scotland. With these subjects out of the way, Domenica suggested that they walk to the National Gallery of Modern Art for the exhibition entitled *Scottish Treasures: Paintings at the Heart of Scotland*. She had received an invitation to the private viewing, which would be at the unusually early hour of five in the evening.

"I've had an invitation," she said, "as a Friend of the Gallery and Angus had his own—*ex officio* as a trustee of the Scottish Artists' Benevolent Fund. Mine says, *Domenica Macdonald and Partner . . .*" She paused. "Two observations there, I think, Nicola. Firstly, I'm officially Dr. Domenica Macdonald—not that I make a great thing about my PhD. But if somebody has a PhD and you don't use the title that could mean that . . ."

"That you cast doubts on their PhD?"

"Yes, or that you think that they're showing off. Which they may not be doing at all."

"What about all those other titles?" said Nicola. "Monsignor. Very Reverend. Provost. Dean. Professor. Sir. The Right Honourable. The ordinary Honourable. Sister. Matron . . ."

Domenica laughed. "Grand Pooh-Bah. Yes, it's Ruritanian, isn't it? But they may serve a purpose—especially the last two you mentioned."

"Sister and Matron?"

Domenica said that both were, in her view, titles of particular honour. "I have the greatest possible respect for nurses," she said. "That is, for nurses who sit by your side and wipe your brow or give you water to drink—that sort of nurse. They're the real heroines. And if they've reached sister status, then that's a great title to give them. Sister. Wonderful—richly deserved. And it says so much in moral terms. I am your sister—I am *with* you. I'm here to be your sister in your time of need."

"And matron?"

"We need to bring her back," said Domenica. "I was talking to Big Lou the other day and she said she had had somebody in her coffee bar—a doctor—who was making that point. He said that a hospital without matron was like a ship without a captain."

"I agree," said Nicola. "My father had a friend, a doctor, who used to run the Victoria Infirmary over in Glasgow. He ran it with a wonderful matron. He looked after the medical side, and she looked after the nursing. They would never have tolerated—not for one second—the sort of neglect that we've heard goes on these days in hospitals. Patients lying on trolleys for hours. Patients in dirty beds and so on. And he did the hospital rounds with his dog, would you believe it?"

"I can."

"The dog went everywhere with him when he went around the wards. The only place it wasn't allowed to go was into theatre—it had to sit outside the door and wait for him to come out."

"And the patients loved it?"

"Of course they loved it," said Nicola. "It cheered them up. It helped them get better. As did matron. The sight of her starched uniform was a complete tonic."

"We need these figures," reflected Domenica. "We need bank managers who dress like bank managers and give you a cup of tea while discussing your overdraft. We need dentists who wear blue jackets buttoned up at the front. We need head-waiters in white jackets. We need people who occupy roles and wear clothing to prove it. It's a form of social reassurance. It represents order, and we need order. We don't need chaos and confusion. In short, we need civilisation, and if you chip away at any of its pillars—in the name of informality or whatever—you also weaken the underpinnings. At the end of the day you have what Hobbes warned us about—the opposite of civilisation."

"The opposite of civilisation . . ."

"Yes, a society—if one can call it a society—in which the sense of what binds people together is absent. A society in which there is no community. A society in which we are strangers to one another, and unconcerned about the fate of those about us. A society that is selfish and greedy and doesn't care about public goods. A society that doesn't believe in public libraries or in helping the sick. A lonely place, a cave of ice, a soulless desert."

Domenica finished her warning before returning to the invitation she had received. "A second point," she said. "*Partner* is confusing. A lot of people these days interpret that as being your *bidie-in*, but some don't. Some think it's just partner as in 'friend' or person who happens to accompany you to things, or dances with you: *Take your partners for the Dashing White Sergeant.*" She paused. "Of course all these Scottish dances are going to have to change. *Gay Gordons* is obviously not inclusive enough; that'll have to change. When it comes to the *Duke of Perth*—elitist if ever there was an elitist name for a dance."

Nicola laughed.

"Don't laugh, Nicola," warned Domenica. "Remember that we are surrounded by New Puritans these days. You'll only have to apologise if you're found laughing. *Ms. Nicola Pollock deeply regrets laughing at an inappropriate comment passed by Ms. Domenica Macdonald and wishes to ensure people that she will not laugh at anything very much in the future.*"

Nicola made an effort to look contrite. "I'm going to miss tasteless jokes," she said ruefully. "Once humour is sanitised, it becomes pretty dull, doesn't it?"

Domenica agreed. "We shall just have to remember them and laugh without any explanation of why we're laughing. We shall have *memory jokes*—things that we once thought funny but can no longer admit to finding amusing. Like that one about the two Glaswegians, the Pope, and crème de menthe. How we all laughed."

"But nobody could take offence at *that*."

Domenica frowned. "If you come from Glasgow you might. It suggests that some Glaswegians drink too much."

"So we can't tell that joke any more?"

"No."

"Why?"

"Because those Glaswegians who drink too much won't like it."

"But what about Edinburgh? There must be plenty of people in Edinburgh who drink too much."

"There are," conceded Domenica. "But somehow it's not so funny."

27

Clare Talks to Bruce

Clare Hodding was pleased that Bruce was paying such attention to her story.

"You know something, Bruce?" she said, as they lay side-by-side on the sofa of her Newington flat. "Some men don't listen to what you tell them. No, I'm not saying you're one of them, but . . ."

"Of course I'm not one of them," interrupted Bruce. "I'm a new man, Clare baby: I always listen to women. I *feel* for women."

Clare glanced at him. "Don't come the raw prawn with me, Bruce," she said.

Bruce smiled. "I'd never do that. Mind you, I do like your Aussie expressions. Raw prawn? That's great. Very expressive. Any others?"

Clare looked up at the ceiling. It made her sad to think of Australia, of home, of her friends, of the casual friendliness she missed so much; of the smell of the bush and the sound of the wind in the eucalyptus trees, like waves upon a shore.

"Other expressions? Oh yes, there are plenty of those."

"Give me one."

She tried to remember. "Well, do you know

what it means if you say somebody's got kangaroos loose in the top paddock?"

Bruce thought for a moment. "I'd say they were a sandwich short of the whole picnic," he said.

"More or less," said Clare. "And what's 'to take a Pommie shower'?"

Bruce shook his head. "No idea."

"To use deodorant," said Clare.

"Very unfair," said Bruce.

Clare laughed. "Slang always is, isn't it?"

Bruce wanted to get back to Clare's story. "So you enjoyed being an air stewardess?"

Clare corrected him. "Cabin attendant," she said. "Yes, I did. It was great. I had some terrific runs: there was a period when I went to Bali a lot. We often had lay-overs in Bali—a day or two before going back to Perth or Brisbane." She paused. "And LA. We went to LA quite a bit. I liked that. I went to Hollywood, you know. You can go there. It's a bit tacky when you get close up, but you see some extraordinary things."

"Such as?"

"I saw one of the stars once. I was in a coffee bar and this guy came in—all natural, same as anybody else—and ordered a *latte*. And everybody was looking at him—I swear the whole place stopped talking and stared at him."

"A celeb?" asked Bruce.

"More than that—a star. An actual star."

"So what happened?"

"Well, they gave him his *latte* and he took it to a table."

"No!"

Clare dug him in the ribs. "Don't be sarcastic. Do you want to hear this or not?"

"I'm all ears," said Bruce. "This star took his coffee to his table. And then?"

"He sat down and started to drink it. Then his phone went and he answered it. He cupped his hand round it so people couldn't hear what he was saying."

"He was probably talking to another star," suggested Bruce.

Clare agreed. "Probably. Anyway, after a while he left and everybody started talking again. They were all talking about him, I think."

"Who was he?" asked Bruce.

"I can't remember. Anyway, I asked somebody at the table next to mine and she said, 'Oh, it's so-and-so.' She was surprised I didn't know. Apparently he acted the part of somebody or other in something big. She said that he had been nominated for an Oscar but hadn't won because his eyebrows weren't quite right."

"So that was LA," muttered Bruce. "Quite the place."

"Yes, but as I said, there's a tacky side to it. If you go into a restaurant there are all these wannabe actors hoping that somebody will notice them. Apparently if a director comes in for a meal there is always a massive fight to see who can serve at that table. Sometimes it gets really nasty."

"People want to be in the movies," said Bruce. "I turned down offers, you know."

Clare was impressed. "To be in the movies?"

"Yes," said Bruce. "I've been asked."

Her incredulity showed. "And you said no?"

"Yup. Got other things to do."

Clare leaned over and delicately licked the tip of his nose. "You're so cute, Bruce. Seriously cute. You would have been great on the screen."

Bruce nodded. "I suppose so. But there we are." He paused. Why did she keep licking the tip of his nose? Nobody had ever done that to him before and he was not sure how to react. Did she want him to lick the tip of her nose? He was not sure that he wanted to do that.

"Tell me what happened," he continued. "Why did you leave the airline?"

Clare laughed. "It left me, actually. It was such a stupid thing. It should never have happened. And it wasn't my fault."

"I didn't think it would be," said Bruce.

"We were on a long-haul flight," Clare said. "The plane was going from London to Sydney, via Singapore. I had flown up on a different flight from Melbourne to Singapore, and I had two days there before I was due to fly back down to Sydney. Have you ever been to Singapore, Bruce?"

Bruce shook his head. "Not yet. It's on the list, though."

"It's a great place," said Clare. "It's really hygienic, you know. You can go and eat at a roadside stall and be absolutely confident that you won't pick up something. Try to do that in some places and you're dead. Big time." She grimaced. "I had a friend, you know—somebody I worked with on the airline—who went somewhere dodgy and ate rice from a buffet. I think it was in Vietnam. Anyway she was in a perfectly good hotel somewhere or other—one with good TripAdvisor ratings—and there was this buffet, see, and she took some rice from it. Bad mistake. Never, ever eat rice from a hotel buffet in places like that. The reason? You know the reason?"

Bruce shook his head.

"It's because rice is an ideal breeding ground for the organisms that cause food poisoning. They love it. They get in there and they say *let's multiply* and they do. And then what do the hotel staff do, Bruce? I'll tell you. When all the guests have had their lunch and there's still a lot of rice left on the buffet, the waiters take the rice back to the kitchen and they keep it for use the next day. So when the next lunchtime comes round, what have you got? You've got whole colonies of bacteria and viruses too. Viruses like rice as well—a virus *loves* rice, Bruce."

Clare drew breath. "So this friend of mine

151

ate some of this rice and she started to feel sick about four hours later. And she became sicker and sicker and ended up in hospital. She was on a drip, Bruce, because, well, not to put too fine a point on it, she was pretty dehydrated by having to go off to the dunny all the time. And you know what? They said she could have died. Actually died, as in dead, Bruce."

"As in *dead* dead?"

"Yes. But she didn't die. She lived."

"As in *alive?*"

"Yes."

28
On the Flight Deck

"So there you were in Singapore," said Bruce.

"Yes, ready to go on duty," said Clare. "So we were collected from the hotel and taken out to the airport. It was all pretty straightforward. Briefing from the Purser, signing for the supplies and so on. Passenger manifest. An absolutely routine flight." She stared up at the ceiling as she continued. "I was on duty in Business Class, which is always better than being in Economy. You don't get as many difficult passengers there—usually. They can be demanding, but you don't get kids being sick all over the place or nuns with guitars—only joking. I actually had a nun with a guitar on board once, you know—the real thing. When I saw her I thought she must be an actress, but she was an actual nun. If we'd got into difficulty—if the plane started to go down or anything like that—I'm pretty sure she would have calmed the passengers down by singing something appropriate.

"Anyway, I was in Business Class and everything was going smoothly. We had served drinks once we took off and were taking orders for lunch. I was working the first few rows and one of the others was doing the next ones. You know the sort of thing—*Are you going to be having the salmon or the beef en croute?* Not exactly rocket science, but you have to make people think you really care about what they're going to have.

"Everything was going fine—and then we hit turbulence. Now most turbulence, Bruce, is not too bad. The plane just bumps about a bit, but nothing serious happens. This was like that— it was pretty mild, but the Captain decided to switch on the seat belt sign and everybody had to return to their seats. No big deal.

"I went up to the front and began to work back down the cabin to check up that everyone was belted in. We suspended cabin service, naturally, until the Captain gave the say-so.

"Well, there I was, going down the rows, and in the third row there's this guy sitting there without

153

his belt on. So I ask him to fasten his seat belt and he ignores me. He completely ignores me. So I tell him that he really needs to do it because the fasten seat belts sign is on. And then he gets up and sort of brushes past me to go and talk to this friend of his a few rows back.

"I say to him, *Listen sir, you have to get back to your seat—the Captain has switched on the seat belt sign.*"

Bruce was wide-eyed. "And did he do it?"

Clare shook her head. "He completely ignored me."

"So what did you do? Tell the Captain?"

Clare sighed. "That's what they said I should have done. But I didn't. I grabbed him and tried to push him back towards his seat."

Bruce whistled. "Well . . ."

"He didn't like it," Clare went on. "He started to kick me—he really did. And so I hit him in the stomach and when he bent forward I gave him a sort of karate chop on the back of the neck. He didn't like that one bit."

"He wouldn't," said Bruce.

"Then the Purser came along and calmed him down. He led him to his seat and crouched down and talked to him for a while. Then he came back to where I was standing and he said, 'You know who that was?' I said, 'It was an unruly passenger—that's who it was.' And he said something about not trying to be

154

smart—something like that, and then he said, 'That's the Prime Minister of New Zealand.' "

Bruce let out a hoot of laughter. "You didn't! The Prime Minister of New Zealand!"

"Not the current one," said Clare. "This was someone called Jones. He didn't last very long, but he was Prime Minister at the time. How was I to know? Who can be expected to know who the Kiwi Prime Minister is? They keep changing them."

"You were in the right," Bruce observed. "You can't have people walking about planes when the seat belt sign is on. Anarchy."

"Too true. But did the airline think that? Oh no, the Purser went off to the Captain and he asked to speak to me right away. It was like being sent to the Principal's office."

Bruce sympathised. "Poor you."

"So I go up to the flight deck and there's the Captain sitting there reading a magazine while the plane flew itself. The First Officer was painting his nails. I'm not making this up, Bruce—I swear I'm not. And the Captain says to me, 'I hear you've hit the Prime Minister of New Zealand.' And then he wags his finger at me—like this—and says, 'Naughty! Naughty!' "

"Bizarre," said Bruce.

"And then the First Officer pipes up and says something like, 'You're for the naughty stool, sunshine!' "

"I can't stand it when people call me *sunshine*," said Bruce. "It gets right up my left nostril."

Clare considered this for a moment. "I don't like being called *doll*," she said. "There was this passenger once who kept calling me *doll*. It really got to me. So I . . ." She hesitated.

"Go on," said Bruce. "Tell me."

"Well, this is a secret of the trade, so to speak. Don't spread it around, but you know how cabin crew sort out people they really don't like? They open the luggage bin above the passenger's seat, pretending they have to rearrange things, and then they drop a case on the person's head. They say *Oops!* and make out they're really sorry, but it's always intentional."

Bruce stared at her in astonishment. "So you did that?"

Clare shook her head. "No, that's the nuclear option. I opted for the response just below that. I spilt a drink on his lap."

"Going back to the Captain," said Bruce, "what did he do?"

It was evident that the recollection was painful. Clare lowered her eyes as she spoke. "He suspended me from duty. I had to go and sit right at the back of Economy for the rest of the trip. It was like being a prison warder and being sent to prison. I was right there among them. I felt seriously ashamed."

"And that was the end of your career?" asked Bruce.

"Yes."

"And then?"

"I came to Scotland." She paused. "I met you and . . . and the rest is history."

"I'm glad we met," said Bruce.

She looked at him fondly. Then she leaned forward and very gently and precisely licked the tip of his nose.

29

More Things in Heaven and Earth

While Clare was relating her past to Bruce, out at Nine Mile Burn Elspeth and Matthew were closely examining Rognvald, one of their triplets.

"I can't really see in this light," complained Elspeth. "Get a torch, Matthew. Then we can shine it right into his mouth."

They were in the kitchen at the time, and Rognvald, who was just beginning to take his first uncertain steps, was struggling to free himself from his mother's parental grip.

"Don't let him fall over," said Elspeth when Matthew returned with the torch.

"He won't stand still," said Matthew. "Rognvald's much steadier on his feet."

"This *is* Rognvald," Elspeth pointed out.

Matthew blushed. "I meant to say Tobermory," he said hurriedly.

Elspeth assured him that she was not criticising him. "I can get them mixed up too," she said. "But I've worked out a way of telling them apart. I think Rognvald's ears are a little bit smaller than Tobermory's. And Fergus has got a little mark on his chin, a freckle—not very big, but the others don't have it."

She took the torch from Matthew and then gently parted Rognvald's lips. Shining the torch into his mouth, she peered at a small circular mark. "It's very red," she said.

Matthew leaned forward. "It's difficult to tell," he said. "Mouths are naturally red."

"Yes, but not that red. And look, there's another one."

"Mouth ulcers?"

"I think so. And it would explain why he wouldn't have his food at lunchtime. He threw it down on the floor. All of it—which is unlike him, as he's normally a little hog."

"What did Patty say when you phoned her?"

Patty was a cousin of Elspeth's who was a paediatrician at the Sick Kids' Hospital.

"She said we should look for any other spots. She said to watch him and take him to the doctor if we find anything or if he seems really unwell."

"Where?" asked Matthew. "Where should we look for spots?"

"She said the hands," answered Elspeth. "Also the soles of his feet."

"And what did she think it was?"

"I wrote it down," said Elspeth. "Over there. That piece of paper."

Matthew picked up the piece of paper lying on the table and began to read it. "Hand-Foot-Mouth disease," he read. "I thought that was what cattle got."

"They get Foot and Mouth," said Elspeth. "Different virus. I've written down the name of the virus. It's there."

Matthew read on. "Coxsackie virus. Is that it?"

Elspeth had now taken off one of Rognvald's socks and was flashing the torch on the sole of his foot.

"Matthew!" she exclaimed. "Hundreds of them. Spots. Look."

Matthew peered at his son's foot. "Oh dear," he said. "That must be uncomfortable. Poor wee boy."

"He doesn't seem to be noticing them," said Elspeth. "Little stoic!"

"Brave boy," said Matthew, tickling Rognvald under the chin.

Elspeth stood up. "Patty offered to drop by," she said. "I'm going to ask her."

She left Rognvald with Matthew while she

made the telephone call. The other two boys were with Birgitte and Anna, playing in the garden before it was time for bath and bed. Her cousin, who lived in Fairmilehead and who therefore did not have a long journey to make, assured her that it would be no trouble to call round. She was at a loose end, she said, as her fiancé, with whom she lived, was an engineer on an oil rig and was away for the entire week.

Half an hour later she was with them, drawing up to the front door in the battered red coupé she had bought at medical school in Aberdeen and that had served her well since then. Matthew greeted her and took her through to the kitchen, where Rognvald was being entertained with a set of brightly coloured building bricks.

Patty knelt down to join him at his play.

"Well now, young Rognvald," she said. "Who's heading for the building industry?"

Rognvald looked at her briefly, and then, in the casually rude manner of all small children, returned to his play. Patty looked at the exposed soles of his feet.

"Yes," she said. "Typical."

She managed to turn his head briefly while she expertly examined his mouth.

"Yes," she said. "Probably what I said over the phone." She moved to the sink to wash her hands. "It's not very infectious to adults. It can be highly contagious, though, with infants.

Spreads like wildfire. Are the others all right?"

Elspeth said she thought they were.

"Have you taken his temperature?" asked Patty.

Elspeth nodded. "It's up."

"It has a febrile effect," said Patty. "I mean, it can lead to fever. But the main symptom is those spots in typical places—hands, feet, and mouth. Hence the name." She paused. "But it's not really anything to worry too much about. He'll probably be fine in a week or so. The others will probably come out in spots soon."

Elspeth and her cousin sat down to a cup of coffee while Matthew took Rognvald off to join the other two boys. There was a certain amount of family news to be exchanged: the illness of an uncle in Dunfermline, the graduation of another cousin who had been studying to become a dental hygienist, and the arrival of Patty's brother's second baby. Those details exchanged, Elspeth asked Patty about her work. She had recently sat a further set of professional examinations and was awaiting the results.

"But we're all busy," Patty said. "It doesn't get any quieter. Particularly in the summer, when children get out a bit more. Our casualty department can be worked off its feet at times."

"I suppose there are also lots of children swallowing things," said Elspeth. "I've always imagined that must form a major part of the business at the Sick Kids'."

Patty laughed. "We had a very strange case a couple of days ago. A three-year-old was brought in by his mother. She said that she had seen him swallow a 2p coin. She was adamant that it had gone down. So we said that she should take him back and wait for nature to take its course— it usually does, and the coin can be recovered when it's gone through the system. Fairly straightforward."

"And all went well?"

"Well, this is the extraordinary thing. She telephoned and said that she'd been vigilant and, lo and behold, the money eventually appeared. But—and listen to this—it was now two 1p coins! Can you believe it? Change!"

"Surely not . . ."

"The doctor in charge was flabbergasted. She's going to write it up for the *British Medical Journal*—perhaps for their Christmas issue, which likes cheerful little articles."

"But . . ." began Elspeth.

Patty shrugged. "What does Hamlet say to Horatio?" she asked.

30

On the Success of Others

Matthew had taken Rognvald back to join his as yet uninfected brothers, leaving Elspeth to see her cousin out to her car.

"We must see more of one another," said Patty. "It's ridiculous—we live within a few miles of one another and yet we hardly ever meet."

"Yes," agreed Elspeth. "But I know how busy you are. And your job must make it difficult to have much of a social life."

Patty sighed. "I cope. And what about you? You must have your hands full with the boys. One's hard enough—but three!"

"I manage. I've got those Danish au pairs, you see . . . and Matthew's a very hands-on dad."

"Yet boys . . ."

It was Elspeth's turn to sigh. "You know, I look at my friends who have girls and I think, *How easy it must be for you.* Girls play quietly with their dolls; they don't rush around destroying whatever's in sight. There's no kicking, shoving, pushing. No testing the breakability of things."

Patty smiled. "Yes, boys are different. And men too."

"Yet we're expected to deny it. We're so busy

trying to promote the notion that there are no differences . . ."

Patty took this up. "Thereby ignoring the evidence of biology. Men and women are different—they just are. That's not to say that some of these differences aren't socially constructed . . . of course they are, but you can't deny certain basic attributes."

"Yet they do," said Elspeth. "The deniers, that is. They make the fundamental mistake of saying that what they want to be the case *is* the case." She paused. "And have you noticed something else, Patty? Have you noticed how people think it's all right to run down men? To say that men are dim or insensitive? That women are far more competent at all sorts of things?"

She looked at her cousin, and saw that her words resonated. She knew that she had to be careful: to express a view contrary to the received opinion, the policed consensus, could be dangerous. As in Stalinist Russia, in contemporary Scotland even a cousin might turn one in . . .

"Oh, I've noticed that," said Patty. "People think they can say anything derogatory about men—things they'd never dare say about women—and rightly so. It's called gender defamation, I think—something like that."

"Poor men," sighed Elspeth. "Discriminated against. Condescended to. Labelled as incompetent."

"All the things that used to happen to women," murmured Patty.

"Two wrongs don't make a right," said Elspeth.

Patty did not disagree. But she remembered something. "I saw a report in the paper of a visit a well-known politician made to an all-girls' school."

"Are there any left?"

"One or two. Anyway, he went there to give prizes at the speech day—you know, the usual thing. Where a girl called Flora Thompson, or whoever, gets all the prizes—tennis, mathematics, poetry, art and so on; awful girl . . ."

Elspeth stopped her. "Flora Thompson?"

"I was just making up the name. She could be called anything . . ."

"But she *was* called Flora Thompson. I remember her. She was in my year at school. She won everything—*everything*. She used to sit at the desk in front of me and when we had tests she would always finish twenty minutes before the rest of us. She'd put down her pen and look round at us with a look that said *What's taking you so long?*"

"I really wasn't talking about anybody in particular. Flora Thompson's a very common name."

Elspeth assured Patty that she understood that; there were numerous Flora Thompsons, she said. There was more, though, that she wanted to say about *her* Flora Thompson. "She had a bag that she used to carry round," she said. "She kept her books in it. And her pen. And her gym shoes. It was made of blueish canvas-type stuff. And it had *Flora Thompson* sewn on it. And underneath, in smaller letters, was *Ravelston Dykes*. That's where she came from, you see—Ravelston Dykes."

Patty laughed. "I can see it. I'm sure that there are plenty of entirely unobjectionable people who come from Ravelston Dykes, but somehow . . ."

"Exactly."

"What happened to her?"

"After she left school? After she had finished being head girl?"

"Yes. She must have had a brilliant career somewhere. After all, if you're Flora Thompson from Ravelston Dykes . . ."

"She went to Oxford. Somerville College."

"Of course. Of course. Where she got a first?"

"Yes. In something like Sanskrit."

"And then?"

Patty waited.

"So you really want to hear?" asked Elspeth.

"Yes, of course."

Elspeth smiled. "Do you want to hear about her fall?"

Patty did not conceal her delight. "I knew it! I knew that something awful would happen to her.

Nemesis never lets these people get away with it."

"But what if there's no fall? Would you be disappointed?"

Patty's grin faded. "You're going to tell me she found a wonderful man? You're going to tell me about her meteoric rise in the City of London? You are, aren't you?"

"I read about her wedding in the former pupils' mag. There was a picture of Flora with a very handsome man. Really handsome . . ."

Patty winced. "To die for?"

"Yes, to die for. He raced vintage cars down in the Borders. He had a house somewhere near Kelso, I think. And his family had a marmalade factory. You see their marmalade in the supermarkets. They're big marmalade people."

"I don't want to hear about that. I just don't."

"I looked very closely at the photograph," Elspeth went on. "I wanted to see if there was something wrong with his looks—just anything would do. Some flaw. A weak jaw. Even a mole would have helped."

"And there wasn't?"

"No, he was perfect. He was just so beautiful."

"Rats!"

"Well there's more," Elspeth continued. "She got herself into the *Guinness Book of Records*. The fastest ascent of Ben Nevis by any woman— ever. There it is: *Flora Thompson*."

Patty closed her eyes.

"Why do we resent the success of others?" asked Elspeth. "We should be glad for Flora Thompson."

They were silent. They stood on the drive outside the house and were silent.

"Perhaps we need to forgive her," said Elspeth.

"Or ourselves," added Patty. "We need to forgive ourselves for not being Flora Thompson ourselves."

Elspeth looked up at the sky. She felt that she had been vouchsafed a profound insight in what Patty had just said. She needed forgiveness as much as anybody else—but it had never occurred to her that this forgiveness might come from herself. How, she wondered, did one forgive oneself? By some sort of formal act—by words addressed to oneself? Or by trying to forget?

She said goodbye to Patty and then watched her cousin's car drive away. She waved, but Patty did not see her, and soon disappeared, anyway, into the rhododendrons and their hidden green tunnel.

31
Not in the Ordinary Sense of the Word...

It took Matthew some time to settle Rognvald, but at last the small boy, relegated to a cot in a spare room so as not to disturb his brothers, fell asleep. Returning to the kitchen, Matthew found Elspeth preparing *boeuf bourguignon*, snipping at rashers of bacon with a large pair of kitchen scissors.

He seated himself at the scrubbed pine table. "Poor little boy," he said. "He was a bit uncomfortable, I think. He wasn't scratching, though—just niggling."

Elspeth dropped the trimmed bacon into the pot. "And the others?"

"Sleeping like logs," answered Matthew. "I shone a torch on their faces to check for spots. Nothing."

Elspeth thought it possible they might escape infection. "Patty said it's pretty contagious amongst children, but she didn't say it was a foregone conclusion that they'll get it."

"Nor that we would," observed Matthew.

"I suppose we should tell Birgitte and Anna.

169

They're going to have to help me nurse them. Have you said anything yet?"

He said that he had not.

"I think you should call them in."

Matthew nodded. "They're in Anna's room. I heard them moving about."

Elspeth frowned. "Moving about?"

"Yes. There were various sounds. I couldn't make out exactly what was going on."

Elspeth stirred the stew thoughtfully. "Go and knock on the door," she said. "Remember to knock. Don't go in."

"What shall I say?"

"Tell them that Rognvald's not well and we need to talk to them."

He left, and a few minutes later returned with the two Danish girls. One of them, Birgitte, was wearing a dressing gown wrapped around and secured with a broad purple belt; the other had on an outfit that looked like a Scandinavian traditional costume: an old-fashioned, aproned dress in plain red and white.

Elspeth surveyed their unusual garb, but left it unremarked upon. "Rognvald's ill," she said.

Birgitte, who was usually the more assertive of the two, spoke first. "Matthew said." She paused, looking at Matthew in a slightly accusing way. "So, what's wrong with him?"

"It's something called Hand-Foot-Mouth disease."

Birgitte gasped. "Foot and Mouth?" She turned to Anna, and said something in Danish. Anna now gasped.

"Well, that's its common name," said Elspeth. "It's caused by a virus. Coxsackie virus."

Birgitte screamed. It was a sudden, high-pitched scream that caught Elspeth unawares, causing her to drop the spoon into the *boeuf bourguignon*.

"It's not serious," blurted out Matthew. "Highly infectious, but not serious."

Birgitte spun round to face Matthew. "Infectious? Highly infectious?"

Matthew looked to Elspeth for help.

"My cousin dropped in," she said. "She's a paediatrician. She said . . ."

She did not finish. "Infectious?" screamed Birgitte. "We'll get it too? We'll get this Foot and Mouth?"

Matthew tried to calm her. "It's not the Foot and Mouth you're thinking of," he said.

Birgitte was having none of this. "When cattle get Foot and Mouth," she said, "they shoot them. That's what happens. They shoot them. And yet you say that it's not serious?"

Elspeth, having failed to extract the spoon from the *boeuf bourguignon*, was becoming increasingly irritated. "Listen, you stupid girl," she began. "It's not the same disease."

Birgitte stared at her through narrowed eyes. "Who's stupid?" she shouted.

Matthew moved forward. "There's no need for anybody to get upset," he said. "Nobody's stupid."

"Your wife said I was," shouted Birgitte. "She called me a stupid girl."

"Well you are," muttered Elspeth. "And what do you two do in that room all the time? You lock yourselves away. What are we to think?"

Birgitte looked at Anna as if to confirm the magnitude of the insinuation. Anna began to cry.

"Look," said Matthew. "Let's all just calm down. Birgitte, Elspeth didn't mean to call you stupid—not in the ordinary sense of the word."

"Yes I did," muttered Elspeth.

"See!" yelled Birgitte. "Did you hear that?"

Matthew gave Elspeth a reproachful look. "She didn't mean that. She's upset. We're all upset."

"I am very calm," said Birgitte. "I am listening to all these insults, but I remain very calm. Look at me—am I not calm?"

"Actually, your face is all red," said Elspeth.

The effect of this on Birgitte was instantaneous. "You hear that, Matthew? You hear what this wife of yours says?"

Matthew tried again. "Let's just forget it. The important thing is to think of the boys. We'll probably need help with nursing them tomorrow—Elspeth won't be able to cope on her own."

Birgitte drew in her breath. "That's a great pity,"

she said. "Because Anna and I are not going near them. We're not going to get Foot and Mouth."

"But you must," said Matthew. "You can't just ignore them."

"Yes, we can," snapped Birgitte. "Very easily."

"Then you're fired," said Elspeth. "Thank you very much for your help in the past, but now you're fired. You can go back to Denmark tomorrow. We'll get you both a ticket."

The effect of these words was to bring about complete silence. As Elspeth delivered her blow, Matthew opened his mouth to speak, but no words came. Birgitte froze, as did Anna, while Elspeth herself, the deed done, looked down at the floor, as if ashamed.

Brigitte's nostrils flared. "I resign," she said.

"Too late," said Elspeth. "You've already been dismissed."

"No," said Birgitte, her voice rising. "Don't try to beg us to stay. It won't work. Anna and I are leaving right now."

"You pigs," whispered Anna. "You Scottish pigs."

Elspeth laughed. "Coming from a Dane, I take that as a compliment."

Matthew looked at his wife in dismay. This was no time to make jokes about Danish bacon. "I'm very sorry it's come to this," he said gently.

Birgitte gave him a dismissive look. "Too late," she said.

The two young Danes swept out of the room. Elspeth looked at Matthew and shrugged. "I didn't start that," she said. "I really didn't."

"Nobody said you did," said Matthew.

"I'm not going to get another au pair in a hurry," Elspeth said. "Those two . . ."

"Anna was all right," said Matthew. "She was led astray by Birgitte. We should never have allowed it."

32

The Pronunciation of Gullane (Part 72) . . .

Nicola looked at her watch.

"I don't want to break the party up, so to speak," she said. "But I was thinking of taking a walk. Interested?"

Domenica had enjoyed their conversation over tea and was happy to continue it on a walk. Their discussion had ranged widely, and Nicola was a good listener. Domenica appreciated this because she found that Angus, although prepared to listen, often appeared to lose the thread while she was speaking. This resulted in his asking questions that may have had a bearing on something she had said much earlier rather than on the point she had reached. At tea that afternoon, they had skirted round politics—"So confrontational, so bitter," Nicola had remarked—and were delicately discussing the affairs of the Pollock household. Domenica was cautious: she sensed that Nicola and Irene were at odds, but did not want to say anything critical of somebody who was, after all, her guest's daughter-in-law.

She need not have worried.

"I don't wish to be disloyal," Nicola remarked, "but I find I have nothing in common with Irene."

Domenica raised an eyebrow. "I see."

"I tried," said Nicola. "I tried right from the beginning."

"I'm sure you did."

Nicola gazed out of the window. "What alternative does one have as a parent? Your son or daughter brings home somebody you can't abide: what do you do?"

Domenica shrugged. "I don't know: I've never had that experience."

Nicola hesitated. She understood the sensitivity of those who had not had children. People could go on about their offspring without realising that the childless might find such conversations painful.

But Domenica had no such feelings as she now went on to speculate on just how difficult such a situation might be. "You can't tell them, can you? You can't tell your child that you don't like his friends, can you?"

"In general, no," said Nicola. "Most parents encounter that at some stage—the child gets in tow at school with the wrong sort—what do you do? One thing you shouldn't do is come out with it outright. That can have the opposite effect."

"It makes the disliked friend seem more attractive? Forbidden fruit tastes sweeter?"

Nicola nodded. "Exactly. And that's particularly serious if the child is at the rebellious stage—or thereabouts. That's asking for trouble."

"In such circumstances," suggested Domenica, "perhaps you say the opposite of what you feel. You say, *How I like your new friend!* And that then makes your offspring think there's something wrong with the friend, and go cool on him or her."

"I tried that," said Nicola. "Right at the beginning—when Stuart turned up with Irene—I tried that. I told him how much I approved of her. I told him that she seemed just right for him."

"And it didn't work?"

"It didn't work at all. So then I tried the opposite. I said that I wondered whether he and Irene were entirely compatible. I said that there was nothing wrong with her, but was she right *for him*."

"And?"

"He was too smitten. I don't think he took in what I said. I could have said that she was wanted for murder and he wouldn't have noticed."

Domenica smiled wryly. "Love is blind, isn't it? All the clichés about love are absolutely true. Love is blind."

"Or at least partially sighted," said Nicola.

"Partially sighted in the sense of being partial in the way it views *things*—yes, of course it is." She was about to continue and say that she assumed that Nicola meant *partly sighted* but she did not: there were some battles that had been lost a long time ago and only the most diehard pedant would still fight: the confusion between partially and partly; the splitting of the infinitive; the distinction between *hopefully* (in the sense of *with hope* or *hoffentlich*) and *it is to be hoped*; the whole issue of whether Gullane was pronounced *Gullun* or *Gillin* (the latter, of course, being the correct pronunciation). On that last point she had recently heard a friend talk of *Gullun* (sic)—a friend who should have known better. She had remonstrated with him in vain and had been rebuffed; he had thrown in the towel, it seemed, unwilling to stand any more in the way of those who regarded the correct pronunciation as somehow elitist. She had felt sorry to see one of the few remaining bastions topple and fall, but had realised that those who pandered to the enthusiasms of the moment just wanted to be loved—as everybody did—and had chosen this form of identification with error to strike the pose that would, they hoped, bring them love and acceptance from those who pronounced Gullane incorrectly. And her understanding of this brought with it another insight: those with whom one seeks to curry favour will never accept one fully. Those who pronounced Gullane incorrectly would never accept as one of them those who had in the past called Gullane by its correct name. No amount of ovine clothing brought the wolf an invitation to the family occasions of sheep.

But Nicola was not thinking about Gullane; she was remembering Stuart's wedding, an occasion at which she had struggled to contain her tears. She recalled Irene's insistence that it was she who would wait at the altar for Stuart rather than, as was customary, for the bride to make her entrance. She remembered the guests' confusion, and how this was replaced by titters as they incredulously took in Irene's version of the Scottish Episcopalian wedding service. She remembered the intake of breath as the congregation heard the revised vows: the older form of service, controversially had the wife promising to "love, honour and obey"; the obedient element had been dropped by even the most ardent traditionalists, but now it appeared again, at Irene's instance, in the man's vows: if there was to be obedience, it was to come from him.

"How completely and utterly embarrassing," whispered one guest. "Why does she think she has to make a political gesture at her own wedding?"

The guest to whom this aside was addressed was not so sure that it was a gesture.

"Perhaps she means it," he whispered back.

Nicola had kept her eyes firmly closed throughout the service. *Was it for this the clay grew tall?* Those desolate words of Wilfred Owen came to her mind; was it for this she had raised her son? Was it for this that she had loved and nurtured him—to see him delivered into the hands of a woman like Irene?

Now, so many years later, there was a chink of light; the very slightest sign of promise. Now there was a chance that the curse that descended upon him on that fatal day might be lifted and Stuart might be freed of that which had oppressed him for the past ten years.

Nicola felt guilty thinking this, but thought it nonetheless. That which we think we shouldn't think may be just the thing we should think. *Go for it, Stuart,* she muttered, lapsing, just this once, into an over-used colloquial exhortation that normally irritated her, but that was, in these circumstances at least, just right. Go for it. Find a woman who appreciates you. Find happiness before it's too late . . .

33
Domenica and Nicola Walk to Stockbridge, and Beyond

Their walk led them along Cumberland Street in the direction of Stockbridge. At the bottom of the brae, where St. Vincent Street completes its short, cobbled journey, Domenica pointed out St. Vincent's Chapel.

"A small church," she said. "But very high. Incense and so on."

"If God exists," said Nicola, "do you think he cares how he's worshipped?"

"Or if he's worshipped at all?"

Nicola thought about this. She had the vaguest of theologies; a childhood in the embrace of the Church of Scotland meant that she had been imbued with the moral seriousness that the Kirk professes, but she no longer found it in herself to believe the claims of institutional religion. Now, like so many others, she did not know what she believed; there might be some designing power, or there might not be—frankly, how could anybody possibly tell? "It's ritual, isn't it? Ritual has nothing to do with God—it's about ourselves and how we feel about the world."

"Interesting," said Domenica. "I used to be

more intolerant of ritual than I am now. I used to think it was meaningless. I used to think it absurd that people forbade certain foods, walked in circles or recited nostrums. But now, well, I suppose I've moderated my views. I see it in a very different light."

"Which is?"

"I suppose I see rituals as an expression of value in a world that can be indifferent, or even downright hostile. The performance of rituals makes us members of something, and that can be important, don't you think?"

Nicola said that she thought it could—if you needed the consolation of membership.

"But many people do," said Domenica. "It's all very well for us—we've been brought up in a dominant identity, but there are plenty of people who haven't had that privilege. Membership might mean much more to them." She paused. "But it's not just about being part of a group. Rituals may have an intrinsic meaning: they affirm things."

At that moment, they had reached the corner of North-West Circus Place, and a figure had appeared at a window just above eye-level. A smiling fair-haired woman waved a hand, and Domenica returned the greeting.

"My friend Suzie," she said. "They bought that place recently. It's what we call a pavilion flat—a corner flat looking out onto two streets."

Nicola looked up at the handsome Georgian building. "This city is so beautiful," she said. "Living here is like living in an opera set."

Domenica nodded. "I don't want to go on about ritual," she said, "but in performing the ritual, you're saying something about ultimate reality. You're saying that something—some idea, some association, has real worth."

Nicola was not convinced. "But you can express all that in words, can't you? Why do you need rituals?"

"Because acts make you pause for thought. The ritualistic act is the act beyond one—it is greater than the individual; it's significant precisely because it's nothing to do with our immediate purposes."

"Oh."

"Yes."

"I see."

They walked on into Stockbridge and then began to make their way along the small river that runs through the city, the Water of Leith. "Over there," said Domenica, nodding to a street on the other side of the tiny rapids, "is Ann Street. I have friends there. Do you know anybody who lives in Ann Street?"

"I did," said Nicola, "but not any more—since I went to live in Portugal I'm so out of touch."

"It's become frightfully expensive," said Domenica. "It's very fashionable these days."

She remembered something. "I used to know a man who dressed very formally," she continued. "He was an elder of the Kirk and a member of the Merchants' Company—very Edinburgh, as we used to say. Anyway, I remember I once went to a drinks party in their house—they lived on the South Side—in the Grange, I think—and one of the other guests lived in Ann Street. When he heard this, our host just looked at him over the top of his half-moon specs and said, 'Rather narrow staircases in the houses down there— awful houses to get a coffin out of.'"

"Hah!" said Nicola. "Edinburgh at its finest."

"Quite," said Domenica. "It says a lot about the slight air of disapproval that's a vital component of the Edinburgh outlook on life. Ann Street may think itself fashionable, but try to get a coffin down those stairs!"

Under the Dean Bridge, they stopped and looked up at the stone arches, so high above their heads. *"Where the iron spikes curiously repel the suicides,"* said Domenica. "Ruthven Todd wrote that, you know. He found it strange that tiny iron spikes on the side of the bridge would deter those who wanted to end it all."

"I read something by him a long time ago," said Nicola. "Something about being on Mull."

Domenica knew the poem. "That was called 'In September.' He remembers stacking peat on Mull as the clouds of war gathered in Europe. And he wishes he'd stayed on Mull. There was something about the Atlantic flowing in sluggishly past Jura, and the hills being like lions crouched against the autumn gales . . ."

Nicola closed her eyes. "Oh, I can see it," she said. "The slow movement of the sea, the sense of being on the edge of a continent . . ."

"While all the time it's September, which is a month that evokes ideas of . . . ideas of what? Of change, thinning out, the gradual attenuation of warmth and light?"

"All of that," agreed Nicola.

"Or even a time. A time can be made to sound ominous. Remember Lorca's poem about the death of a bullfighter? There was that insistent refrain *A las cinco de la tarde* . . . At five in the afternoon, at five in the afternoon. It's rather like a drumbeat. Now the gangrene comes . . . at five in the afternoon."

Domenica looked at Nicola and for a few moments they said nothing, sharing, in silence, a sudden glimpse of the sadness of life. Of course life was sad; just below the surface, like the pulse of an artery, life beat out a rhythm of impermanence and regret.

"September," said Domenica, breaking the silence. "There's Auden's 'September 1, 1939.' He tells us he's sitting in what he calls one of the dives on Fifty-Second Street . . . That poem haunts me, you know."

"I wish there were more voices for love," said Nicola suddenly. "I wish that hate hadn't seized all the song sheets."

"So do I. So do I."

They stopped. A man was standing a few hundred yards away from them, looking down into the mill pond in the Dean Village. Nicola gripped Domenica's arm.

"Stuart," she said.

Domenica saw that she was right.

"He mentioned he was going for a walk," said Nicola. "But he implied it would be somewhere different."

"People change their minds."

"Yes, but . . ."

Stuart was now beginning to walk on. Nicola peered after him intently. "I want to see where he goes," she suddenly declared. "Do you mind if we follow him?"

"Not at all." Domenica readily agreed but looked sideways at her friend. Why should any woman want to follow her adult son round Edinburgh—in broad daylight? Was this some fantasy of Nicola's?

"I'm sure he's going to meet his lover," said Nicola, lowering her voice although there was no danger of being overheard.

"His lover? How exciting!"

"And I want to see what this woman looks like," said Nicola. "I want to embrace her. I

185

want to thank her. I want to say that however clandestine their relationship, it has my blessing."

"How very unusual," remarked Domenica. "How very remarkable for a mother to be quite so enthusiastic about her son's . . . how shall I put it? Adventures?"

"Bid for freedom," said Nicola. "That's what I call it." She paused. "And I wouldn't describe it as remarkable. I'd say it was progressive."

"*Quot matres, tot sententiae,*" quipped Domenica.

Nicola glared at her. "Meaning?"

"As many mothers there are, so too are there maternal opinions," explained Domenica.

"Then why didn't you say that?" asked Nicola accusingly.

"Clothe a mundane observation in Latin and it sounds so much more impressive," *Domenica dixit.*

34

Irene as Termagant

The two women followed Stuart at a sufficient distance that he would not notice them should he turn and glance over his shoulder. But he did not do that, seeming intent on reaching his goal rather than meandering in the way in which one on an innocent afternoon walk might do. As he reached the top of the narrow lane that led up from the Dean Village, Stuart increased his pace, and it was difficult for Domenica and Nicola to keep him in sight. But by breaking into the occasional trot they still had him in view when he eventually reached the gates of the Scottish National Gallery of Modern Art.

"We can take our time now," said Nicola.

Domenica nodded, but said nothing. She felt vaguely foolish: there was something ineffably discomfiting about following another person— there was an element of concealment, of subterfuge, that sat ill with an open, honest approach to life. If you wanted to find out what somebody was up to, you should ask him. If he chose not to answer, or to lie, then that was to his discredit rather than yours.

"He'll be meeting her there," went on Nicola. "I'm sure of it."

Domenica looked away. She regretted agreeing to accompany her friend on this ridiculous mission, but it was now too late to withdraw. And in spite of these misgivings, there was still a bit of her that shared Nicola's curiosity. Over the years she had seen Stuart's sufferings, and now here was a chance to witness his attempt to snatch some happiness in life. Poor man, she thought; to be married to . . . she tried to think of metaphors for Irene—a *shrew?* That was a common insult applied to women who were argumentative and difficult, but it had sexist connotations that she did not like. Men were never criticised for shrew-like qualities, even though they often had them. No, shrew was not quite right for Irene. Harridan? That had connotations of age and crustiness that were not quite appropriate; Irene was too contemporary to be a harridan. Termagant? Now there was a word. Irene was definitely a termagant in so far as that term suggested an overbearing nature. But it also was suggestive of harshness, which again did not quite suit Irene. Deities were represented as termagant if they were harsh and punitive, and that was exactly what some deities were conceived to be.

She thought of some of the Greek gods—they were termagant in their spitefulness, their cruelty, and their willingness to inflict punishment on hapless mortals, only some of whom deserved their fate. How strange it was, she thought, that people had been prepared to attribute to their particular deity a nature that was so unpleasant— and some religions still did conceive of God as cruel and unforgiving, ready to smite those he identified as worthy of his hostile attentions. Whereas in liberal western religions, the Supreme Being was seen as distinctly emollient, as cuddly even, possibly looking a bit like Liberace, and behaving in like manner, a bit given to displays of candelabra and glitz. Though one became too familiar with the Supreme Being at one's peril, thought Domenica, remembering Auden's tale of the denizen of Fire Island who, hearing thunder, said "There's Miss God up to her tricks again" only to be immediately struck by lightning. Supreme beings, perhaps, disapprove of archness, however much they may have liberalised in other respects.

However one might describe Irene, whatever metaphor captured most accurately her domineering traits, her political and social posturing, her absurd ambitions, the fact remained—at least in Domenica's mind—that Stuart's wandering was entirely understandable and now that it was beginning to manifest itself, *even the ranks of Tuscany could scarce forbear to cheer* . . . And in one respect, Nicola, as mother-in-law in that marriage, represented the Tuscan ranks who felt so tempted to disloyalty when they saw Horatius survive his plunge into the swollen waters of the Tiber.

But this was not the time for further thoughts of this nature, as they had entered the hallowed portals of the Scottish National Gallery of Modern Art. They had crossed the threshold over which a piece of installation art, in blue neon tubing, spelled out the message *Everything will be alright* (sic). Domenica had gasped at the sight. By *alright* the artist presumably meant *all right*. She had drawn Nicola's attention to the solecism but had been given the answer, "Deliberate, I imagine. The National Gallery *must* know that no less an authority than the late Kingsley Amis described *alright* as 'gross, crass, coarse and to be avoided' and Bill Bryson, hardly a fuddy-duddy, describes its use as 'illiterate and unacceptable.' So they must be making a populist, subversive gesture by refusing to use the correct spelling, *all right*. The tyranny of orthodoxy, the straitjacket of orthographic correctness, are both challenged—at a stroke! How tremendously clever!"

Domenica nodded. "I feel very old-fashioned," she admitted, "in taking the view that people should know how to spell. I find myself so out of step with forward-looking, progressive people who have abandoned the accusative case when it comes to the first person singular. It makes *you and I* look so pedantic."

Nicola laughed. "Oh, very good," she exclaimed. "Indeed, that's a lesson for *we*."

"On a serious note," said Domenica. "Does it matter? Think of our petty concerns and then look up at the night sky, at the stars in the firmament, and think: do any of our petty little concerns really make one jot of difference? Do they mean anything in the context of this great spinning universe—*if* universes spin, which I am not at all sure they do . . ."

"They explode," said Nicola. "Or implode. I can never quite remember which it is."

"It must make quite a difference, though," said Domenica. "But in essence, our smallness, our irrelevance in the cosmic context, should make us less petty, more accepting, less attached to small and ultimately meaningless things."

"And make us embrace our fellow human beings more warmly," said Nicola. "Reflections on human smallness have often prompted me to think that. What do divisions between people matter? What does it matter if somebody is English or Scottish or whatever?"

Domenica thought about this. "*Sub specie aeternitatis*, it matters not at all," she said. "But specific human culture *does* matter. I don't want Scotland to stop being Scottish. I know it may not mean much when you look up at the night sky, but it means a great deal in the actual living of our lives in the here and now. Small things seem big when you're right up against them, but you have to distinguish those that mean something, and those that don't."

"So we should worry if people write *alright* rather than *all right*? Or if they write *Scottish National Galery* rather than *Scottish National Gallery*?"

"Maybe not. Maybe that's not quite important enough."

Nicola had thought of something else. "Or worry about how they pronounce Gullane?"

"Oh, that's different," said Domenica. "Some things are *really* important."

35

All About Hipsters

That morning, Bruce Anderson, now in his late twenties, former pupil of Morrison's Academy, Crieff, surveyor, exponent of clove-scented hair gel, owner of an attractive north-facing flat in Abercromby Place, golf handicap 14, was gazing into the eyes of Clare Hodding, former pupil of Presbyterian Ladies' College, Perth, Western Australia, sometime cabin crew member of Qantas, enthusiast of extreme sports, and tenant of a shared flat in Newington, Edinburgh, where the mutual eye-gazing was now taking place, over a breakfast of 25% extra fruit luxury muesli, croissants, and Java-roast coffee.

Bruce said, "I really like your eyes, you know. I'm not just saying that, I really like them. They look like . . ." He transferred his gaze to his muesli where, swimming in a small lake of semi-skimmed milk, were two tiny pieces of dried papaya. "Like papaya," he concluded.

Clare acknowledged the compliment with a

smile. "You're really sweet," she said. "I like your . . ." She searched her mind for a few seconds. His hair? She liked the *en brosse* hairstyle that Bruce affected; she liked running her fingers over it; it reminded her of a scrubbing brush. "I like your hair," she said at last.

Bruce touched his head. "People do." He paused. "And do you like my hair gel? I buy it online, you know."

"It's strange," she said. "It reminds me of the dentist. The smell of the dentist's."

"Hah!"

"And I like your face," Clare continued.

"I like your face too," responded Bruce.

They each took a spoonful of muesli.

"This muesli's great," said Bruce.

"It's got more fruit than the usual stuff. I like muesli that has lots of fruit." She paused. "You know what I don't like, Brucey?"

"You tell me, honey-pants."

"I don't like that muesli that's really sweet— you know the stuff? It's so sweet that it actually tastes sharp. And then you look at the amount of sugar it has in it and I swear it goes off the scale. Pounds of sugar—pounds of it. Added by the muesli people. And then they expect you to think it's healthy, but actually it's not. Who do they think they're fooling?"

"*Pas moi*," said Bruce.

"Is that Latin?" asked Clare.

Bruce shook his head. Then he added, "I think it's great that we like the same things."

There was a brief silence. Then Bruce continued, "When I'm with you, you know, I don't want to be anywhere else. Strange, isn't it?"

"I'm cool with that," said Clare. "I like it when you hold me. You know what I thought when you grabbed me that first time—remember, when we were in that pub and you came up behind me and grabbed me, and I thought, *Hey, this guy's like grabbing me!* And then I thought, *And I really like it!* That's what I thought, you know."

Bruce laughed. "I thought, *Gee, this girl's got what it takes.* Those were my exact thoughts, you know. And then I thought, *Search over.*"

"You didn't!"

"Yes," said Bruce. "You see, I'd been looking for a long time for somebody like you, and I thought I'd never find her—and then, bang, you walk into my life, and I thought, *Search over.* True. I did. I thought that."

"I'm really happy for you, Bruce," said Clare. "But . . ."

He looked at her in alarm. "But what?"

"Oh, but nothing important . . . Just but . . . but you know how it is when you meet somebody you really like?"

Bruce was hesitant. "Yes?"

"Well, you meet somebody you really like

194

and you think *He's just perfect*. That's what you think, but then you realise that nobody's *absolutely* perfect, and you work out why they're not quite perfect."

Bruce put down his spoon. He was not sure what to expect, and he was concerned that he was not going to like whatever it was that Clare was going to say.

"I never said I was perfect," he said. "We all have some flaws . . . even me . . . I fully accept that there'll be some things that I need to work on." He could not help but grimace. Was it possible that he was not everything she wanted when it came to . . .

"Oh, it's not you in the sense of *you*," said Clare. "It's just that . . . well, this place . . ."

They were in Clare's kitchen, and Bruce cast an eye about it. As a surveyor he would have rated it in need of redecoration, but why should that have anything to do with him?

"We could spend more time in my flat," he said. "It's much nicer than this."

"Oh, I'm not talking about the flat," said Clare. "I'm talking about Edinburgh. About Scotland."

Bruce frowned. "What's wrong with Edinburgh?"

Clare smiled tolerantly. "It's a bit . . . How shall I put it? Conventional."

Bruce was relieved that the fault was

Edinburgh's rather than his. "Oh, yes, it's full of square people. Squaresville, Midlothian. Really square."

"And all this old stuff," said Clare. "These old buildings. Museums and so on."

"Some people like that," said Bruce.

"Oh, I know, it's more about being in touch with what's going on. You see, I think people in Scotland get the message really late. They're not in touch with the vibe."

Bruce shrugged. "I don't know. Glasgow's cool, you know. There's a lot going on in Glasgow. Would you like to go over there some time?"

But Clare was not listening. "Have you heard of hipsters?"

Bruce smiled. "Sure, everybody's heard of hipsters."

"They wear beards," said Clare. "Quite large beards, but well-tended. Nothing scruffy. And these really nice jeans—really tight round the legs."

"I've seen them," said Bruce. "There's a shop down on Queen Street for hipsters; they sell stuff for beards and moustaches. Clippers for trimming nasal hair. Pomade. Notebooks. Speakers. Hipster stuff. And the guys who run it have beards."

"Interesting. Just for guys?"

"Yes. It's just for guys. But women can go in there to buy stuff for guys, if they like. But they shouldn't expect to find anything they like for themselves."

"Hipsters don't cause trouble for other people," said Clare. Her remark had no bearing on what had gone before, and Bruce struggled to see the relevance.

"I never said they did," he said.

"They ride bikes too," said Clare.

"Yeah, sure, hipsters ride bikes. Other people ride bikes too."

"Hipsters like bikes without brakes," Clare continued. "You stop the bike by pedalling backwards. Hipsters don't go for bikes with all sorts of extra stuff on them, like brakes."

"Oh well . . ."

Clare reached across the table and touched his wrist gently. "Could you and I go shopping?"

Bruce nodded. "What do you need?"

"It's more a case of what *you* need," answered Clare.

"Oh? What do I need? You tell me."

"New jeans," said Clare. "For starters."

36

You've Got Great Contours

Bemused but not unwilling, Bruce accompanied Clare to a shop on Princes Street that she said was just the place "for what we need."

"You said it was for what *I* need," Bruce pointed out.

"Same thing, Bruce," said Clare. "You, me— we're an item, aren't we? What you wear reflects on me."

"And vice versa?" asked Bruce.

Clare was thoughtful. "Possibly. Not that I like being arm candy, if you don't mind."

"And yet . . ." He left his reservation unfinished. There was something about Clare that discouraged argument, and yet this did not really diminish his enthusiasm for her. She was . . . what was the word? Spirited? Yes, that was it. It was something to do with her being Australian, he thought. Scottish girls were all very well, but they could be a bit given to looking on the negative side. It was something to do with cultural expectations of being miserable. Australians had that optimistic, can-do approach that he found so refreshing.

He would not have agreed to being led off

to Princes Street by a Scottish girl; until the advent of Clare, he would never have so much as considered letting somebody choose his jeans. But now, like some neutered suburban male, dragged off by a domineering wife to buy a cardigan, Bruce agreed to follow Clare into the retail no-man's-land of Princes Street—the home of bland chain stores, places of mirrors and glass and materialism.

She seemed to know where she was going and they stopped outside a shop that announced itself simply as M*N.

"What does the * stand for?" asked Bruce.

Clare looked up at the sign. "Oh, I don't think that means anything," she said. "It's just a cool name for a shop."

Bruce was not convinced. "I think it might be *E,*" he said. "As in *MEN.*"

Clare was unconvinced. "Oh, I don't think so," she said. "You don't want to read too much into these things.

"They've got a good selection of jeans in this place," she said, as they stood at the entrance to a shop at the west end of the street.

They went inside. Clare seemed to know her way about, and led Bruce to a rack on which pairs of blue denim jeans were displayed. *Tight fit,* proclaimed a sign.

"Intimate question, Bruce," said Clare. "What's your waist measurement?"

199

Bruce gave her the figure. "I'm 34 inches," he said.

"Right," said Clare. "32."

Bruce corrected her. "No, 34."

Clare shook her head. "We're not talking about comfort here, Bruce," she said. "And denim gives. You need to get a slightly smaller size so that the material can *mould* to your shape."

"I thought denim shrank," said Bruce.

"It both shrinks *and* gives," said Clare. She selected a pair of jeans and handed them to him. "We'll try these to start."

Clare led Bruce to a fitting room.

"Give them to me," he said. "I'll go and try them on."

"Oh, we're all coy all of a sudden, are we?" said Clare. "I'll help you."

Bruce looked embarrassed. "I can do it myself."

Clare shook her head. "You're going to need help," she said.

He did not argue, but followed her meekly into the cubicle.

"Right," said Clare. "Put these on."

Stripped to his shorts, Bruce took the proffered pair of jeans. He now saw just how slender were the legs—a thin sleeve of material no thicker, he thought, than his forearm. "I don't know if I'm going to get into those," he said doubtfully. "Maybe a larger size . . ."

"Don't be defeatist," said Clare, manipulating

the foot that Bruce had tentatively pushed into the leg of the jeans. "Just push. Straighten out your foot—like a ballet dancer—and push."

Bruce did as he was told. Even with his foot straightened unnaturally, tendons strained, it was only just possible to penetrate the tight embrace of the trouser leg, and then only with Clare reaching in at the other end to grip his foot and pull it through.

"There we are," she said, as his left foot burst through to freedom. "I told you it would be fine."

Bruce wiggled his foot. "It's going to cut off the circulation further up," he said. "It's gripping me like a vice."

"No it won't," said Clare.

"It will," insisted Bruce. "My legs already feel numb."

"That's natural," retorted Clare. "When you get new jeans, your legs feel numb to begin with. It wears off."

Bruce struggled with the zip. He prided himself on his lean stomach, but even breathing in, it was difficult for him to do up the jeans. Eventually he succeeded, but found that breathing had become painful and could only be managed in short, determined bursts.

"Great fit," said Clare, standing back to admire him. "Look how they follow the contours of your body, Bruce." She paused. "You've got great contours, you know, Bruce."

Bruce looked in the mirror. He tried to take a step forward, but he found this difficult.

"I can't walk," he muttered.

"Of course you can walk," snapped Clare. "Don't be such a girl, Bruce."

Bruce looked at her in astonishment. "I'm not a girl," he muttered.

"You're behaving like one," repeated Clare.

Bruce bit his lip. "You're one to call me a girl," he said. "You're one yourself."

Clare looked at him belligerently. "You calling me a girl?" she asked.

Bruce thought better of it. "No," he said. "And anyway, let's not argue. It's just that I think these jeans are too tight. I'm not criticising you or anything, I'm just saying it's really hard to walk—and it hurts."

"What hurts?" asked Clare.

Bruce looked away. "Walking hurts."

"You'll get used to it," said Clare. She drew back the fitting room curtain and signalled to the shop assistant hovering outside. "We'll take these."

"Great fit," said the assistant.

"He'll just keep them on," said Clare. "Can you wrap up his old gear?"

"Sure," said the assistant, throwing Bruce an admiring glance.

They made their way slowly out of the shop.

"Shoes next," said Clare.

"I don't need shoes," said Bruce.

"Yes you do. You need some colour on your feet. You know those soft leather trainers that people wear? They make those in red. Red's what you need."

Bruce sighed. In normal circumstances he would long ago have resisted—and dispatched—this gross interference in his life, but circumstances were not normal. He looked at Clare. He wanted her more than anybody he had ever wanted. He yearned for her approbation. He hung on her every word. He was completely and utterly in thrall to her. So this was what it was like to be . . . He searched for the right expression. *In love?* Was this what it was like to be in love?

He thought: *I'd do anything for you.* And as he was thinking this, struggling to walk in his new, impossibly tight jeans, he looked at her and felt a by now familiar melting. *She dissolves me,* he thought.

Clare turned to him and smiled.

"This is fun, isn't it, Bruce? Buying clothes for you. It's like . . . it's like I'm dressing a doll."

Bruce tried to laugh.

"And flannies next," said Clare.

"Flannies?"

"Flannel shirts. They're the thing, Bruce."

She looked at him, as if to discern signs of resistance. Satisfied there were none, she smiled.

"Good on you, Bruce," she said. "You're a real sport, you know."

37

They Simply Cried

Angus Lordie was relieved when Domenica returned from her walk at half past four that afternoon.

"You've taken your time," he said. "You haven't forgotten about the lecture, have you?"

"*Making Sense of the Twentieth Century*? No, I'd remembered. It is at six, isn't it?"

Angus nodded. "Yes. It's just that I wasn't sure that you'd remembered."

She reassured him. "I'm looking forward to it. I'm not sure if I'm currently able to make much sense of the twentieth century—the lecture will no doubt help."

Angus looked thoughtful. "Oh, it was quite a century. Massive culling by humanity of itself. Degradation of the planet. Close shave with complete destruction . . ."

"The Cuban Missile Crisis?"

He nodded. "We came within two minutes of the end, I gather. Some American naval vessel had a Soviet submarine in its sights. The commander was getting ready to fire, and if he had . . . then the sub would have replied with torpedoes. And that would have been the beginning of the third—and final—world war."

For a few moments they were silent.

"What would it have been like?" Domenica asked.

"A rushing wind. Unimaginable light. Then darkness." He paused. "How did Robert Oppenheimer put it? He was said to have quoted from the Bhagavad Gita: *If the radiance of a thousand suns were to burst at once into the sky, that would be the splendour of the mighty one . . .*"

Domenica looked doubtful. "I'm not sure that anybody would have said anything quite so striking, don't you think?"

Angus was not sure. "Well . . ."

Domenica explained. "You see, when something remarkable or important happens, people tend to come up with something very simple. They say *Oh no!* Or, these days, with strong language being so pervasive, they say something scatological. They tend not to say anything very profound."

"So it's mostly *oops*-type responses?"

"I think so. In fact, I read somewhere that some of the people who witnessed the first explosion at Los Alamos simply cried. They just cried." She paused. "By the way . . ."

"Yes?" said Angus.

She hesitated. She did not like gossip but she

felt that what one said to one's spouse was, in a sense, privileged and was exempt from whatever moral constraints limited gossip.

"Well, my walk with Nicola . . ."

Angus waited. "Yes? Something happened?"

They were in the kitchen of their flat in Scotland Street, and Domenica now crossed the floor to look out of the window. Across the street, perched on the roof of the tenement opposite, a couple of large seagulls preened themselves in the late afternoon light.

"Gulls," muttered Domenica.

"Arrogant birds," said Angus. "Your walk?"

Domenica turned round. "Stuart downstairs . . ."

"Yes?"

She swallowed hard. ". . . is having an affair."

Angus frowned. "Stuart Pollock? Mr. Irene? Having an affair?"

Domenica nodded. "Nicola and I saw him in the Dean Village. We were down there on our walk and we saw him in the distance. She wanted to follow him; I was reluctant at first, but I didn't think it was my place to disagree with her."

Angus's frown changed to a look of incredulity. "You actually followed him? Like a private detective?"

"Well, it wasn't quite like that, but we did keep him in sight. He went up to the Gallery of Modern Art." She paused. "I know how ridiculous this sounds."

He nodded. "It certainly is a bit ridiculous, but if you did it, then you did it."

"We did. We went inside and we saw him in one of the galleries—with a woman." Angus absorbed this information.

"There are many reasons why a man might be with another woman," he said. "She could be a relative, for instance—a cousin. He might be showing her round."

Domenica shook her head. "No, she wasn't a relative. And you can tell, you know, Angus. You can tell from the body language that people have with one another."

"Tell what? Whether they're related?"

"No. You can tell whether they're lovers or not."

Angus was silent as he absorbed the news. He had always felt considerable sympathy for Stuart, and he felt not the slightest tinge of disapproval. Irene was impossible—everyone knew that—and most people knew, too, of the tyrannical way in which she seemed to keep Stuart under her control. Most men, he imagined, would have revolted against this a long time ago, but Stuart seemed strangely passive. Some men, perhaps, wanted wives or partners who were domineering; some men actually *liked* to be treated like little boys. Perhaps there was something of that nature going on and Stuart was not at all unhappy with his lot.

But now there was this apparent lover, and

that suggested that underneath it all, Stuart may well have been seething. He was a bit mild to have an affair, Angus felt, although the most unlikely people have secret love lives in which they do things you would never imagine they would do. There had been several cases of that in Edinburgh, and the city's collective jaw had hit the table when details emerged—as they eventually did in most cases of this sort.

Having thought about it along these lines, Angus ventured an opinion.

"I don't blame him," he said. "If it's true, as you suggest . . ."

"It's true," said Domenica.

"Then she has only herself to blame."

Domenica had to agree. "She's pushed them all around so much. It's what keeps her going, I think."

"I was rather hoping that she'd stay in Dubai," Angus said wistfully.

"So was I," confessed Domenica. "It's a very uncharitable thought to have of a neighbour, but it would have been a very satisfactory outcome. But I gather that she was too much of a match for the Bedouin sheikh in whose harem she was confined. She started a book club for his wives, you know. It went down very well, but when the wives started to discuss books that their husband didn't exactly approve of, it was time for Irene to return to Scotland."

Angus looked thoughtful. "I wonder what those books were," he mused.

"Oh the usual thing," said Domenica airily. "*The Oasis of Loneliness*, for example. *Fifty Tents of Grey . . .*"

Angus burst out laughing. "What fun we have," he said.

Domenica nodded. Then she said, "Oh, Angus, could you open that window for me? I think it's stuck. Rain must have got in somehow."

He rose from his chair and began to struggle with the recalcitrant window. Suddenly the sash moved and the window, to which Angus had been applying his shoulder, flew wide open.

Angus was defenestrated.

38

Scottish Defenestrations

It happened so quickly. One moment he was in the kitchen, struggling to open a window and thinking: water has penetrated the wood and it's swollen and I should have had the outside painted when we last had the painter in . . .

Defenestration, properly so-called, should be distinguished from falling from a window through inattention or a loss of balance, or any of the factors that precede accidental descent. Those who jump out of windows voluntarily, either in pursuit of self-destruction or to escape from pressing threat, are not, according to ordinary usage, defenestrated: that occurs when a person is ejected out of a window by force, human or natural. In the case of Angus Lordie, defenestrated from his kitchen window in Scotland Street, the force was a natural one—the window to which he applied his shoulder was less firmly stuck than he had imagined. Thus it was that he was defenestrated, even if no human agency was involved in the mishap.

He had no idea how he suddenly came to be upside down. He saw the sky above him, and his immediate thought was of its indifference. Something important was happening to him, and the sky was neutral to it. And then he thought: if I believed in something—anything—then I wouldn't experience this abandonment, because the sky would be part of a world in which I am not as insignificant as I now feel . . .

Defenestration has a long history in Scotland, even if there is nothing in Scottish history to match the Defenestration of Prague—actually the Second Defenestration of Prague—a famous event that achieved a notoriety quite out of proportion to its actual, immediate impact; after all, nobody died, at least not through the actual defenestration: the Catholic dignitaries who were in this way so discourteously treated survived their ignominious fall, landing, partisan pamphleteers claim, in a dung heap. That was the Protestant version of events—the victims of the defenestration being Catholic. According to Catholic accounts, those defenestrated were unharmed because they were caught by angels on the way down. The First Defenestration of Prague, which occurred in 1419, involved the fatal throwing out of the Town Hall of a number of members of the City Council.

Generations of schoolchildren were exposed to the exam question: "What were the consequences of the Defenestration of Prague? Do you think that the Defenestration was the most important cause of the Thirty Years' War?" These issues, along with those raised by the Schleswig-Holstein Question, and indeed the West Lothian Question, circulate endlessly in the dim corridors of half-forgotten historical knowledge, ready for picking by any examiner short of a question.

Angus thought: Prague, Prague. I've never been to Prague—I meant to, but never got round to arranging it because there were so many other things . . . and who would have looked after Cyril? Cyril, my unquestioning friend, in whose eyes I am omnipotent—the founding principle of his canine universe. Cyril, who loves me so, and whose heart will be broken beyond repair . . .

The major Scottish defenestration was perpetrated by King James II. James was born in a time in Scotland when simply to be a member of a particular family would constitute a destiny of plotting, fear and bloodshed. He was not the best of hosts: the famous Black Dinner of 1440 saw the entertaining of two young members of the Douglas clan at his table in Edinburgh. Following the last course of the meal, the guests were dragged from their chairs, taken outside, and executed. James was only ten at the time, and there must have been an adult hand in the background, but it was not a good sign. If he picked up bad habits as a youth, he was to show them again when he murdered Lord Douglas when he was his guest in Stirling Castle. According to the *Auchinleck Chronicle*, a contemporary manuscript source, James stabbed his guest twenty-six times when Douglas refused to decouple himself from an alliance that would have challenged royal authority. He then defenestrated him, much to the delight of his secretariat, who joined in the fun, removing the Earl's brain with an axe.

These were colourful times in Scottish history, and we must be careful not to judge by contemporary standards. Everyone of any significance in Scotland, we may assume, had either got to where they got through violence, or kept their position by the same means. But this sort of thing did set an unfortunate precedent for Scottish hospitality—a reputation that was to be reinforced by the behaviour of the Campbells towards their MacDonald guests at that fateful dinner party in Glencoe. The Massacre of Glencoe, as that incident used to be called, is now more politely referred to as the Misunderstanding of Glencoe, although there are those who continue to harp on about not murdering one's dinner guests.

The Defenestration of Stirling Castle is relatively well-known; other Scottish defenestrations are more obscure. There was the Defenestration of Colonsay, a small Hebridean island—a defenestration that is still talked about today, although nobody knows who was thrown out of the window, by whom, or when it happened. There has been speculation as to the cause, but there is no authoritative view on that. What is agreed, though, is that it would not have had serious consequences, as all the buildings on the island were, at that time, only one storey high.

Moreover, in keeping with the architectural style of croft houses in that part of Scotland, they would not have had large windows—if they had windows at all, being known as *black houses*. The Defenestration of Colonsay therefore probably involved no injury to anybody, and may indeed have been no more than an attempted defenestration—foiled by an absence of windows.

More recently, the Defenestration of Hawick involved the throwing out of a window in a municipal building of a large section of the Conservative faction on the Borders Council. Accounts of this are confused, but press reports of the time suggest that being tired of bickering, the combined factions of the Liberal Democrats and the Scottish National Party threw the Conservatives out of a window, again on the ground floor. The Conservatives were then chased by the *keelies* of the town, who hurled insults before dispersing into local bars. This incident is still talked about in the Borders, but probably never took place.

Angus Lordie, however, was defenestrated and . . .

> Why am I not dead? he thought. And why am I in this tree, suspended upside down, with that terrible pain in my leg; and the sky is darkening, and who will give Cyril his dinner . . . ?

39

Mist-covered Mountains

He was dimly conscious of the sky. There was cloud and a shaft of buttery sunlight. But the light, it seemed to him, was going the wrong way, and it was replaced by haze. There was grey, that was stone, and there was white somewhere that was detached from any object—just white. And then the light and colours became confused, as if he had been peering into a kaleidoscope that had been given a good shake: triangles, shards, diamonds; glowing liquid pools, like watercolours running into one another, without edge; this, perhaps, was how an artist died, among the colours that had been his life.

He did not mind. He felt no regret, or pain, or feeling that what was happening to him was anything but that which had to happen, was right to happen. The self was a small thing, a tiny but insistent illusion that was now being gently awed into silence. It did not matter; it did not matter . . . He was aware of movement; some pressure on his arms, as if somebody were pulling him, and for a few moments he resented that there should be this intrusion. But then he felt sleep claim him, and all sensation drained away, faded, and he no longer cared. So this was what it was like to die: it was an abandonment, a giving up, an allowing of life to drain away. It did not matter, he thought. It did not matter.

There was silence, and then a voice, clear and resonant, and it was talking about Angus. "His work was highly regarded. I remember how, when we were at the Art College together, he was already in demand as a portrait painter, painting friends and relatives at first, and then getting small commissions to paint others. How we envied him that—nobody would buy our work, of course—not at that point, because in those days one had to have talent to call oneself an artist and we were still learning. Years of hard work lay ahead of us in which we would practise our skills before we could presume to call ourselves artists, whereas now . . . oh dear, if you can move a few objects around and stack them one on another then you are greeted with the most enthusiastic encomia and the world beats a path to your door. And you win the Turner Prize if you're outrageous or superficial enough, and you go around talking about your *practice* rather than your art. And the more deliberately provocative or obscure you are the better because *you know* and others *do not know* because they are old-fashioned, or reactionary, or they simply don't understand what the function of art is and they're hung up on the naïve notion that art is somehow connected with the concept of beauty. The concept of beauty! In a world of pain and exploitation—to talk of beauty!

"But Angus would have none of that, and throughout his life he saw his role as an artist to be one of showing us those qualities of truth and beauty—the two are interchangeable concepts, to an extent—that lie beneath the surface of our world. It was his job to reveal the character of the person whose portrait he was painting, to allow the beauty within that life—no matter how mundane a life it may seem—to emerge. In other words, he saw it as his job to allow the least of men the chance to demonstrate in some way the value of their lives, their moments of splendour . . ."

And Big Lou, seated by herself at the back of the church, held her handkerchief in her hands and twisted it in her sorrow, and then looked up because the eulogy had drawn to a close and his friend, his old friend from Art College days, who had delivered it, was stepping down and going back into the body of the kirk; stepping down in his old black suit, in places shiny through wear, at the elbows, at the seat of the pants, his starched white shirt flecked at the collar with tiny specks of blood from where he had nicked himself on the chin while shaving that morning, dressing with such care for the farewell to an old friend, but shaky with emotion ...

And then the sound of the pipes—two pipers, long plaids draped over their shoulders, a green tartan, and *Mist-covered Mountains* played with all the heart, with all the emotion that comes from the love of country that the pipes can express, it seems, as no other instrument can; a wail from the heart, the sound of tears distilled, the sound of the broken heart that grieves not just for one man but for a whole country ...

And there, outside, a dog, held on a lead, confused, but knowing that something momentous was happening, and this momentous thing was about loss and separation, that dogs know only too well, although they have no words for such things.

"Angus?"

A voice penetrating through layers of drowsiness.

"Angus?"

He was confused. Somebody had been talking about him and his work. Somebody had said something about portrait painting. And he had seen Cyril, who seemed to be upset about something; perhaps because dogs can find the sound of the pipes disturbing. Cyril hated *Scotland the Brave*, he always had, and would howl and howl if he heard it played on the pipes. That, Angus said, was the tailored hell that awaited Cyril if he were to become a bad dog and die unrepentant ...

Another voice said, "He's confused, but everything seems to be going in the right direction."

And Domenica said, "What a relief!" and repeated, "Angus, can you hear me?"

He nodded. "Yes. Loud and clear. I was dreaming. Pretty odd dreams."

"Well, you're in the Infirmary now and they say you haven't broken anything, which is something of a miracle."

"A tree . . ."

"Yes, you fell into a tree. Thank heavens."

He opened his eyes to see a nurse peering at him. "You feeling better, sweetheart?"

He opened his eyes wider. "Sweetheart?"

40

The Association of Scottish Nudists

"Two years of disputes," said the Secretary of the Association of Scottish Nudists to the Chairman over lunch in the Scottish National Portrait Gallery. "What did we do to deserve all that aggravation?"

The Chairman, who had taken a mouthful of quiche, took a few moments to reply. Then, reaching for his glass of cloudy lemonade, he said, "Nothing at all, my dear chap—nothing at all. Everything was going perfectly well until those tiresome people from Glasgow . . ."

"It wasn't just Glasgow," interrupted the Secretary. "The Weegies were the ringleaders, of course, but they had plenty of collaborators. There was that woman from Perth—I forget her name, but I can just see her . . ."

The Chairman closed his eyes. Perth? And was the Secretary envisaging the member in question clothed or unclothed?

"She was a shocker, that woman—so strident," continued the Secretary.

"Well, we've put their gas at a peep," said the Chairman.

"We certainly have," agreed the Secretary with a grin of satisfaction. "It's a wonderful feeling to have returned to normality, isn't it? Edinburgh back in control; upstarts back in their box."

"Skulking in their tents," said the Chairman.

"Hah!"

The issue to which the two principal office bearers of the Association of Scottish Nudists were referring was the constitutional battle that had shaken the Association to its core. This had arisen when a substantial group of members had voiced their opposition to the Association's constitution, a document drawn up by an Edinburgh solicitor in the nineteen fifties and distinguished by its unusual voting structure. This gave an unequal number of votes to the various categories of member, with Edinburgh members receiving three votes each and members from other towns and areas having two, one, or, in some cases, half a vote. This had proved unacceptable to members living outside Edinburgh, who had not been persuaded by the committee's defence of the existing arrangements—a defence based entirely on the notion that this system had provided stability for years and should not be disturbed just because some felt disenfranchised.

The uprising by non-Edinburgh members had proved irresistible, and after an undignified vote of no confidence, the existing Edinburgh committee had been replaced by a geographically more representative one. It was only through a cunning scheme dreamed up by the former Chairman and former Secretary that the coup had been reversed and the old committee re-established. This had been achieved through the recruitment of a large number of new Aberdeen members whose votes were effectively controlled by the *ancien régime*. Once that had been done, there had been a very effective splitting off of the old Association, leaving dissatisfied members from Glasgow and elsewhere with their newly renamed but under-funded association, Nudism Scotland—previously the Scottish Association of Nudists which was too easily confused with the Association of Scottish Nudists.

The victory had been Edinburgh's—there was no doubt about that, but it had left the nudist movement in Scotland with a serious divide. Who spoke for the Scottish nudist community? Was it the older, much better endowed—in the financial sense—Association of Scottish Nudists, or was it the more recently formed but more contemporary-sounding Nudism Scotland?

It was this question that had prompted the Chairman to invite the Secretary to join him for discussion over lunch. In spite of their satisfaction that the constitutional wrangles were over, there were grounds for concern over two matters that had recently arisen. The first of these was the issue of who would be entitled to a European Union grant for the furtherance of nudist objectives. This had recently been advertised amongst offers of breath-taking largesse for a variety of causes, and had already attracted the attention of Nudism Scotland, who had applied for a grant of three hundred and twenty thousand Euros for a variety of projects. These included a survey of public awareness of nudism, a research project on the production of nudist-friendly public signage, and a publication grant to support the translation into Gaelic of a number of books on the ideology of the nudist movement in Europe.

"Can you believe it?" exploded the Chairman. "Twenty-five thousand Euros to translate one book into Gaelic. Why? How many people are waiting to read *The History of Nudism in Western Europe* in Gaelic? There was that chap in Stornoway, of course—he was a member for years . . ."

"He's no longer with us," said the Secretary. "Hypothermia . . ."

"Poor fellow," said the Chairman. "But is there anybody else who will read it?"

The Secretary shrugged. "Is that the point? How many Gaelic speakers are there in Aberdeenshire? And yet we spend an awful lot of money translating things in that part of the country."

"That involves making a political point. That's to show the English that Scotland is different. And we're using Scottish money for that—this is getting the Germans to pay for it, effectively. Should we use German money to show the English that Scotland is different? I'm not at all sure about that."

They both continued with their quiche, deep in resentment at the pushiness of Nudism Scotland in applying for these grants.

"One possibility," said the Chairman, "is for us to write to Brussels and tell them that Nudism Scotland has no right to speak on behalf of Scotland's nudists. We could point out that we are the older body . . ."

"And that we're based in Edinburgh,"

interjected the Secretary. "Those bureaucrats in Brussels understand about capitals. They'll know that we're the capital of Scotland. Nudism Scotland is using a Glasgow address, you know. Somewhere in Bearsden, I believe."

"The thought of it!" said the Chairman.

"We could suggest that they are really Nudism Glasgow," continued the Secretary.

"Hah!" said the Chairman. "That would show them over in Brussels. Perhaps we could point out that it's the equivalent of some group at Ostend claiming to speak for all Belgian nudists."

The Secretary smiled. "You're right—they'd understand that. Mind you . . ." He was looking out of the window, as if remembering some-thing. "Mind you, I remember my wife and I had a very enjoyable weekend over near Ostend some years ago. There's a nudist colony in the dunes there—a lovely set-up. They had very comfortable little chalets and a wonderful sing-song round the camp-fire in the evening. We enjoyed ourselves immensely."

"It's good to have memories like that," said the Chairman. "The movement is quite strong over there, I believe. And they're very welcoming. It's a reminder of what the European ideal is all about, isn't it? That instead of fighting with one another, we should simply . . ."

The Secretary finished the sentence for him. ". . . simply take our clothes off together."

"Exactly," said the Chairman.

For a few moments they both reflected on these visions of social concord, but then the Chairman remembered the second matter that had been troubling him and he raised this with the Secretary when the latter came back from the self-service counter with two cups of Assam tea. Over this tea they now talked about something that was far more troubling than anything Nudism Scotland or the European Union could send their way.

"It really is very vexing indeed," said the Chairman.

"Quite," said the Secretary. "And what on earth are we going to do?"

41

A Meeting in a Bistro

It had been agreed between Stuart and Irene that on Saturdays Bertie would have at least some time with Stuart's mother, Nicola, while Stuart looked after Ulysses. This gave Irene the opportunity either to have a long lie-in, or, as she had recently taken to doing, to go to the National Library of Scotland on George IV Bridge, where she was working on a short guide to the works of Melanie Klein. Stuart had encouraged her to embark on this project as he felt that the more energy she put into it, the less she would have for what she occasionally referred to as the Bertie Project, her name for the parental task of bringing up their seven-year-old son.

He disliked that name almost as much as he disliked the project: why could Bertie not be left alone to grow up in the way that suited him? He was, after all, a particularly appealing little boy, free from any discernible character defects, obliging, gentle, and, most remarkably of all, utterly without guile. Unlike most small children, who can lie without the slightest element of self-reproach when they think it is in their interests to do so, Bertie was completely truthful. He described the world exactly as he saw it; he expressed in a completely open way the thoughts that went through his mind; if asked what he was doing or thinking he answered in a way that concealed nothing, held nothing back. Why, wondered Stuart, should such a self-evidently balanced and engaging boy be subjected to what could only be described as an unremitting programme of psychotherapy, yoga, and intense tutoring in everything from Italian *conversazione* to calculus?

In Stuart's view, little boys needed room to grow up at their own pace and in their own way. That is not to say that they did not need guidance and discipline—of course they needed that—but there had to be space for the green shoots of the emerging personality to grow. Bertie did not have that, but Stuart had been unable to insist on its provision. He was not a coward, but he was, to a very great extent, in awe of the exceptionally powerful and domineering woman he had married. It was all very well for people to think that he should stand up to Irene, but he was the one who was married to her; he was the one who had to live with her enthusiasms and disapprovals. And that was far from easy.

On that particular Saturday—the Saturday on which Angus Lordie was discharged from the Royal Infirmary following his defenestration—Irene had announced that she would not be going to the National Library and that she would therefore look after the children until lunchtime, after which Stuart and Nicola would take over. Stuart had planned his day accordingly, but had suddenly changed his mind and declared, to his mother rather than Irene, that he had other plans and would she mind taking both Bertie and Ulysses for the entire afternoon?

Nicola had immediately suspected that Stuart's plans involved a meeting with his lover. This would have bothered some mothers, but not her: as far as she was concerned she was only too delighted to facilitate his affair. "By all means, my dear," she said. "And don't bother to hurry back from . . . from wherever you're going—I'll be delighted to look after the children for as long as you want me to."

"You're so kind, Mother," Stuart had replied. "It's just that there are various things I need to attend to and Saturday afternoon's a good time to tackle them."

Nicola tried to keep a straight face. "Of course, dear. Nothing like a Saturday afternoon for . . ."

Stuart shot her a glance, which she fielded with equanimity. "For catching up," she finished.

Bertie, of course, accepted the situation with his usual stoicism. "Do you think we could go to the Botanic Gardens this morning?" he said. "We've been studying cactuses in class and I thought it would be nice to see all those cactuses in the greenhouse there—you know the one."

"Some other time," said Irene. "I was planning to go to Glass & Thompson for a cup of coffee. That'll be a nice outing for you and Ulysses. You can have one of those foamy cappuccinos with no coffee. And Ulysses can lick your spoon. He'll love the outing."

Bertie said nothing. He understood that it was futile to argue with his mother, although he knew that Ulysses would definitely not enjoy the outing. He would be sick, as he always was, whenever he went on any expedition with his mother.

"When we come back, can I watch some football on the television?"

Irene pursed her lips. "No."

"I just thought I'd ask," muttered Bertie.

"Well that's your answer, Bertie. We have far better things to do with our time than watch football, *carissimo*. You could do a painting, for instance, to take with you to your grandmother later on. You could read that little Italian book I bought for you, *La famosa invasione degli orsi in Sicilia*. There's so much to do, Bertie."

They set off, although their departure was delayed by the need to give Ulysses a complete change of clothing. This was necessary, as the infant had been copiously sick when Irene had picked him up to tell him they were going on an outing. Once this was done, though, they set off, with Bertie pushing Ulysses in his pushchair, walking confidently ahead of his mother.

Bertie noticed that his mother seemed distracted as they approached Glass & Thompson. He had asked her a question that she appeared not to hear at all, and when he remarked that he thought that Ulysses might like an ice cream, the retort that he might have expected in usual circumstances simply did not materialise.

The bistro was quiet; there were a couple of people at the table near the door and several more in the small snug to the side. But then Bertie noticed the man sitting at one of the tables at the back, and he caught his breath.

"Look Mummy," he whispered. "There's Dr. Fairbairn."

Irene gave the impression of being surprised. "Dr. Fairbairn? Well, well, Bertie, there's a thing."

Bertie pointed to a table nearby. "Shall we sit down here, Mummy? Then we won't need to disturb Dr. Fairbairn."

Irene laughed. "Oh, come now, Bertie! It would be very rude for us to sit at another table. Poor Dr. Fairbairn—he'd think we were avoiding him."

Which is precisely what Bertie wanted to do. In his view Dr. Fairbairn was a dangerous madman who, if he had not already been admitted to Carstairs State Hospital, would certainly be going there shortly. Did his mother know the risk she was running in sitting at the same table as such a person? Did she have the slightest understanding of just how unstable the famous psychotherapist was? Clearly not, thought Bertie.

42

Ulysses Reacts

Dr. Hugo Fairbairn, now also known as Professor Hugo Fairbairn, having been translated to a chair in Aberdeen, was the author of that classic of child psychotherapy, *Shattered to Pieces: Ego*

Dissolution in a Three-Year-Old Tyrant. His reputation was based not only on that book, but on a slew of frequently cited papers, including his major essay on one of his patients, Wee Fraser. This patient, years later, had head-butted the psychotherapist on a bus destined for Burdiehouse and was roundly chastised in return. This altercation was not mentioned in the paper, but Dr. Fairbairn had never got over it; it was, he confessed, his *rucksack of guilt*. All of us carry such a rucksack; all that differs is the contents.

For more than two years, Dr. Fairbairn had been Bertie's psychotherapist, seeing him each Saturday for an hour. Bertie did not enjoy these visits to Dr. Fairbairn's consulting rooms in Queen Street and saw no reason for their continuation. His mother, however, was an exponent of what she called *preventative psychotherapy* and believed that it would be easier for Bertie to negotiate his way through the shoals of adolescence if he had been set on the right course at an earlier age. She also frankly enjoyed seeing Dr. Fairbairn, and often used up half of Bertie's hour in talking about herself while Bertie paged through old copies of *Scottish Field* in the waiting room. There was much to entertain Bertie in *Scottish Field*; it gave a picture of a life that he would love to have been able to lead: a life of parties and walks in hills, of Highland games and salmon fishing; of vintage racing cars and pedigree dogs; it was all there, tantalisingly out of reach and, what was more, thoroughly disapproved of by his mother.

Dr. Fairbairn's departure for Aberdeen had been somewhat sudden. It occurred shortly before the birth of Ulysses and was as welcomed by Bertie as it was viewed with dismay by his mother. Bertie had hoped that this would be an end to psychotherapy, but all that happened was that he was taken on by the therapist who acquired Dr. Fairbairn's practice—a younger therapist, from Melbourne. Dr. Sinclair had initially proposed that Bertie be discharged, as he could find no evidence of psychopathology of any sort, but this had been strongly resisted by Irene, and the sessions had continued.

Now as they joined Dr. Fairbairn at his table in Glass & Thompson, Bertie's heart sank. Would he have to sit there in public view and tell Dr. Fairbairn all about his latest dreams? That, he thought, was the only subject that Dr. Fairbairn enjoyed talking about, and Bertic could not imagine that living in Aberdeen would have changed anything for the psychotherapist. Presumably they had dreams in Aberdeen, thought Bertie, although they would be much more down-to-earth dreams, and certainly less wasteful than the sort of dreams people had in Edinburgh.

Dr. Fairbairn smiled at Bertie as he sat down.

"So, Bertie, this is a very pleasant surprise for me," he said. "My goodness, you've grown—you're quite the young man now, I see."

"Thank you," said Bertie. "I hope that you're enjoying Aberdeen, Dr. Fairbairn."

"Oh, I am, Bertie," said Dr. Fairbairn. "It's a very good place to live."

"Are there many people needing psychotherapy up there, Dr. Fairbairn?" asked Bertie.

Dr. Fairbairn laughed. "One or two, Bertie. Same as here, I suspect." He turned to Ulysses. "And here's young Ulysses." He glanced at Irene; and Bertie noticed that his mother suddenly looked abashed.

"Ulysses doesn't speak English yet," said Bertie. "I think he understands some words, but he can't use them. Mostly, he screams."

"He has a very good grasp of the situation," said Irene. "I suspect he's gifted. We'll find out, no doubt."

Ulysses glanced at his mother and then immediately looked away. His gaze fell on Dr. Fairbairn and the effect was instantaneous. Breaking into a broad smile, Ulysses threw open his arms in a gesture of delight and acceptance. At the same time, he started to coo—a sound that was clearly expressive of the most profound pleasure.

"Look," cried Bertie. "Look at Ulysses, Mummy! Look how he likes Dr. Fairbairn!"

Irene fixed her gaze on the floor; Dr. Fairbairn, flushing deep red, inserted a finger into the collar of his shirt to loosen it.

Ulysses at this point was still strapped into his pushchair. Stepping forward, Bertie released him from his restraining harness, picked him up and passed him over to Dr. Fairbairn. Squealing with delight, Ulysses waved his arms about and kicked his legs, clearly desperate to embrace the psychotherapist.

"You see!" crowed Bertie. "You see how much he likes you, Dr. Fairbairn. Look at him! Just look at him!"

"Well . . ." began Dr. Fairbairn.

"Normally, he's sick when Mummy picks him up," he said. "But he's not being sick all over you, Dr. Fairbairn. He really likes you."

Ulysses was trying to kiss Dr. Fairbairn, and eventually succeeded. Then he wound his small arms firmly round the psychotherapist's neck and held on tightly.

"He doesn't want to let you go," said Bertie. "Do you see that, Mummy? Ulysses wants to hold on to Dr. Fairbairn."

Irene made a non-committal sound. Then, turning to Bertie, she said, "I don't think we should let Ulysses monopolise Dr. Fairbairn, Bertie. I think you should put him back in his pushchair."

"But he's so happy with Dr. Fairbairn," said

Bertie. "It would be unkind to take him away."

"Bertie," warned Irene. "You heard what I said."

Bertie sighed, and started to prise Ulysses away from the now very embarrassed psychotherapist. This was the signal for Ulysses to protest at the top of his voice and to tighten his vice-like grip on Dr. Fairbairn's neck.

"You know something," said Bertie as he tried again to detach Ulysses. "I think that the reason why Ulysses likes Dr. Fairbairn so much is because he looks so much like him—and even a little baby like Ulysses can see it."

This remark brought a gasp from Dr. Fairbairn and a furious, hostile look from Irene.

"Bertie, Ulysses does *not* look like Dr. Fairbairn," she scolded. "You really mustn't say such ridiculous things."

"But he does, Mummy. He really does."

He turned to Dr. Fairbairn. "Did you see his ears, Dr. Fairbairn? Don't you think they look like yours?"

"Bertie!" Irene hissed.

"I don't think so, Bertie," said Dr. Fairbairn. "I really don't, you know."

Ulysses had quietened down now, and was sitting in his pushchair staring intently at Dr. Fairbairn.

"Da . . ." he said. "Da . . ."

"Ulysses is trying to say something," said Bertie. "What do you think it is?"

"Bertie," said Irene, her voice steely. "You know very well that Ulysses can't talk yet. He merely makes noises. Noises like *da*, which doesn't mean a thing."

"I know, Mummy," said Bertie. "But he has to start some time, and maybe he's started now. Maybe his first word is going to be *dada*. A lot of babies begin that way, I'm told."

43

What Ulysses Almost Said

Bertie could not understand why his mother should be so cross with him. As they made their way back home, she said barely a word, and by the time they climbed the stairs at No. 44 Scotland Street her displeasure was showing in her stiffness and coldness.

"I'm so sorry, Mummy," he began. "I don't know what I've done wrong, but I'm sorry for it anyway."

Irene bit her lip. "Bertie, I've told you a hundred times—if not more—that you should never, ever comment on how a baby looks. It's not for the sake of the baby's feelings—it's for the mummy's sake."

"But why should you be upset if I say that Ulysses looks like Dr. Fairbairn? Can't people just look like other people? Tofu says that Larch looks like that Australian film actor—you know the one . . ."

"I certainly don't know any Australian film actors," snapped Irene.

"Well, he does, and he doesn't get angry with people who say it. Why should people worry about their photograph going in the paper—unless it's taken when they're doing something rude?"

"That has nothing to do with it," said Irene. "You're really going to have to follow the rules here, Bertie—and the rules say: don't talk about how babies look; it just isn't worth it. Do you understand, Bertie?"

Bertie was silent. "Sorry, Mummy."

Irene bent down and kissed the top of his head. "That's all right, Bertie. Just don't do it again, please. And here's another thing, don't mention that you and I met Dr. Fairbairn. Let's just keep that as our little secret."

"And only tell Daddy?" asked Bertie. "It could be secret to everyone else, but not to Daddy."

Irene drew a deep breath. "No, Bertie. Let's not get Daddy involved in this. Daddy doesn't need to know about Dr. Fairbairn. He's nothing to do with Daddy."

Bertie looked down at the floor. "Whatever you say, Mummy."

"Well, that's what I say. So let's just get on

with our day. In an hour or so you'll be going to Granny—with Ulysses, so let's just get little Ulysses ready. What colour of sweater should we dress him in today? What do you think, Bertie?"

"White," said Bertie. "Or maybe white and yellow."

"White and yellow? Why those colours, Bertie?"

"So that it won't show when he's sick."

Ulysses was dressed and in due course he and Bertie were taken round to Nicola's flat by Stuart, Irene preferring to minimise contact with her mother-in-law. Bertie was relieved that Stuart made no enquiry as to what they had done that morning. Had he been asked, he would have had to answer truthfully and he sensed that Dr. Fairbairn was not somebody his father wanted to talk about. It would be far simpler, Bertie felt, for the psychotherapist to stay in Aberdeen until such time, of course, as he was committed to Carstairs. Perhaps they could take Ulysses to visit him once he was there; perhaps they had a padded visitors' room where they could have tea together, with nurses ready to seize Dr. Fairbairn should he start to talk about dreams. Ulysses, of course, would not understand, but Bertie would explain it all to him once he learned English. And that did not seem to be happening too quickly; perhaps Ulysses was a Gaelic-speaking baby and some of the sounds he had been making were really Gaelic. Bertie had worked out that if there were roughly fifty-seven thousand speakers of Gaelic in Scotland out of a total population of just over five million, then the chance of a baby being Gaelic-speaking was one in eighty-seven. It may be unlikely that Ulysses was Gaelic-speaking, but it was, he thought, at least possible.

Nicola gave them her usual warm welcome. "How fortunate I am to have them both this afternoon," she said to Stuart as she opened the door of her Northumberland Street flat.

"Well," said Stuart, "I hope it won't be too much."

"I'm sure Bertie will help me," said Nicola, smiling at her grandson.

"Of course I shall, Granny," said Bertie. "And I don't think Ulysses will be difficult. He only screams and is sick when Mummy tries to pick him up. He's fine with other people."

Nicola glanced at Stuart, who did not react.

"Well, here we all are," she said once Stuart had left. "Perhaps we can start off with a little sleep for Ulysses. Look, his little eyes are closing—it's certainly rest time for him."

With Ulysses off to his rest, Nicola and Bertie settled down to a game of Monopoly. Bertie enjoyed this game, which Irene did not allow him to play on the grounds that it encouraged a *rentier* outlook.

"So," said Nicola, as she dealt out the crisp

notes that made up each player's capital, "what did we do this morning, Bertie?"

Bertie hesitated. He never lied and he did not want to start by lying to his grandmother. If he were to do that, then he would rapidly become like Tofu, or Olive, or indeed Pansy, all of whom lied without compunction.

"We went to Glass & Thompson," he said. "You know the place, Granny? That place on the corner of Dundas Street?"

"Oh, I know it, Bertie. How nice. You and Mummy and wee Ulysses?"

"Yes." He was not going to tell any untruths, but he would not volunteer information.

Then came the question he had been dreading. "And who did you see there, Bertie?"

Bertie swallowed hard. "We saw a friend of Mummy's," he said, hoping that this answer would end his grandmother's questioning.

"Oh?" said Nicola. "And what was her name?"

Bertie fixed his eyes on the Monopoly board. "It wasn't a *her,* Granny. It was a *him.*"

Nicola picked up the dice shaker. "Really, Bertie? Who was it then?"

"It's a person called Dr. Fairbairn. He's a psychotherapist. He keeps asking people about their dreams."

Nicola shook the dice, but did not spill them on the board. The rattle was like a drum-roll that precedes a theatrical revelation.

"Dr. Fairbairn?" she said.

"Yes," said Bertie. "And you know something, Granny—Ulysses looks just like him. And you should have seen Ulysses when he saw him—he went . . ." He searched for the right word. "He went ballistic, Granny. He really liked him."

The rattle of the dice grew louder. "Did he, Bertie?"

"Yes. And I think he started to talk. I'm not absolutely sure, but I think he did."

"Oh yes, Bertie? And what did Ulysses say?"

Bertie told her.

44

Extreme Sports

Bruce had not been seen in the Cumberland Bar for a few weeks, having spent most of his spare time with Clare, who had different haunts. She, however, had gone to London for a couple of days to meet up with friends from Western Australia, leaving Bruce to his own devices. At a loose end, Bruce had drifted down the hill from his flat in Abercromby Place and found himself in the bar a few minutes before Matthew arrived. Matthew was due to meet Angus Lordie, whom he had not seen since his defenestration; he himself had not been in the Cumberland for some time because of domestic pressures following the storming out of their two Danish au pairs. Elspeth was coping, but only just, and Matthew was trying to get home before four each afternoon in order to make it easier for his wife.

Elspeth was understanding. "You have to have a bit of a life yourself," she said. "When did you last go to the Cumberland?"

"Oh, that doesn't matter," said Matthew. "You don't have to worry about me."

But she was insistent. "Go on Friday evening. Treat yourself. I'll come in and collect you at eight. I've got Mrs. Macildownie coming that evening—she'll look after the boys."

He had accepted, and after closing the gallery at six had walked down the hill to the bar on the corner of Dundonald Street and Cumberland Street; he had agreed to meet Angus at six thirty.

Bruce greeted him effusively. "So, Matthew," he enthused. "Where have you been?"

Matthew stared at Bruce. There was something different about him, but it took him a few moments to work out what it was. Then it dawned on him. Bruce had become a hipster.

"Bruce," he said. "You've . . . you've signed up to hipsterdom."

Bruce frowned. "What do you mean?"

"Your gear. Those jeans."

Bruce grinned—in a slightly forced way.

"Change of style, Matt," he said.

"Can you walk in those?" Matthew asked, pointing to the jeans.

"Ha, ha!" said Bruce.

"I wouldn't bend over," continued Matthew. "Not if I were you. Something might give."

Bruce ignored this. "So where have you been?"

Matthew explained about the departure of the two Danes. "They were becoming increasingly difficult," he said. "Especially Birgitte. She had a real attitude problem."

Bruce laughed. "Tell me about it. I've known Danish girls before. They have major issues."

Matthew sighed. "I rather liked them to begin with, but then . . . somehow it changed."

Bruce shook his head. "Hopeless."

Matthew remembered about Clare. "I hear you've got a new . . ."

"A new main squeeze," said Bruce, smiling. "Yes. She's an Aussie."

"So I've heard," said Matthew. "And I gather she's . . . quite a girl."

Bruce winked at him. "You can say that again, Mattie. Still, can't complain."

Matthew smiled. Bruce was so predictable. And he spoke in clichés—ancient clichés, for the most part. Did anybody still refer to their partners as *main squeezes?*

"Is it true she's into extreme sports?"

Bruce nodded. "She's a great skier. Off-piste, of course. She's going to take me heli-skiing in

243

Canada next winter. You go to places nobody's ever skied before. None of your Whistler stuff—this is serious Rockies."

Matthew was a cautious skier. He had skied at Aviemore and once or twice in France, but the idea of heli-skiing in the Rockies struck him as highly risky.

"We're going up to Skye soon," said Bruce. "We're going to be doing some para-mountain-biking. It's the latest thing, apparently."

"Para-mountain-biking?"

"Yes. You have a mountain bike and it's fitted with a sort of flexible wing device—like a hang-glider wing. When you ride downhill you can launch yourself as if you're launching a hang-glider."

Matthew was puzzled. "But the bike . . . ."

"It's strapped to you—so you can use it to land again and ride off."

Matthew was wide-eyed. "Have you done it before?"

"No," said Bruce.

"And Clare? Has she done it?"

"Not as such," said Bruce. "But she's got a video of it and she's going to get somebody to show us. Then it's off to the Cuillins for us."

He ordered a beer.

"And tell me, Matt," he said. "Are you getting somebody to replace the Danish girls?"

"I hope so," said Matthew. "We're going to go

to an au pair agency. They fix you up. There are lots of Spanish girls looking for jobs these days. Jobs are pretty tight in Spain."

"A consequence of the new German Empire," said Bruce.

"I'm keen to learn Spanish," Matthew continued. "If we get a Spaniard, then she can give me Spanish conversation lessons."

Bruce looked thoughtful. "It's just occurred to me," he said. "Clare is looking for something. She doesn't have a job at the moment."

"Do you think she'd like to help Elspeth?"

"I don't see why not. She was complaining about not having enough to do." He paused. "She wouldn't need to be paid a lot—she gets money from her old man in Australia each month. He's loaded."

Matthew was cautious. "Has she had experience with children?"

Bruce answered without hesitation. "Yes. In fact, she was training to be a physical education teacher and then she moved on to something else."

"What happened?"

Bruce was vague. "Oh, she just moved on."

It was at this point that Angus Lordie came in with Cyril. News of his defenestration had spread, and there was a cheer from many in the bar when he entered. Angus acknowledged the compliment with a small bow. Cyril barked.

Bruce bought Angus a whisky and signalled to the barman to pour a dish of non-alcoholic beer for Cyril.

"Well, Angus," said Matthew. "That was a narrow escape, I gather."

Angus nodded. "I never thought I'd be defenestrated," he said. "But who would? I imagine that everybody who's ever been defenestrated must think that it could never happen to him."

"Well, wrong," said Bruce. "You think accidents are for other people? Wrong! They're for you as well."

Matthew thought of para-mountain-biking. There must be at least some risk attached to that. How many para-mountain-bikers made it to the bottom? he wondered. Did Bruce know the answer? Did anybody?

Angus raised his glass to Bruce. "*Sláinte*," he said.

"Chin-chin," said Bruce. And to Angus, he said, "Happy landings!"

Angus glanced at Matthew. "You know, I had the most extraordinary dreams when I was out for the count. I thought I was at my own funeral at St. John's on Princes Street. I heard my eulogy, I heard the pipes playing *Mist-covered Mountains*. I saw Cyril sitting outside, looking dejected."

Matthew said nothing.

"*Mist-covered Mountains*," said Bruce. "Jeez, I

love that tune. It gets me here—right here, every time." He pointed to his chest.

"It's left me feeling different," said Angus. "About everything." He hesitated. "Well not absolutely everything. But I've changed my views on conceptual art. On the Turner Prize, for instance."

"And the Venice Biennale?" asked Matthew.

"Yes," said Angus. "That too."

"And?" asked Matthew.

"I'm in favour of the whole thing," said Angus. "It's as if scales have fallen from my eyes."

Wrong, thought Matthew. *It's you who's fallen. You fell from a window, not scales from your eyes.*

"Are you telling me," Matthew asked. "Are you telling me that you approve of all that pretentious banality?"

"It's not banal," said Angus. "It's exciting. It's challenging. And a great deal of it's happening right here in Scotland. New, ground-breaking stuff."

And with that, Matthew realised how profound was the damage his friend had suffered.

45

Among the Watsonians

"Today's a very important day," announced Bertie to Irene as their bus, the 23, bound ultimately for Morningside, laboured up the Mound. As a concession to Bertie, Irene had agreed that they could sit on the top deck, where they were afforded a view of Princes Street Gardens, of the Castle, and, to the north, of the New Town's eccentric skyline—a vista of spikes and crenellations and the distant hills of Fife.

Irene was attending to Ulysses, who was struggling to free himself from her grip, and she only half-heard what Bertie said.

"A what sort of day, Bertie?"

"An important day, Mummy," repeated Bertie. "We're going to hear about the school play. We're going to hear what Miss Campbell has chosen for us."

"Oh yes," said Irene. "And what are the possibilities, Bertie?"

"She says it will probably be Shakespeare."

Irene rolled her eyes. "How very contemporary," she muttered.

"I'd like to do *The Merchant of Venice*, Mummy. Have you heard of that one?"

"I have, Bertie. And I suppose it has some sort of message for us in view of the banking crisis, but I do wish they'd choose something with *bite*."

Bertie asked his mother what she would prefer, and she waved a hand airily. "There are plenty of plays you might attempt, Bertie. There's a play about the unequal division of wealth in Scotland—*The Cheviot, the Stag, and the Black, Black Oil*. That speaks to inequality. I'm sure that they could do a simplified version for children." She paused for a moment. "That's just one; there are many other socially engaged plays."

Bertie looked out of the window. He was hoping for something with a bit of excitement in it. He had heard, for instance, of *Peter Pan*, and he rather liked the plot. He would have liked to be Captain Hook if at all possible, although he imagined that Tofu would try to get that role. He could be Peter Pan himself, of course, or one of the Lost Boys. And there was a dog in the play, too, a large sheepdog called Nana. He would love to be in a play with a dog. Perhaps Angus Lordie's dog Cyril might audition for that role.

"Have you heard of *Peter Pan*, Mummy?" he asked.

Irene gave a dismissive snort. "Sentimental nonsense," she said. "The product of an infantile imagination, Bertie. Barrie himself clearly never grew up."

"But it has pirates in it," said Bertie. "And a crocodile."

"Highly unlikely, Bertie," said Irene.

Bertie looked out of the window again. Edinburgh seemed so safe, and it was precisely this that may have lulled his mother into an unrealistic view of the world; there *were* pirates and crocodiles; they may not be juxtaposed, but there was no doubt about their existence.

Bertie waved goodbye to his mother at the school gate. Unlike most children, Bertie was not embarrassed by his parents, and he tolerated even his mother's more extreme tendencies. This was a product partly of his good nature and partly of the realisation that other people's parents were objectively far more embarrassing than his. Tofu's father, for instance, a well-known figure in Scottish vegan circles, drove his son to school in a car that had been converted to run on olive oil, with the result that it belched olive-scented exhaust fumes as it stuttered its way up Spylaw Road. He also wore strange clothes, most of which were made from hemp and dyed with turmeric and other natural substances. Tofu was in denial of these paternal characteristics and resorted to the simple expedient of spitting on anybody who made any reference to them.

Olive's mother was arguably even worse. She wore a Che Guevara T-shirt, the same T-shirt she had possessed since her student days, and only changed it to don another faded garment bearing a photograph of Mao Tse-tung. That was a matter of some awkwardness for Olive, but any embarrassment she felt paled in comparison with that felt by her friend Pansy, whose father never appeared at any school function in anything but his kilt and a white-horsehair sporran and whose mother, who bore a strong resemblance to the late Marilyn Monroe, habitually wore a pink shift dress with slits up the side.

Just a block or so away was George Watson's College. Physical proximity, though, could not disguise the gulf that existed between the Steiner and Watson's parents. The Steiner parents often walked their children to school, or accompanied them on self-propelled scooters, whereas the Watson's parents drove their children to school and later collected them in Range Rovers, many of which were identical in colour. This had consequences in that it was only too easy for the parents to get into the wrong Range Rover once they had retrieved their offspring and then drive off quite unaware of the mistake they had made. Of course, this did not matter too much, as the other parents would simply climb into what they imagined was their Range Rover and indeed might never discover what had happened. It was widely known in Edinburgh that there were at least twelve Range Rovers in the hands of the wrong Watsonian parents, and one Range Rover in particular had been driven by no fewer than five sets of parents before anybody discovered the mistake.

There were differences, too, in the names favoured by the two sets of parents. Watson's fathers, usually themselves Watsonians, tended to be called Finlay, Iain, or David, while Steiner fathers preferred names such as Edwin, Theodore, or Pax. Watsonian fathers were, virtually without exception, followers of the Scottish rugby team and had debenture seats at Murrayfield, while Steiner fathers tended to view rugby as a barbaric pursuit, explicable only in tribal terms, engaged in by clearly non-cerebral types from the Borders or New Zealand, and best viewed as a pro-longed homo-erotic encounter starting with close clinches on the pitch and ending with communal showers behind closed doors. This view was not shared by the Watsonian fathers.

Bertie had no inkling of these divisions. He would have liked to play rugby himself, and he would have liked to wear a Watson's blazer. But this was not his lot, and he accepted that. He was happy enough at Steiner's, which was a good, gentle school, even if it meant that he had to put up with the likes of Olive and Pansy, both of whom were now staring at him as he made his way up the driveway to the main school building.

"There's Bertie," said Olive, in a loud stage whisper as he walked past. "Poor Bertie! His mother's a cow and his father runs around having affairs with people in museums."

"Yes," said Pansy. "It's so sad, because Bertie would be such a nice boy if it weren't for his face and his pink dungarees."

Bertie tried to ignore this, but he blushed bright red.

"Look," crowed Olive. "Bertie's bright red. Do you think that's the male menopause, Pansy?"

Pansy giggled. "Either that or high blood pressure," she said.

46
The Play's the Thing

"Now then, boys and girls," said Miss Campbell. "Today you're going to learn what play we'll be performing this year. I know how excited you all are about this and how much you've been looking forward to it."

Olive's hand shot up.

"I'll be very happy to have a leading part, Miss Campbell," she said. "I'm good at learning lines."

"Casting will be done in due course," said Miss Campbell. "And I'm sure there are many in the class who are good at learning lines, Olive. We must remember that the talents we have are often possessed by others—in equal or even in greater measure." She looked intently at Olive. "We must remember that, boys and girls."

Olive shook her head. "Not by everyone, Miss Campbell. Hiawatha is hopeless at remembering things. He just can't do it, can you, Hiawatha?"

Hiawatha, a lanky boy with red hair and a slightly puzzled expression, shook his head. "I can remember things, Olive. I don't remember everything, but I still know quite a bit."

"Oh, do you?" taunted Olive. "In that case, tell me your mobile phone number. Go on, tell me."

"Olive!" reprimanded Miss Campbell. "That's no way to talk. Of course Hiawatha knows his mobile phone number."

"He doesn't, Miss Campbell," said Pansy. "I've seen it written on his hand. You don't have to write your mobile phone number on your hand."

"That's because it's so long," said Hiawatha. "Nobody can remember all those numbers."

"*Au contraire,*" said Olive. She had just learned the phrase and had become fond of using it. "*Au contraire,* Hiawatha. I remember mine. And my parents' numbers. And Pansy's too."

Miss Campbell tried to remember if she had ever encountered a child as irritating as Olive, and decided she had not. But she was professional, and swallowed her irritation. As breezily as she could, she clapped her hands together.

"That's quite enough of that," she said. "Let us not forget the play, boys and girls!"

"*The play's the thing*," quoted Olive. "That's from *Hamlet*, Miss Campbell. *Hamlet* is by Shakespeare, you know."

Miss Campbell bit her lip. "I am well aware of that, Olive."

"And there's a lady called Ophelia in it," Olive continued. "I'd be prepared to be Ophelia if you decide to do *Hamlet*, Miss Campbell. I already know some of the words."

Miss Campbell closed her eyes briefly. "Thank you, Olive, that won't be necessary—because we are not going to be doing *Hamlet*, you see." And she thought, *You little madam.*

Olive pouted.

"So you can't be Ophelia," hissed Tofu. "Don't call us, we'll call you!"

Miss Campbell persisted. "So, boys and girls, the play we shall be doing this year is none other than *Macbeth*. Now can anybody tell me: who wrote *Macbeth*?"

Bertie knew, but did not put up his hand.

"Tofu?" asked Miss Campbell.

"Some guy," muttered Tofu.

"Well, in a sense that's correct," said Miss Campbell. "But which guy? That's the question that's buzzing around in our heads, isn't it? So, who wrote *Macbeth*?"

Bertie now felt he had no alternative but to

255

put up his hand. "William Shakespeare, Miss Campbell."

"There you are," said Miss Campbell. "That's absolutely correct, Bertie. William Shakespeare." She paused, surveying the class before her. "Now then, boys and girls, who can tell me anything about Shakespeare?"

Larch held up his hand. "He's dead."

"Who killed him?" asked Tofu.

"Well, I don't think . . ." began Miss Campbell, only to be interrupted by Larch.

"He was shot, I think."

"No," said Miss Campbell. "Shakespeare was definitely not shot."

"Pneumonia," said Pansy. "He died of pneumonia, Miss Campbell."

The teacher made an effort to regain control. "Let's not speculate as to how William Shakespeare met his end." She hesitated—how *did* Shakespeare die? "It was, I think, a natural death. He had a full life, you see . . ."

"Old age," said Pansy. "He was probably really old. Forty or something."

"We shall move on," said Miss Campbell. "Now let me tell you a little about *Macbeth*. Did you know, for example, that there was a real Macbeth? That he really existed? Did you know that, boys and girls?"

"Was he the leader of the SNP?" asked Larch.

"No, Larch," said Miss Campbell. "He had

nothing to do with the SNP. Macbeth, boys and girls, was a King of Scotland in the . . . the . . ." She tried to remember. The problem with being a teacher was that one was expected to know so much and Moray House was so long ago and . . .

"Eleventh century," said Bertie. He had detected Miss Campbell's uncertainty and wanted to help, but wished at the same time to be as tactful as possible. "I bet that was what you were going to say, Miss Campbell."

The teacher looked at him with gratitude. "You're absolutely right, Bertie. It was indeed the eleventh century."

"You think you know everything, Bertie," hissed Olive *sotto voce*. "Well, I'm telling you, Bertie, the days when boys knew everything are over. They're *over*, Bertie. Boys know nothing these days."

"Nothing," whispered Pansy. "You hear that, Bertie? Boys know nothing."

"I never said I knew everything," whispered Bertie defensively. "I never said that I knew everything. You say I did, but I didn't, Olive."

"So you're calling me a liar, Bertie Pollock? Is that what you're saying? You're calling me a liar . . . and you and I are meant to be engaged."

It was a familiar charge, brought up by Olive from time to time, especially when in a tight corner. "We aren't engaged, Olive. I never said I'd marry you. I never said that."

"You did," said Pansy. "I heard you, Bertie."

"There you are," said Olive. "So if you think you can go around promising to marry people and then turning round and calling them liars, you've got another think coming, Bertie. *Au contraire.* The Scottish Government knows about people like you. You're going to be history, Bertie. History."

Miss Campbell, aware that some sort of altercation was taking place at the back of the room, clapped her hands together. It was a familiar resort for her, although she remembered being told somewhere in her training that one should do it sparingly. One could not go through the days clapping one's hands together, tempting though the expedient might be. It was time to think about casting. She had her ideas, but, as she surveyed the class, she realised that it would not be a simple business—or would it? Was there an incipient Lady Macbeth in the class? There certainly was. There was, so to speak, a natural; but should she give the role to Olive simply because she embodied everything that Shakespeare had in mind when he created the character? And what about Macbeth? That depended on whether one had in mind the historical Macbeth, who was very different from the Macbeth of Shakespeare's imagination, or whether one had to go along with the popular misconception.

And then there was Duncan. In the play he

represents goodness. One choice then for that part. Only one. But that would mean Bertie would have to play against Olive, and should one really so direct a school play that it reflected the dynamics of relationships in the real world?

Tofu's hand was up.

"Yes, Tofu?"

"I'll be Macbeth, Miss Campbell."

She looked at him. Something within her gave; some ligament of the mind snapped. "No, Tofu, you can be a tree. There's a forest in this play. You can be one of the trees."

It was a delicious feeling, and Miss Campbell allowed herself a smile.

"And Olive," she continued. "You can be a witch. The play starts with some very nasty witches. You can be one of them. First witch, in fact."

47

The Isobars of Guilt

Stuart looked at his watch. He had left the office at twenty past five, and it was now almost six o'clock. He had told Irene that he would be back later than usual, possibly even slightly after eight, as he had a meeting. She had not been paying particular attention and had nodded in a vaguely irritated way, as she usually did when he addressed her. As it happened, she was on the phone when he spoke to her; Stuart found this a good time to address her about anything, as she would wave a hand slightly dismissively on such occasions, as if to imply that her telephone conversation was infinitely more important than anything he might have to say. In this way Stuart could tell her virtually anything without provoking much of a reaction, and could later claim—if challenged—that he had told her about whatever it was he was being accused of not having told her.

"But I spoke to you," he would say. "I distinctly remember. I told you."

"I have no recollection of it," Irene would reply.

"Well I did," he would claim, and with all the conviction that came from knowing that what he said was true.

And that counted for something with Stuart, who had been brought up to believe that truth really mattered and that one should not tell lies. If Bertie was scrupulously honest, and if he inherited that from either parent, then it was from Stuart, who had brought it home to his young son that no matter how mendacious the rest of the world might be—and it *was* mendacious, as Stuart had discovered in the course of his career—you should always try to tell the truth.

This had become a slightly old-fashioned view—almost quaint. For many people the truth, it seemed, was what you wanted it to be, and if you asserted a falsehood long enough with sufficient conviction, then it would be believed, not only by those whom it was intended to deceive, but by you yourself. This enabled you to protest with real feeling when the fact was called into question.

Stuart had never felt comfortable with this, and he had experienced even greater misgivings about the argument that the truth simply did not matter. This was an aspect of living in the post-factual age, an age in which the difference between believing and knowing was being eroded. In a post-factual age, it did not matter if you had no evidence for what you asserted—the important thing was to believe it. So, even if all the evidence pointed in the direction of x, you did not have to say that x was the case—if you preferred y, then you denied x and asserted y.

He had thought about this once when walking down from the Lawnmarket to the Tron Kirk and had reflected on the fact that the stone on which he was walking was the very stone on which David Hume and Adam Smith had trodden in that special moment of the Scottish Enlightenment, and that now, and not for the first time in the last hundred years, those Enlightenment values were being assailed. And not just from one quarter—not just from proponents of ideological or religious obscurantism—but from all sorts of enthusiasts who had simply stopped listening, who were not interested in the facts as determined by empirical observation. So those who did not like the implications of Darwin had a simple remedy: deny what he said, just deny it. And those who did not think that global warming existed could do the same in relation to the evidence of thermometers. What, after all, are thermometers in the face of *belief?* And on the coat-tails of those who ignored the facts there travelled all sorts of sinister enthusiasms and social infections: arrogance, intolerance, indifference to need. After all, even the facts of gross injustice could be rejected if one were in full denial mode, as things you did not want to see simply did not *need* to be seen.

Stuart looked at his watch again, and for a moment he wavered. He had said to Irene that he had a meeting, and for that reason would be late. That had not been a lie, because it was indeed true that he did have a meeting. He had *not* told a lie. He had not. And from that fact he drew comfort. He would not have liked to lie to Irene.

But there was a problem, and this problem, like many of the problems we face, philosophical or otherwise, concerned the meaning of words. What exactly did the word *meeting* mean?

Stuart had noticed that meeting covered a

multitude of . . . He paused in the dialogue with himself. *A multitude of sins* was a common enough expression, but its use in this context was unfortunate, because, well . . . is what I'm doing a *sin?* No. Not at all. Sin is something you have to sign up for; you have to accept the whole shooting match of religious belief to start talking about sin. Wrong, yes; you could talk about moral wrong, but not sin. So what I am doing is not a sin because I don't believe in sin. Or so he said to himself.

Let's start again, he thought. People often got others to claim they were in meetings when yet others phoned up and they did not want to talk to them. *He's in a meeting at the moment.* That phrase, so beloved of those whose job it was to answer the phone, could cover almost anything, from obeying a call of nature to enjoying an extended lunch to . . . well, in a few cases perhaps, to being in an actual meeting. In this case, though, the extended meaning of the word meeting was not even an issue. He *was* going to be having a meeting, in the sense that he was going to be meeting somebody—and that, surely, was a meeting even if it was not a meeting at the office. But did any of this matter? He had said nothing about where the meeting would be, and who would be there. Irene assumed that it was at the office and it would be with the usual people—his colleagues in the Scottish Government Office of

Statistics (Creative Section). But if she believed that, that was not because of anything he said, and so it was not his responsibility. We cannot be held responsible for the misinterpretations of others. If they think you're talking about x when in fact you're talking about y, then that's not your fault. Nor do you have any duty to correct them in their assumptions, if those assumptions are incorrect. Or do you?

He sighed. The problem with being brought up to do the right thing, was that it ruined your fun. Forever. He looked up at the sky. Guilt. That was the problem. It lay across Scotland like a blanket. It was as invisible as an isobar, but it was there, and one corner of that blanket, it seemed, was reserved for him.

48

Imagined Interrogations

He walked along Great King Street, a street that he had always found somewhat intimidating. This was Georgian grandeur, the buildings being higher than those of Northumberland Street (comfortable affluence) to the south or Cumberland Street (aspirational simplicity) to the north. And the street itself was wider, giving a whiff of Paris, with its wide boulevards; yet somehow it was not quite so human as other New Town streets where one just felt so *right* . . .

That was such a vague thing to think, thought Stuart, but it was real. One felt right in certain places; one felt that one was where one should be. He had come across this notion when paging through the first chapter of Karen Blixen's memoir, *Out of Africa*, where she had described the feeling of being under that particular sky and feeling that this was exactly where she was intended to be. That passage had stuck in Stuart's mind; he had not read the rest of the book, but those words had remained with him as a musical worm might stick in the brain and repeat itself time and time again. Great King Street was not where he was intended to be, he thought, but Howe Street, which soon came into view as he made his way westwards, was a different matter, because that was where *she* lived, and that transformed it, that imbued it with significance, if not exactly with glory.

At the corner end of Great King Street, he paused. To his left, Howe Street ran sharply uphill; to his right, continuing downhill, it became St. Vincent Street, at the end of which the solid shape of a vast disused church, a sort of compacted, Presbyterian version of Saint Mark's or even Hagia Sophia, made an architectural full stop. Stuart looked neither up nor down, but behind him, throwing a nervous glance back down Great King Street, over his shoulder. He was not quite sure what he was expecting to see. Irene lurking by some railing, following him, determined to break apart whatever alibi he might provide for the hours between the end of work and his guilty return to Scotland Street at eight o'clock?

"Good meeting?" she might say; a neutral opening comment of the sort that all skilful interrogators use before they flick open the cigarette case and offer their victim a cigarette. And then the lighter would be produced and the hand of the victim would shake revealingly as he lit his cigarette, although of course neither he nor Irene smoked.

"Nervous?" the interrogator would say, but half-jokingly.

"Why should I be nervous? I have nothing to hide." Spoken by one, of course, who had everything to hide . . .

"Why were you in Great King Street when you said you would be at the office? Great King Street is not exactly on the way from Victoria Quay."

He would look about furtively, and she would nod to a tough-looking assistant whose fists, he had noticed, were clenching; a woman, not a man, of course, because this was woman's business, this exposing of the meretricious doings of men.

"Were you by any chance going to see some-body, Stuart? You don't mind if I call you Stuart, do you—after all, we've been married for years . . ."

He felt his neck becoming warm, and he loosened his collar. This was absurd, and he would make a conscious effort to control these fanciful, unsettling thoughts. There was no possibility of his being seen by Irene, or by anybody for that matter. He might as well be in Shanghai or . . .

"Stuart . . . well, well, good evening. And what brings you here?"

He looked up sharply. It was Angus Lordie, who had walked round the corner from Howe Street, with his dog, Cyril, panting on his lead. Cyril liked Stuart, who had, from the canine point of view, a particularly attractive smell, and he jumped up appreciatively to lick Stuart's hands.

"Down, Cyril!" commanded Angus, and the dog obeyed, sitting quietly at Stuart's feet, looking up at him with undisguised olfactory adoration.

"Good dog," muttered Stuart, and then, to Angus, "Just taking a walk. It's such a nice evening." And that, he thought, was not a lie either. He was taking a walk, even if he had a clear destination in mind.

Now he remembered that Angus had just been discharged from hospital after his defenestration.

"I'm so glad to see you back on your feet," he

said. "After what happened. It must have been a terrible shock."

Angus smiled. "The actual process happened very quickly," he said. "One moment I was standing at the window, trying to get it open, and the next . . . well, I was upside down, and then I was vaguely conscious of the tree and of being manipulated. Then I was in the Infirmary."

"Where they looked after you well?"

Angus nodded. "Extremely well, apart from an initial shock. The nurse called me *sweetheart*. I'd never met her before and there I was, more or less out for the count, and she called me *sweetheart*."

"She was probably trying to be friendly—trying to reassure you."

"Perhaps. But do you think that in a formal setting like that—nurse and patient, after all— terms like that shouldn't be used?"

Stuart shrugged. "Oh, I don't know . . . *Sweetheart* is like *darling,* I suppose, or *love*. That's what people call one another. Or *pal,* if you're addressing a man. Or *Jim*. One of the security guards down at the office calls me *Jim*—it's a sort of honorific here, don't you think?"

Angus wondered whether nurses should call patients *Jim*. "This won't hurt, Jim, I'm just going to take a wee blood sample." To which the patient might reply, "Oh dinnae bother about that, hen"—in the case of a female nurse, or, in the case of a male nurse, "You go right ahead, pal." He had always liked the term of address *hen,* common between women in Scotland but becoming less so. There was something reassuring about it—an assumption of comfortable intimacy, the equivalent of the English term *ducks* or *ducky.* But this was not the point: the point was that the state—in the shape of a nurse or doctor—should not address you as a sweetheart; it just shouldn't. What was wrong with *sir,* or *madam?* Those terms indicated respect, and surely the state—or its health service in this case—should respect those for whom it cared, even if they were vulnerable, or confused, or, as in his case, recently defenestrated. But perhaps that was an old-fashioned view.

Stuart looked at his watch. "I must dash," he said. "I have to see somebody."

It slipped out, but Angus, of course, was not to know. Or so Stuart thought, at least for a second or two; he reckoned without Nicola's having told Domenica and Domenica's having passed the information on to Angus. So he knew, and his expression showed he knew. "Of course," he said, and smiled—a smile of patent disbelief. And Stuart, noticing this, knew that his secret was no secret, and his heart sank, as does the heart of anybody whose fond illusions are destroyed before his eyes.

49

A Cry of Freedom and Defiance

Stuart almost turned back, but did not. As Angus said goodbye and continued his walk, Cyril glanced over his shoulder and gave Stuart one of those canine glances into which one might read either nothing or everything. Looking into the eyes of an animal may be like looking into a mirror: one usually sees nothing but the returned stare; or it may, for a brief and wonderful moment, be like looking into the soul of the world. The eye of the animal is nature; is the world itself, stripped of the human meaning with which we clutter everything around us. Pure being. Simplicity. Acceptance.

Stuart was ready for reproach. He had realised that Angus had sensed—though heaven knew how that had happened—that he was engaged in a clandestine errand. Perhaps it was the guilt that he felt; perhaps that shone out of him— if guilt can shine. Of course the light that guilt generates is a low one; it casts a weak beam, one that requires that we look hard to see its features; whereas confidence and self-satisfaction glow with bright, unambiguous light.

Cyril had looked at him and, in so far as a

dog might smile, he had done just that. And as he did so, the sun had caught his gold tooth— that rare attribute possessed by no other dog in Scotland—a gold tooth implanted one memorable evening by a dentist in the Scottish Arts Club after a convivial dinner. Cyril's tooth had broken and he was in some discomfort, and the dentist, who happened to have his emergency repair kit in the downstairs cloakroom, had fashioned the tooth from a small brooch donated there and then by one of the party. That gold tooth now sent a small flash of reflected sunlight back to Stuart, and it was the signal that he needed.

I shall not turn back. I shall not go home to the servitude imposed upon me.

Servitude, he realised even as he mentally uttered it, was too strong a word for his circumstances. There was real servitude in the world— it was still the lot of countless millions—and it should not be cheapened by those whose condition was infinitely better than theirs. No, he was not in servitude, but his position was still one of . . . of what? Of restriction? Of humiliation?

Perhaps that was it. It was humiliating to be disagreed with on almost everything. It was particularly humiliating to be told what to think; to be told that everything you said—or almost everything—was somehow wrong—an inadmissible view that was somehow inferior to the set of opinions held by Irene. That set of opinions had an imprimatur from some body, some grand council as it were, of the enlightened. These were the people who told other people what they might think and say. These were the people who told you what words you could use, what opinions you could express, what views you might form of the world about you. And if you deviated from this imposed consensus, then you were roundly condemned, ostracised, denied a hearing. How subtly and with such stealth did freedom of speech drain away.

That was what Irene stood for. She stood for intolerance and domination. She stood for those people—those nameless people, who would dictate to others. She was a tyrant, just as all those people who crushed others into silence were tyrants.

And then a terrible realisation dawned on Stuart. It came to him naturally, perhaps even inevitably, once he had dared to entertain those first thoughts of rebellion. He was married to a fascist.

He felt immediately ashamed. He could not think that, even if the word came to him unannounced, unsought-out. But it was true: Irene was a fascist. She wanted so many of the things that fascists wanted—the same powerful state, the same unanimity of opinion and purpose, the same imposition of ideology, the same suppression of free debate that those grubby bullies wanted. There was little difference when you were on the receiving end as to whether such hectoring and oppression came from left or right. Herbert Marcuse, who preached the silencing of those who disagreed with his agenda, was a name that crossed Irene's lips with approval. What company did Marcuse keep?

He heard a strange sound. He knew it was not there, not in the real world that was the corner of Howe Street and St. Vincent Street on this innocent Edinburgh evening; it was there somewhere in his mind. It was a rushing sound— the sound of a waterfall or a wind. It came upon him like some divine and benign tinnitus, and for a few moments obliterated much of the other evidence of his senses. It consumed him, and strengthened him. It clothed him with resolve.

Why, he thought, should I accept it? Why should I sit there and listen to her going on? Why should I let her push my son around, making him the receptacle of her views, her prejudices, her enthusiasms? All that psychotherapy, that yoga, that Italian *conversazione* . . . all of that being forced down the throat of a little boy who really wants to go fishing, to own a Swiss Army penknife, to take the train to Glasgow. *Glasgow!* In Bertie's mind Glasgow was some sort of promised land, a place where freedom existed; a place free of psychotherapy and Italian *conversazione*; a place where every boy, or almost every boy, possessed a Swiss Army penknife. It was the shining city upon the hill that was denied him, but he would take Bertie to live there, in a metaphorical sense, of course, although there could even be real trips to Glasgow on the Queen Street train, father and son together, going to Glasgow just because they felt like it. And Bertie could bring that little friend of his, Ranald Braveheart Macpherson, that rather wistful little boy with his spindly legs, but who seemed so loyal and appreciative. The three of them could go to Glasgow for the afternoon and eat unhealthy food before returning to Edinburgh.

But that was not the immediate issue. The immediate issue was whether or not to walk fifty yards or so up Howe Street and ring a particular doorbell that would sound in a particular flat. He hesitated for a further minute or so, and then made his decision. The pressing of that bell would be an act of resistance, a cry— or perhaps a ring—of freedom and defiance.

It was the bell of the young woman whom Stuart had met in Henderson's Salad Bar when he had spilled his soup and she had offered him a handkerchief; a young woman with whom, in the space of less than four minutes, he had fallen completely in love.

50

Hipster Pyjamas

In general, the demands of the hipsterdom into which Bruce had been propelled by Clare were not such as to make much of a difference to his daily life—except for the extremely tight jeans, of course: these were an important part of being a hipster, it appeared, and as such could not be exchanged for something more comfortable. Even more challenging were hipster pyjamas, a pair of which were ordered online by Clare. The sizing chart for hipster clothes is unlike that of normal clothes; there is no S/M/L and XL with which most people are familiar, rather there is SC/C and XC, standing for Slightly Cool, Cool, and Extra Cool. This option was to be combined with a further choice, pertaining to size, which was H/2H and 3H. Bruce was initially puzzled by this, but Clare knew exactly what it meant. "H stands for *hunk*," she said. "It's simple, really. You're an XC/3H. No probs."

Bruce was unsure about pyjamas. He normally slept in boxer shorts and a T-shirt that bore the legend *Aviemore* in faded print; a comfortable form of night garb. He had had pyjamas when he was a boy in Crieff, but had abandoned them in favour of this new choice when he left home for university. Nobody, he had been told, wore pyjamas at university—except perhaps the *sad,* the *tragic,* and the *lonely.*

"Are pyjamas *in* these days?" he asked Clare. *In* was a convenient code word for *hip,* as Bruce had discovered when he read a newspaper article about hipsterdom.

"Sure," said Clare. "Provided they're cool pyjamas. Nobody wears those old-fashioned ones—you know, the stripy flannelette things our granddads wore."

"I see," said Bruce. "But those flannelette shirts—those shirts you call flannies . . ."

"Different," retorted Clare. "Those are *in,* big time." She paused. "You know, Bruce, sometimes I think you just don't get it. No offence. It's something to do with being Scottish, I suppose. I'm not sure that anybody in Scotland really gets it. Odd, isn't it?"

"Do Australians get it?" asked Bruce. "All of them?"

Clare considered the question. "Some don't, fair enough, but I'd say most Australians get it right from the beginning. We get it as kids and then we carry on getting it as adults. Does that answer your question?"

The pyjamas arrived at Clare's flat in Newington, and Bruce was encouraged to try them on immediately.

"It feels odd getting into my pyjamas in the middle of the day," he said. "Can't it wait?"

"You know something, Bruce?" Clare said. "You've got serious hang-ups. You need to loosen up."

"I don't think you can . . ."

He was not allowed to finish. "I suppose it's not your fault. You've been brought up like that, and you can't help your upbringing. You come from . . . Where's that place? Grief?"

"Crieff," said Bruce. "And it's quite a nice place, actually."

"Oh, I'm sure it is. And that school of yours . . . What was it called?"

"Morrison's Academy. And it's pretty good, actually."

"Oh. I'm sure it is," said Clare.

Bruce decided to fight back. "But what about you?"

She raised an eyebrow. "Yes, what about me?"

"You come from Perth, don't you? Isn't that in the sticks somewhere?"

Clare's eyes narrowed. "You ever been to Perth, Bruce?"

He was undeterred. "And that school you went to? Presbyterian Ladies' or whatever it was. That doesn't sound very cool to me."

"You ever been there?" snapped Clare. "You ever seen it? But, look, let's not argue. You can't help being who you are, and I can't help being who I am. On balance, I'm happy that I'm me and not you, but then you're a man, aren't you, and that's your issue."

"I don't want to fight," muttered Bruce.

"Then try on the pyjamas. Go on. I'll close my eyes. Or go into the bedroom. Be my guest."

He left the room, the freshly unwrapped parcel in his hand. He looked at the label: XC/3H, just as she had said it would be.

The pyjamas were made of a cloth that imitated, but was not, denim. Unwrapping the trousers, he noticed that there were two neat rents in the knees, carefully placed as fashion rents tend to be. And now the lower section of the legs . . . He frowned. These were every bit as narrow as the legs of his new jeans, if not narrower. The night, therefore, would be as uncomfortable as the day. Could he turn in bed in these pyjamas? Probably not: he would have to swing his legs out of the bed, stand up, and then lower himself back on the other side.

He squeezed himself into the new garment and then, walking with some effort and not a little discomfort, he made his way back into the living room.

Clare whistled. "Fab!" she said. "Seriously fab!"

"They're not very comfortable," said Bruce. "They're a bit tight."

Clare sighed. "But I've told you, Bruce—I've

told you hundreds of times: clothes *give.* They start off a bit tight but they're designed to give. You'll be fine in those."

He sat down, with effort—and with a rather alarming tearing sound.

"See," said Clare. "They're giving already."

She looked at her watch. "I think you should go back and get dressed," she said. "Aren't we expected soon at those friends of yours?"

"Matt and Elspeth? Yes. In an hour or so."

He stood up, almost prepared for the further sound of ripping and the feeling of cool air about him. That was better. When clothes gave, one obviously felt much cooler. And he felt cooler yet when, in the vintage Triumph sports car that he had recently acquired, he drove Clare off to Nine Mile Burn, the car-roof folded back, the light air of summer in their hair. He glanced at her as he took the car down the long stretch of road past Flotterstone. I'm lucky, he thought; I have this fantastic girlfriend, this car, this empty road; I could be old, middle-aged even; I could be short and overweight; I could be everything I'm not; instead of which I'm me, here in this car, with this girl, with my future stretching out ahead of me. That's what counted.

51
An Eighty-four Horse-power,
Six-cylinder Narcissist

Elspeth was at the end of her tether. Since the departure of the two Danish au pairs, she had struggled to cope with the sheer physical labour involved in managing three energetic and increasingly mobile young boys. She looked back with nostalgic longing to the days when the triplets were immobile, when they could be placed on a mat and would be unable to do much about it. Even when they worked out how to turn themselves over—a major stage in a baby's life— they were containable; but then came crawling, when they would shoot off at different speeds and in different directions, and finally walking, when she found that she was frankly unable to manage without help.

It had given her cause for thought. She was fortunate: she could afford help in the shape of Birgitte and her friend; there were plenty of mothers of twins or triplets—the vast majority— who had to cope without any help at all, not even that of a nearby grandmother. And it was not just those mothers who had experienced a multiple birth whose life was one long battle; most women who had more than one small child led lives that were dominated by the relentless demands of their offspring; mothers who struggled to find a moment to themselves; mothers who had to develop an ability to deal with one small child with one hand and another with the other hand. Amongst such there must be so many lives of quiet desperation; Elspeth knew that and did not take her good fortune for granted.

Matthew did his best. He had so arranged his work commitments that he could spend as much time as possible at home, but there were limits to what he could do. The Danes had left about a week earlier, and he had managed to take over for two complete afternoons during that period, allowing Elspeth the chance to lie down and catch up on sleep, but for the rest she had been in sole charge.

Now at least there was the prospect of help. She had received with undisguised elation the news that Bruce's new girlfriend was looking for a job and might be interested in helping with the boys. She knew nothing of Clare other than that she was friendly with Bruce, but she was prepared to overlook that fact. Elspeth had little time for Bruce, whom she had once described to Matthew as an "eighty-four horse-power, six-cylinder narcissist"—a description that Matthew had thought a bit extreme. "He's doing his best," he said, trying to convince himself that this was indeed the case. He saw what she meant, but Matthew was one of these people who was prepared to give others the benefit of the doubt even when their flaws were writ large for all to see. He remembered the chaplain at school all those years ago saying, "We are all flawed, boys—in our various and inventive ways." One of the boys had muttered *Speak for yourself, Chaplain* but that phrase had stuck with him— *in our various and inventive ways*—as had the sentiment behind it.

Of course the fact that Clare was associated with Bruce raised at least some issues as to her taste, and possibly also as to her judgement, but Elspeth was very much aware that women found Bruce attractive and that a perfectly sensible, level-headed woman could easily fall for him. She herself would never do that, but she understood the physical realities of these matters and would certainly not hold it against Clare that she appeared to have fallen for Bruce. "You don't judge people by their friends," she remarked to Matthew, and he had nodded his agreement. But then he had looked at her, and they both realized that what she had just said—although the sort of thing we like to say, and feel good and virtuous about saying—was actually quite false. Of course you can judge people by the company they keep, at least to an extent, she thought, and

Matthew thought the same. But neither said it.

And now Bruce and Clare were due to arrive in twenty minutes or so and she was trying to have scones ready for their arrival. Things were not going well; Matthew was looking after the boys, giving her the chance to be alone in the kitchen, but everything was not working out as smoothly as she wished. The scones were quite straightforward and would be baked in time, but she had also been trying to make a pork pie for lunch the following day, and that was not going well. She had made the jelly—using trotters specially obtained from her butcher, Mr. Christie—but she had found it difficult to get this into the pie once the hot-water pastry crust had baked. And then the crust had split at a crucial point, allowing liquid to drain from the filling and compromising the structural integrity of the pie.

She looked at her watch, and decided to leave the pie for the time being. If she could not get the jelly into it, then it would be a pork pie without jelly; nobody would notice the difference, and she could use the jelly to make lentil soup. But did she have lentils? She tried to remember whether she had bought them on her last visit to the supermarket. She thought she had, but could not be sure. And if she had not bought lentils, then what else had she forgotten? She sat down. *I have to get a grip,* she told herself. *Help is on the horizon.*

And over that metaphorical horizon—the drive-way between the rhododendrons in reality—drove Bruce and Clare in Bruce's open Triumph TR3. As they approached the house, Bruce sounded the horn and waved cheerfully to Matthew, who was waiting to greet him at the front door.

"Jeez, Matthew," said Bruce as he emerged from the car, "this is quite some place you've got here. How much did you pay for this?"

Matthew smiled. "Not too much," he said.

"I'd say eight hundred grand," said Bruce, looking about him. "It depends on how much land you've got."

"Six acres," said Matthew.

"Six acres is six acres," said Bruce.

He introduced Clare. "This is my old pal Matthew," he said. "He's not as dim as he looks."

Matthew smiled, and shook hands with Clare. "My wife—Elspeth, that is, is inside. Come and meet her."

"Matthew eventually got somebody to marry him," said Bruce. "Only joking, Matt, old chap."

Elspeth appeared from the kitchen, drying her hands on a dish towel.

"Where are the sprogs?" said Bruce.

"They're having their afternoon sleep," said Matthew. "A rare moment of peace . . ." He stopped himself. They wanted Clare to work for them, and this might give the wrong impression of the boys. "Actually, they're very good," he said.

"Pull the other one, Matt," said Bruce.

"Come along and have some tea," said Elspeth. "And scones. I've made some scones."

Clare smiled. "I love scones," she said. "I had an aunt in Murrumba Downs who made terrific scones."

"Murrumba Downs!" exclaimed Bruce.

Clare looked at him. "So?" she said.

"Scones," said Elspeth. "Let's go and have a scone."

52
The Symbolism of Scones

"Nice scones," said Clare. "Different, though."

"Different from what?" asked Bruce.

Matthew gazed up at the ceiling. "We all have fixed ideas on how things should taste," he said. "Childhood determines that. The way things are cooked at home is, of course, the definitive way."

Elspeth looked thoughtful. She did not want to find out how scones were cooked in Murrumba Downs. "It's the same with religion, don't you think? That comes through childhood exposure."

"Membership, rather," corrected Matthew. "Don't you think religion has become more about group membership these days—rather than theology?"

Elspeth did not entirely agree. "People can come to a position through choice. I know somebody over in Glasgow who was on a spiritual quest . . ."

Matthew smiled. "I know who you're talking about. A very nice man."

Bruce bit into a scone; a light dusting of flour stuck to his lips, outlining them in white. "Went on a quest?"

Clare reached over and brushed away the flour. As she did so, she looked reproachfully at Elspeth—a look that was not seen by anybody else. "Did he go somewhere?" she asked.

Elspeth shook her head. "No, it wasn't that sort of quest. It wasn't a pilgrimage or anything of that sort. He was just looking for something to satisfy himself spiritually. You know the feeling?"

Clare did not. She looked blank. Bruce whispered in her ear: "God—your actual God."

"He tried various options. He went to Catholic Mass. He went to a Church of Scotland service. He even went to a Quaker meeting—but none of them seemed to be quite right for him. Then he went to a synagogue, and liked it."

"But it's hard to become Jewish, isn't it?" said Clare. "I know somebody back in Perth who wanted to be Jewish and got nowhere. You're not exactly recruited."

"It's not a proselytising religion," said Matthew. "They want to make sure you mean it. They don't seek out new members."

"But they do allow them," said Elspeth. "He had to go through a lot of instruction and then he was accepted. It answered his needs. He was very happy. Judaism's a very satisfying religion. I find his story rather inspiring. We all need some sort of spiritual life—otherwise . . ." She thought: otherwise what? Otherwise a pointless, arid life, trapped in an empty materialism. Religion was all about deep meaning—and we all needed that.

"The thing that interests me," said Matthew, "is this: isn't it harder to accept the tenets of a faith when you approach it as a possible convert?"

"Much harder," said Clare.

They all looked at her.

"Why do you think it is?" asked Matthew.

She shrugged. "Just is," she said. "That's the way it is. What you're told as a kid you keep in the back of your mind with all the other stuff you get. You don't go there. You just accept it all."

"Possibly," said Matthew. "Possibly."

Elspeth thought that Clare had a point. "I think Clare's right. We all have a set of attitudes that are part of our deep cultural background. We don't question these. They're just there—like the way you tie your laces; like the way you talk; like the nursery rhymes you're taught."

Matthew smiled. "And some of that stuff is pretty odd," he said. "Did you believe, for example, that if you cut yourself in the web of skin between your thumb and your forefinger you got lockjaw? Remember that?"

Clare did. "And if you put blotting paper in your shoes you fainted. We did that to our gym teacher. We put blotting paper in her gym shoes and waited for her to faint. She didn't." She looked disappointed.

"This chap," said Bruce. "This chap who became Jewish signed up for everything? Special food and all that?"

"Yes," said Elspeth. "The food bit can be very important in a religion."

"I don't see what difference it makes," said Bruce. "Who cares what you eat? Didn't Catholics used to eat fish on Friday?"

"I think they can eat meat on Fridays now," said Matthew. "Things have changed."

"The Pope said you can," said Clare.

"The food part is a ritual," said Elspeth. "It underlines membership. And it's about adherence too. If you don't eat whatever you're not meant to eat, it reminds you that you've accepted the other, more important things."

She saw that her guests had finished their scones, and she passed the plate. "As far as I know," she said, "there's no religious faith that says you shouldn't eat scones."

"Don't say that too loudly," said Matthew. "It's exactly the sort of thing somebody might pick up on. No scones from now on, folks!"

Elspeth laughed. "I suppose that scones do carry a bit of symbolism. They're a rather . . . how should I put it? They're rather a *polite* food. Bourgeois? Lace doilies? Edinburgh?"

"They're definitely Edinburgh," agreed Matthew. "And yet . . . if you go to a small town in Scotland, they'll offer you a scone."

"They like scones in Crieff," said Bruce suddenly. "Boy, do they like scones in Crieff."

"I wasn't thinking of Crieff," said Matthew. "I was thinking of smaller places—where they eat a lot of scones. Places like . . ."

"Auchtermuchty?" suggested Elspeth.

"Perhaps," said Matthew. "Perhaps everywhere in Scotland is . . . is prone to scones. Maybe it's just part of our inheritance."

"Isn't Scotland sometimes called the *Land of Cakes?*" asked Clare. "I remember my father used to call it that. He was Scottish, you know—or, rather, his father was, which made him Scottish, he said, although he was born in Oz."

"And by the same token it makes you Scottish," said Matthew.

"So you won't need to convert," said Elspeth, laughing. "You won't need to do anything else to become Scottish."

"Except accept our prejudices," muttered Matthew. "Do you want me to list those?"

Elspeth gave him a discouraging glance. She did not want Matthew to be misunderstood; he was proud of Scotland, but ashamed of it too. And that, she thought, was how it should be: one should be proud of one's country but ashamed of it as well. "And anyway . . . Clare, Bruce told Matthew that you were looking for a part-time job."

Clare nodded. "Yup. Anything. Baking scones even."

"Hah!" said Bruce. "*Très drôle.*"

Elspeth hesitated. "I've got these triplets, you see, and I used to have a couple of Danish girls . . ."

"Good riddance," interjected Bruce. "You should have seen them, babe . . ."

Elspeth winced. *Babe.* What century was Bruce in? *Babe!*

"Elspeth and I were wondering," said Matthew, "whether you might . . ."

Clare reached for another scone. "Do the job? Yes, no probs. I like kids—always have—even snotty little . . ."

"She's only joking," said Bruce.

53

Metaphorical Falls

Stuart made his way up Howe Street, crossing the road at the corner of which Madame Doubtfire had once run her cat-infested shop, selling winter coats from deceased estates, reminding passers-by, should they need reminding, that she had "danced before the Czar." Here the city's palimpsest had faded, as it had in so many other places where lettering had lingered for so long that the claims of ancient outfitters, upholsterers, pen-makers, and whisky distillers seeped out of the stone. But neither Stuart's eyes, nor mind, were on such matters as he began the short ascent leading to the blue door, with its polished brass Roman numerals, through which he had gone for the first time just a few weeks ago.

A few weeks ago . . . so short a time, and yet for him those weeks constituted one of the great divides of his life, as significant as the first few days away from home when he had started at university. Days when, almost reeling at the possibilities, he had found himself master of his destiny, able to decide what to do with his time, what to eat for breakfast, what clothes to wear; freedom, in short, to live out his life as he wished to live it. Freedom, that state that is as easily obscured by a thousand tiny quotidian constraints as it is by the slamming of a prison door, or, in his case, perhaps, by the contours of an unfortunate domestic arrangement—to put it simply, and brutally, by his wife; by Irene, author and begetter of the Bertie Project, relentless advocate of the correct approach to everything, enforcer of an orthodoxy of Stalinist proportions . . . And yet she was still his wife, still the woman who made a home for him and his children, who loved those children fiercely even if Ulysses was profusely sick whenever she picked him up, who would defend him ferociously if he were ever to be assailed, who was the other party in the pronoun *us* he used when talking about so many things, who laundered his socks and shirts and merino-wool underwear, who did the shopping for sun-dried tomatoes and tagliatelle and Chianti at Valvona & Crolla, who sometimes, even if hardly ever, laughed at his jokes . . .

In spite of all that, he had created a watershed in his life, an occasion that he would forever view as the point at which a new and important phase had started. And that had happened when he had slipped into Henderson's for what he had thought would be a quick bite of lunch. Stuart only very occasionally ate out—Irene disagreed in principle with the idea of being served food by others, which she had labelled as irretrievably bourgeois—an attempt, in short, to recreate the conditions in which people were attended at table by servants. This meant that any sampling of restaurants had to be undertaken by Stuart as a solitary diner, in the eyes of some a slightly melancholic sight, although solitary diners may be quite happy, particularly if they are left to read the book or magazine they are trying to read and are not too often disturbed by over-attentive waiting staff asking them whether everything is all right.

Henderson's, a vegetarian restaurant even in the days when restaurants in Edinburgh were few and far between, and when those that were vegetarian were even rarer, had become an Edinburgh institution, ranking along with such well-known howffs as the Oxford Bar or the Café Royal. Stuart chose it for his lunch that day not just because he liked the atmosphere and food, or because it was widely appreciated for not being too expensive, but also because it was just round the corner from a one-day conference he was attending at the Royal College of Physicians on Queen Street. This was a conference on health statistics, and Stuart had been sent by his department to listen to a variety of papers on the incidence of several conditions, on cost/benefit figures, and mortality rates.

He had enjoyed the morning sessions, but was less interested in the afternoon's offerings, the highlight of which was to be a paper by a Belgian health statistician on the collection of data relating to accidental falls in the home. Stuart was not unsympathetic to Belgians who suffered injury of this type, or indeed of any type, but he felt that it had little bearing on the work that he did for the Scottish Government. People were always falling over and hurting themselves—everybody knew that, and he was not sure whether information as to how often they fell off ladders or stools was going to change all that. Ladders, of course, could be made safer, but that was an issue for their manufacturers, who were all in China, and even if they made these as safe as they possibly could, there were always people who would use ladders inappropriately. Perhaps ladders should carry a warning, as so many other things now did: *climbing a ladder can lead to a fall* would perhaps be the wording, or *use this ladder responsibly.* That would give pause for thought, perhaps, to the reckless and troublesome minority deter-mined to use ladders irresponsibly, and indeed to others, who might interpret such warnings more metaphorically. Falls awaited us, in such a view, even if we never used an actual ladder.

And as for the Belgians, thought Stuart as he made his way towards Henderson's, accidents in the home were surely the least of their problems. They had experienced great difficulty, had they not, in even establishing a government—any government, let alone one that would have the time or inclination to warn its citizens about the inappropriate use of ladders. And they were always bickering amongst themselves about where they belonged, whether they were French or vaguely Dutch; there were times when it must be so hard to be Belgian, thought Stuart; perhaps he should give their domestic accident issues a more attentive hearing than he was currently proposing to do.

He reached Henderson's. The restaurant was busy, and the staff were asking people to share tables; Stuart agreed, and was directed to a table at which a young woman was already sitting. As he placed his soup bowl on the table, he spilled a small amount on the front of his shirt, fumbled, and spilled a further small amount on the sleeve of his jacket.

"Oh," he said.

"Poor you," said the young woman opposite him. "Here, let me wipe it off for you."

"I'll be all right," muttered Stuart.

"Well, take this handkerchief—it's unused. You don't want to ruin your jacket, and you can keep the hanky."

It would have been churlish to refuse, and he took the handkerchief offered him.

"I feel so stupid," he said.

"Nonsense. We all spill soup on ourselves. Everyone does. All the time."

Oddly, he thought of the Belgians. They presumably spilled soup on themselves in the home—and then fell off ladders. That was called piling Pelion upon Ossa. Strange. Ridiculous.

He smiled, and wiped at the stains. Then he looked at her—and fell, metaphorically, of course, and there are no statistics for metaphorical falls.

54

Deceit and Concealment

Stuart felt a certain embarrassment in speaking to somebody when he had a soup stain on his shirt-front. The attempts to deal with it with the donated handkerchief had merely succeeded in spreading the stain across a wider area of fabric, although they had been a bit more effective on the darker material of the jacket.

The young woman looked concerned. "I'm afraid that's only gone and made it worse."

Stuart was quick to reassure her. "But food stains are natural. It's only recently that we started to wear clean clothes. A few hundred years ago everybody was covered in stains."

She nodded. "Well, they didn't have many clothes, did they? Many people had only the set they stood up in."

Stuart agreed. "I read somewhere that a

reasonably prosperous farmer's wife in Scotland back in the . . . seventeen-hundreds, I think it was, would have only one decent dress." He paused. "My name's Stuart, by the way. And I do have another shirt."

"I'm Katie," she said.

As he unfolded the paper napkin encasing his cutlery, he stole a glance at Katie. He felt flushed, no longer anything to do with the soup but with the way he was feeling. He was aware that his pulse was racing. Adrenaline, he thought. But why should he feel that in this perfectly innocent social encounter—in Henderson's, of all places, a restaurant that was synonymous with health and openness, not some place of subdued lighting and seductive couches, some louche dive where every second table hosted a furtive assignation? Vegetarianism did not go with all of that, although vegetarians undoubtedly had their moments, as everyone did . . . The answer, of course, was that if it was a perfectly innocent social encounter, then it had been that only for a minute or two before it had transformed into something rather different.

He looked at her again, and this time it coincided with a look she was giving him—a look of reciprocated interest. And at that Stuart caught his breath and for the briefest of moments closed his eyes. What he experienced then was something he had not experienced for years, a stirring of interest—*that* sort of interest. This was a sexually charged situation. Somewhere, deep in the socio-biological hinterland, some switch had been tripped, some instigator of chemistry had engaged. He breathed out. That made it no better. He breathed in. It was worse.

"I like this place," said Katie.

"Oh, so do I," said Stuart quickly; so quickly, in fact, that she had barely finished speaking before he replied.

"Not that I'm a vegetarian," continued Katie. "I eat quite a lot of fish, but I hardly ever have red meat."

"Me neither," said Stuart. "Although I must admit I miss bacon. We've been told that we shouldn't eat too much bacon or processed meat anyway. Did you see that stuff from the World Health Organization? They said that we ate far too much processed meat—burgers, bacon, that sort of thing."

She nodded. "I read it. And if that comes from the World Health Organization then I suppose indirectly it has the authority of the UN behind it. And we should listen to the UN, I suppose."

"The Security Council is probably going to tell us not to eat bacon or salamis," said Stuart, and laughed. "It's only a question of time."

He relaxed. The burning sensation around his neck had abated now and he felt that his pulse was slowing down. But he was still very much aware of a feeling of excitement—a joy that was close to exhilaration—that had come over him.

"Where do you live?" he asked, and immediately regretted the question. It was not what one should say immediately to somebody one meets in a restaurant. "I mean, do you live here in Edinburgh?"

Katie did not seem to mind the question. "Howe Street," she said. "And you?"

He thought of lying. Could he tell her? Could he utter the words: *Scotland Street?* To do so would be to admit to his actual home in a way that seemed quite inappropriate in this context. But honesty prevailed—at least to some extent—and he replied, "I have a flat in Scotland Street." *I,* not *we.*

It was the first piece of subterfuge, the very beginning. *I have a flat in Scotland Street.* That sounded like a bachelor establishment—a flat occupied not by three other people, one of them his wife and the other two his progeny. He swallowed hard. It was very easy to mislead simply by not mentioning something, even something as important as one's marital status. And then he remembered that he was wearing a wedding ring, and the presence or absence of a wedding ring was something that people noticed; he did not, but then there were things of which men were perhaps less observant than women.

He glanced at her left hand. There was no ring.

And then he saw that she was looking at his hand, even as he had at hers.

"My wife and I . . ." he blurted out. "Well, we're . . ."

He had no idea why he spoke, and he immediately felt a burning sense of disappointment. Why had he mentioned Irene—and what was the unspoken ellipsis meant to signify?

She said: "I understand. Don't worry."

He felt a surge of relief. She had interpreted his Delphic utterance as meaning that he was separated or at least in a marriage that was not working. Perhaps he had sighed, or she thought he had sighed, after saying *well, we're* . . . It was just the sort of moment when people might sigh after saying *Well, we're no longer together* or *Well, we're going our separate ways, you know how it is (sigh)* . . .

He asked her, "What do you do, Katie? Do you mind my asking?"

She seemed pleased that the conversation was going no further into status issues. "What do I do? Well, I suppose that by profession I'm a teacher—or that's what I'm qualified to do. I used to teach English—now I'm doing a PhD in literature. I've just started."

He wondered about her age. Thirty-three, thirty-four? It was difficult to tell.

"And you?"

"I work for the Scottish Government." He

should have said that he was a statistician—he knew that—but it seemed so dull beside a PhD.

But she asked, "What sort of work?"

Now he had to confess. "Figures," he said. "Actually, statistics. I make up figures for them."

She laughed. "I thought they invented them themselves."

"No," said Stuart. "Governments always have people to advise them on how to invent figures." Then he added, "It's not easy to hide the truth. You have to be expert at it."

His words hung in the air, as if in reproach. He looked up, expecting to see them there, flashing in neon, declaring to the world, or at least to that section of the world present in Henderson's, that here was a man embarking on a course of deceit and concealment, and really rather thrilled about doing so.

55

Squtlandiyah

"Why are you doing a PhD?" Stuart asked, and then added, "Actually, I don't mean to be rude. That sounds a bit rude—but why are you doing it?"

She explained that she hated teaching. "The idea of teaching is fine, but the reality, I'm afraid, was quite different. I trained in Scotland, you see, and then went down south. I found a job in Cambridge."

"Why Cambridge?"

She hesitated. "I followed somebody."

"Oh, I see."

"It didn't work out—the relationship, and the job, for that matter. We were both . . . how shall I put it, rather different. I think he wasn't quite sure whether he liked men or women. There are plenty of people like that, you know—they just aren't sure."

"Somerset Maugham had something to say on that, you know. He told his nephew, Robin Maugham, that if he was in any doubt about his inclinations he should just walk down the street and see where his eyes went."

"I suppose that's right. I hadn't thought of that."

"Although," mused Stuart, "one's eyes could go places for entirely innocent reasons. You might be interested in what people are wearing, for example. You might look at them for that reason."

"Possibly. But in his case, I think he decided he liked women—but not me."

"I'm sorry."

"Thank you. Anyway, he went off with a woman who designed handbags. Can you believe it? There he was, an astrophysicist, and she designed handbags!"

Stuart smiled. "Handbags can be much more than . . . than mere handbags. Handbags can be a weapon—look at Maggie Thatcher. Or a protection if you're in the public eye. Look at the Queen—she always carries a handbag, although she doesn't need to."

"She could have somebody else carry it for her, I suppose."

"Exactly," said Stuart. "Like those maharajas who had so many jewels that they couldn't wear it all themselves. There was one who used to dress quite simply—well, in simple silks, put it that way—and he had somebody who walked behind him wearing all his jewellery for him—some retainer who was laden down with massive rubies and so on."

"This handbag woman was a real . . . Sorry, I was about to use bad language—and you mustn't use bad language in vegetarian restaurants."

"Well, you certainly shouldn't say *bloody* . . ."

She laughed. "I won't. But you just did."

"For illustrative purposes. Solely for illustrative purposes."

"I can't stand swearing," she said. "It's such an excuse for thinking. It just fills the air, like radio jamming. And it's an act of aggression. It's rubbing somebody's nose in things."

"Tell me more about the handbag designer," said Stuart.

Katie had been toying with a bowl of pasta,

now half eaten. She pushed it away. "I enjoyed that, but I took too much. The handbag designer? She was awful. She was called, believe it or not, Amaryllis. How pathetic. If you're going to have a botanical name, then you could at least have something that wasn't as . . . as vapid as Amaryllis. You may as well have a Latin botanical name, like *Magnolia stellata* or something like that."

Stuart remembered something. "Bertie has a boy in his class . . ." He trailed off.

She looked at him enquiringly. "Bertie?"

He tried to read her expression, but reached no conclusion. "My wee boy. I have a young son. Bertie. He's seven. Anyway he goes to the Steiner School and the kids there all have unconventional names. There's a boy called Tofu, and then there's a Hiawatha and a Larch. And what made me think of it was your mentioning botanical names. I suppose Larch is botanical enough, but there's a little boy who's just started there—he's in Bertie's class—who's called Knotweed."

"Knotweed! Is he Japanese?"

"No, he's Scottish. You'd think that people would have more sense than to land a child with a name like that." He paused. "But this Amaryllis?"

"Oh, she was tall—very thin—long legs. And she had a sort of drawly voice—you know those voices you come across, those condescending voices that sound as if they're so very bored with

304

everything. Well, that's what she sounded like. And she called everybody darling."

"Actors do that," said Stuart. "Perhaps handbag designers too."

"He fell for her. He said he couldn't help it. He was quite apologetic, actually, but he said that they looked at the world in the same way."

Weltanschauung, thought Stuart. It helps to have the same *Weltanschauung*.

"What were her handbags like?"

"Ghastly. Tiny little things that cost at least eight hundred pounds each—usually more. I saw one that cost two thousand."

"Ridiculous."

He wanted to get off the subject of handbags. "So you taught down there in Cambridge?"

"Yes, I taught English in a senior school. The kids were ghastly—really ghastly. They had no manners at all. None. They looked at you with a jaded, knowing expression on their face. They were illiterate at the age of fifteen. Nobody had taught them any grammar. Nobody had taught them anything, as far as I could make out."

"Oh dear."

"The teachers were all defeated. They sat in the staff room and stared into space, summoning up their energy for the next stage of the fray. I felt so sorry for them."

"You couldn't bear it?"

"No, so I came back to Scotland and decided to

do a PhD. You can call that escapism if you wish, but . . ."

"I'd never call it that," said Stuart. He was curious what exactly the PhD was about.

"Scottish poetry," she said. "I'm looking at images of the landscape in twentieth-century Scottish poetry."

"What poets have to say . . ."

". . . about the earth on which they stand," she supplied. "Yes, how they relate to the Scottish landscape. Do you know MacDiarmid's 'Island Funeral'? He talks about it being a grey world, with the sea and sky being as without colour as the stones. It's a sombre description, and I suppose sometimes Scotland *is* grey. Or dark." She smiled at him. "You might have heard of the description that an Arab geographer gave of Scotland, which he called *Squtlandiyah*. He wrote that back in the eleventh century. He said that Scotland was uninhabited although there had been three towns until the people living there had fought one another to extinction. The sea round the country, he said, was called the Sea of Darkness. 'The waves are enormous and the sea is deep. Darkness reigns continually . . .' That's what he wrote."

Stuart laughed. "It's dangerous to describe a place you've never been to. He might at least have tried to verify his description."

"Too perilous," said Katie. "Too dark."

"*Spirit of Lenin, light up this city now,*" mused Stuart. "Who wrote that again?"

"MacDiarmid. I suppose that he was momentarily forgetting that Lenin encouraged the public hanging of recalcitrant kulaks. He wrote some wonderful things, though, and then—well some not so wonderful, contrary stuff—during his *Rubbish Period.* I have a theory that many great artists have a *rubbish period.*"

"And perhaps some never get out of it," ventured Stuart.

"Perhaps," said Katie. And then she said, "Look, I have to go. I've got the electrician coming to the flat. Would you like to continue this conversation there? In Howe Street?"

It was a choice between the Belgian health statistician and . . . and what? Freedom? Stuart felt his pulse race. *It's not my fault,* he thought. *I've tried and tried to put up with Irene. But now I've had enough. My rubbish period is about to end.*

56

Shed Issues

Stuart walked back to Howe Street with Katie, barely conscious of where he was or where they were going. He left Queen Street behind him with scarcely a thought of the conference he was abandoning in the Royal College of Physicians; printed versions of the papers had already been distributed to the delegates—a fatal mistake at any conference, particularly for those presenting their contributions after lunch. There would be an audience, of course: not everybody would have met somebody in a restaurant and failed to return to the conference; nor would more than a small proportion of the audience be asleep.

His lack of awareness of his journey was not so much distraction as sheer elation. His conversation in Henderson's with Katie had been a brief one, but it seemed to him that every word had been blessed, had been weighted with significance. And then there was that other factor—the undeniable current of physical attraction that ran between them, that crackled and sparked like a live wire detached from a terminal. It was a current that ran both ways: although he was quite unaware of it, Stuart was considered good-looking. One might have expected his face to be lined with anxiety, as the face of one who is sair hauden-doon by domestic circumstances can be. But this was not the case; the years of living with Irene had made no real impact on the way he looked, and he could still pass for somebody in his late twenties—in the right light.

That was Stuart. As for Katie, regularity of features, a clear skin, and something in the colour of her eyes all served to resonate with Stuart, as did the timbre of her voice. He was used to Irene's tones, which were sharp, strident and, of course, utterly politically correct. Katie's voice was very different; she spoke softly, but with an intonation that was almost seductive, that would be quite capable of saying flattering things about men. Complimentary remarks about men normally incur derision; but even withering scorn does not change the fact that many men secretly want women to admire them and to whisper that they find them strong and decisive. Of course nobody will actually *say* that any more, but men so yearn for it, hopelessly, nostalgically. Listen carefully to what men mutter to themselves, *sotto voce*, as they gaze into the shaving mirror in the morning: *My name's Bond* . . . Many wives and girlfriends do not realise this, but listen they should and they will hear it slip out, this strange, laughable fantasy that men have.

In no time at all—or so it seemed to the newly

struck Stuart—they were in Howe Street and climbing the stair to her top-floor flat.

"I live in an eyrie," she said apologetically. "I haven't dared count the stairs."

"It keeps one fit," said Stuart. "I'm a couple of floors up in Scotland Street."

Once again he had used the first person singular, but this time he had not reproached himself.

"You know," said Katie, "I've just read somewhere or other that the average New Yorker walks four miles a day. Four miles! That's why they're all so slender in New York. They walk."

"We walk in Edinburgh too," said Stuart. "I love . . . just walking about. I don't have to have somewhere to go, I just like walking."

"Do you have a car?" asked Katie as she searched for her keys.

Stuart hesitated. Their car was an issue. Over the last couple of years, it had suffered quite remarkable—and mixed—fortunes. It had been left by mistake in Glasgow, and had been stolen. Recovered by the new friend that Stuart and Bertie had made in Glasgow, Lard O'Connor, † RIP, the car had been returned to Edinburgh, where it was subsequently mistaken for a conceptual art installation, sliced in two, and sent down to London, where it won the Turner Prize. That had been unfortunate, but the insurance money had allowed for the purchase of a slightly better car, currently parked in . . . Stuart hesitated. Where

310

had he parked it? Or had Irene been the last one to drive?

"Yes, I have a car," he said. "I'm not very interested in them, though."

"Me neither. I don't run one."

"Very wise."

She unlocked the door and led the way into a large entrance hall.

"Flagstones," said Stuart.

"I love them," she said. "This flat actually belongs to my parents, who live in Skye now. They kept the flagstones."

My parents live in Skye now . . . Absurdly, Stuart thought of how that line might have come from some condescending colonial story, where a speaker of halting English, perhaps an orphan on some distant South Sea island, says sadly to the traveller, *My parents live in sky now* . . . Mind you, one lived *on* Skye rather than *in* Skye; not that he wanted to correct her. He wanted, rather, to embrace her, to smother her with kisses, to tell her how he felt and how he felt about the way he felt.

"The drawing room's through there," she said. "Go through. I'll make some coffee."

He noticed that she said *drawing room*. Not lounge. Not living room. And this gave him a sudden thrill, because Irene had interdicted the use of the term. "Drawing room," she said scornfully, "is irretrievably bourgeois. Not only that, it's patriarchal. Women used to withdraw to the drawing room—can you believe it? Leaving the men at the table after dinner. Outrageous."

Stuart had said nothing. He would willingly have withdrawn altogether—just to escape the barrage. Perhaps men could start withdrawing—going off to their sheds, if they were lucky enough to have a shed. Or were sheds patriarchal too? Were sheds now forbidden as a locus of clandestine male networking? *Come round to my shed for some networking.*

Was it wrong for a man to want a shed? Or a lover? There were men, he thought, who had all three things: a shed, a drawing room, and a lover. Some of them had even more: a motorbike, perhaps, that made their metaphorical cup run over.

He stood by the window, looking out over Howe Street, aware that he felt alive in a way that he had not experienced for years. Alive. Here in this lovely city, in the flat of this beautiful, intriguing woman, with her drawing room and her twentieth-century Scottish poetry. He closed his eyes and quietly thanked whatever gods had guided his step into that particular restaurant at that particular hour, and thereby changed his life.

57

Snakes and Ladders

Poor wee Bertie . . . but no, Bertie had never bemoaned his fate, had never complained about the mother whom the Fates had allocated to him, never once wondered whether there had been some terrible mix-up in the maternity department of the Royal Infirmary of Edinburgh resulting in his being given as a new-born infant to the wrong mother—to Irene rather than to the woman in the bed next to hers who might, for all he knew, have been a circus acrobat, or an aviatrix, or the owner of a puppy farm on the Lanark Road, or even a *Glaswegianess* (and therefore much, much more fun) . . . there were so many possibilities that would have been infinitely preferable, but being loyal, he had never allowed himself to think of them. So Bertie would never have thought of himself as poor in any sense, and would, moreover, have defended his mother against the slings and arrows directed against her by people like Tofu and Olive, who both took a dim view of her and had described her at various times in the most uncomplimentary language. Only Ranald Braveheart Macpherson saw no fault in Irene, and never suggested that Bertie was unfortunate in

313

his choice—if one could call it that—of parents.

"What people say about your mummy isn't true," said Ranald one day when Bertie was visiting him in Church Hill.

They were playing Snakes and Ladders at the time, and Bertie's counter, having just landed on the head of a particularly long snake, had slid down to a lowly square near the start of the board. His position was very discouraging, and Ranald's comment, although intended to be helpful, did not make it any better.

"What do they say, Ranald?" asked Bertie.

"Oh, everything," said Ranald airily. "They talk about her face sometimes."

"Her face?" asked Bertie. "What's wrong with her face, Ranald?"

Ranald shrugged. "I don't think there's much wrong with her face, Bertie. She looks much the same as most grown-ups to me—you know, all saggy and lined—a bit like a prune. You know how grown-ups look."

"Do you think she looks like a prune, Ranald?"

Ranald shook his head. "No, I don't, Bertie. I didn't say that. I said that most grown-ups look like prunes, but I didn't say that your mummy was particularly like one. I never said that."

Bertie was silent for a moment. It was his turn to throw the dice and he needed a three, a four or a five to avoid further snakes. With a sigh of relief, he threw a three. Turning to Ranald, he asked, "What *do* they say, then, Ranald?"

Ranald thought for a moment. "It depends who you're talking about. You see, there's Tofu . . ."

"I never listen to anything he says," pronounced Bertie firmly.

"Just as well," said Ranald.

Bertie bit his lip. "What does Tofu say, Ranald?"

Ranald hesitated. He lowered his voice. "He says she's a cow. He says that she forced your dad to marry her. He says that when they got married, they had to carry him into the church and then lock the door to stop him escaping."

Bertie listened to this wide-eyed. "I don't think that's true, Ranald. I really don't."

"Good," said Ranald. "I thought it probably wasn't—but I thought I'd just check."

Nothing was said for a few turns. Ranald landed on a snake, but only a short one, while Bertie's counter landed on a moderately good ladder which partly retrieved the situation for him.

"I don't think what Olive says is true either," volunteered Ranald. "She's such a liar, isn't she? People say she's one of the worst liars in Scotland."

Although Bertie thought there might be some truth in this, his kind nature prevented his saying it. So he said nothing.

"So what she says is probably not true," continued Ranald. "At least I don't believe it. Others may, but not me."

Bertie's voice was small when he next spoke. "What did she say, Ranald?"

"She says that your dad's planning to run away. She says that he's digging a tunnel so that he can escape. She says that it's like that film where those people who are caught by the Germans dig a tunnel and get away."

"That's just not true," said Bertie. "And where's this tunnel meant to be, anyway?"

"She said it's in your flat—in the kitchen. She said he's covered up the entrance to it by putting a table over it. She said that he takes the earth outside by putting it in his pockets. She said your mummy's probably German and is just pretending to be Scottish so that nobody's suspicious."

"That shows how much Olive knows!" shouted Bertie. "Our flat in Scotland Street is two floors up. How could my dad dig a tunnel?"

"Those were my thoughts entirely," said Ranald. "And your mother isn't German, is she, Bertie? Although I can see how some people might think she is."

"She's not German," said Bertie. "And it's jolly unfair to accuse her of being German."

"I agree," said Ranald. "Germans can't help it. They didn't decide to be Germans, did they? It's not their fault. You can't blame them just because they're German."

"No, you can't," said Bertie. "And I don't think

there's anything wrong with being German. It's just like being Scottish. We can't help it, can we, Ranald?"

"No," said Ranald. "That's what my father says about the English. He says they can't help it. Did you know that my father's a Scottish Nationalist, Bertie? He says that Scotland will be free one day. He says that once we've beaten the English at rugby, we'll be free and we'll have the Euro and everything. He keeps Euros in his safe, you know, Bertie. I've seen them. A whole pile of Euros. He showed me once and said, 'Those are my Euros, Ranald.' Has your dad got any Euros, Bertie?"

Bertie shook his head. "We're quite poor compared with you, Ranald. I think he's only got about twenty pounds."

"That's all right, Bertie," said Ranald. "I know you can't help it. Maybe when Scotland is free again you'll have a bit more. More Euros, that is."

"But if we beat the English, what about the Queen, Ranald? What will the Queen do?"

"Now, she's German, Bertie," said Ranald. "I think they're all German. That's what my dad says, anyway. He's a Jacobite, you see. He believes that the Stuarts are going to come back one day. He says they're in France at the moment, but they'll come back. And bring lots of Euros with them."

Bertie laid the dice down on the board. "I don't want to play this game any more, Ranald," he said. "Can we go out and play in your garden?"

Ranald, too, was ready to abandon Snakes and Ladders. "We could dig a tunnel," he suggested. "We could escape that way."

Bertie looked wistful. "Do you think we really could escape, Ranald? Do you think we could escape and go and live somewhere else? Maybe Glasgow? We could share. I'd be your best friend and you'd be mine. Do you think we could do that, Ranald?"

Ranald thought for a moment. "Would you like that, Bertie?"

"Yes," said Bertie. "I would."

Ranald looked at his friend. Then he reached out and put a hand on his shoulder and left it there for a moment before taking it away again to put away the Snakes and Ladders set.

58

Chez Macpherson

Bertie had been taken to Ranald Braveheart Macpherson's house by his grandmother, Nicola, who usually looked after him—and sometimes Ulysses as well—on Saturday afternoons. On this occasion, Ulysses remained with Irene, as she had booked him into a three-hour psychological assessment at the Institute of Infant and Child Psychology, the purpose of which was to determine whether or not he was gifted, and in what area his talents lay. These assessments were normally carried out at the age of five, but Irene had insisted that Ulysses should be tested early—before his first birthday, in fact—in view of his likely precocity.

While Irene was thus engaged with Ulysses, Nicola took Bertie off to a pre-arranged play session with Ranald Braveheart Macpherson at the Macpherson house in Church Hill. She dropped him off there after a prolonged visit to the Royal Scottish Museum in Chambers Street, where an exhibition of Celtic artefacts engaged the attention of both of them to the extent that they both forgot about lunch altogether.

"There'll be sandwiches at Ranald's," Bertie said. "Don't worry, Granny. They'll have some for you as well. There's bags of stuff at Ranald's."

"I'm sure there is, Bertie," said Nicola. "But you, in turn, shouldn't worry. I shall go off and find a cup of tea somewhere in Morningside. And a scone. Morningside is just the place for scones."

She left him at Ranald's and found herself a tearoom on Morningside Road. It was actually a coffee bar, but one that served more tea than coffee, and did, in fact, have cheese scones under a glass bell. Sitting there with her scone and tea, she allowed her mind to wander, and thought of Stuart and his affair. Would he have the courage to make something of that? She was not sure. Irene was powerful, and nobody should underestimate her ability to intimidate. What would she do if she were to discover that Stuart was seeing somebody else? Shc started to imagine the scene, but stopped herself. Her son would not stand up for himself; he just wouldn't. But what if she—Nicola—were there? What if she were to stand up on his behalf? She saw that scene clearly enough. *You have oppressed my son—that's what you've done. No, don't you glare at him like that and yes, it is my business, you ghastly, ghastly woman* . . . The trouble was that the scene deteriorated too quickly and became something like the Battle of Monte Cassino . . .

She returned to collect Bertie at half past five. Ranald's father was as hospitable as ever, and invited her to join him in a martini.

"The boys are still playing," he said. "Let's give them a wee while more."

She accepted. She liked Ranald's father, who was a good conversationalist with a tendency to make slightly arch remarks.

"Winston Churchill is my inspiration when it comes to martinis," he said. "Apparently Churchill said that the way to make a martini was to pour in gin, and then bow in the direction of France. I suppose it should be the south of France."

"Hah!" said Nicola. "Whence comes our *Noilly Prat* . . ."

"And Lyndon Johnson liked the in-and-out method. You pour the French into the glass, then you chuck it out and fill the glass with gin."

"*Michty me!*" said Nicola. "That would be too strong for me."

She saw that Ranald's father approved of the *faux* vernacular.

"*Michty* indeed," he said, smiling. "So I shall stick to a very conservative approach. Seven parts gin to one part of Vermouth."

"Oh goodness!"

The drink was mixed and passed to Nicola. "My wife is out at her Pilates class," said Ranald's father. "She will come back, no doubt, much stronger than before, if that's what Pilates does. Positively Amazonian. Who knows? But in the meantime—chin-chin!"

"*Sláinte!*"

"Of course," he corrected himself. "*Sláinte!* How remiss of me! It's just that Gaelic and martinis don't exactly mix, so to speak."

He raised his glass to Nicola afresh. They were standing in the drawing room of the Macpherson house in Church Hill; out of the large, south-facing windows they could see the garden sloping down towards Morningside and the Pentlands beyond.

And in the garden, huddled under a rhododendron bush, but only partly concealed, they
could see Ranald and Bertie engaged in some
game. Viewed from the Macpherson drawing
room, the two boys appeared to be digging.

"How innocent they look," said Nicola.
"Playing whatever it is they're playing. Digging
for something or other. Treasure perhaps?"

"Playing Robert Louis Stevenson," suggested
Ranald's father. He glanced out of the window.
"Mind you, perhaps not as innocent as you
might imagine. You know what Ranald told me
the other day? He said that he and his friends at
cub scouts had been playing Ebola. I asked him
what it was and he said it was a game in which
one person has Ebola and can pass it on to the
others if he catches them. What a distasteful
game!"

"Little horrors," said Nicola.

"I sometimes think that Golding had it right,"
mused Ranald's father. "You know—the *Lord of
the Flies* thesis—that boys left on their own will
revert to savagery."

Nicola looked thoughtful. "I think there was
some sort of experiment. I read about it." She
searched her memory. "Yes, that was it—the
Robbers Cave experiment. I think that was it.
Some American sociologists, or anthropologists
perhaps, took a group of boys off to a camp in
the country and divided them into two groups.

Then they watched how the groups related to one another."

"And?"

"Rivalry. Raids on each other's tents. Fights between the groups. In other words, *Lord of the Flies.* Golding wasn't writing fiction."

"Should we be surprised?" asked Ranald's father. "Isn't it ever thus?"

Nicola looked around the room. It was expensively furnished, but comfortable in a way in which expensively furnished rooms often are not. One wall was home to an impressive library; another was hung with paintings. One of these caught her eye—a rather desolate Highland scene.

Ranald's father noticed her gaze. He reached for the gin bottle to refresh his glass, his first martini having enjoyed a very brief shelf life. He looked enquiringly at Nicola, but she had taken little more than two sips.

"So dry," she said, declining. She approached the Highland painting and read the title lozenge at its base: *Culloden.*

"Are you interested in art?" asked Ranald's father.

"Of course."

"That was painted barely a year after the defeat," he said. "It was in a Macpherson house in Badenoch, but it came down to me. They say that the artist's tears are dissolved in the oil paint."

Nicola studied the battle scene: did oil and tears really mix? As she was doing so, she heard Ranald's father mutter something.

"I'm sorry," she said. "I missed that."

"We shall rise again," said Ranald's father.

"Really?" asked Nicola.

"Yes," said Ranald's father. "As surely as night follows day, we shall rise again." Then he said, "Haven't you noticed?"

59

Bring Back Matron

The morning rush—such as it was—at Big Lou's coffee bar tended to be over by the time that Matthew made his way over from his gallery for his customary cappuccino. When he arrived, he found Lou standing idly behind the counter, her green cloth in her hand, looking up at the ceiling in a thoughtful way.

"Not a busy morning, Lou?" he asked.

Lou gave the counter a desultory wipe. "Just thinking," she said.

"About what?" asked Matthew, perching on one of the stools at the counter.

"Life," said Lou.

She turned to her coffee machine and began to foam a small jug of milk.

Matthew was concerned. "Are you all right, Lou?"

She nodded quickly—too quickly, thought Matthew. "Aye, I'm no bad. Same as usual. Getting by."

Matthew looked at her sideways. She was definitely *not* all right, but he knew that he would have to handle things carefully. Big Lou was independent; she was strong. She had opened up on things in the past, but only in a self-controlled way, and self-pity, so enthusiastically indulged in by others, was anathema to her. It was something to do with being brought up on that farm . . . Matthew tried to remember its name. *Snell Mains*. Cold Farm in Scots. He gave an involuntary shiver. He could picture it, with the wind from the North Sea sweeping up over the coast and penetrating inland, seeking out farmhouses to whistle about, to chill . . . *Snell Mains*—what a thought!

It was that man, he decided. There had been another man, as there always was. Poor Lou—she had terribly bad luck when it came to men. Every one of them was unsuitable in some way. There had been that ridiculous half-deluded plasterer, that Elvis impersonator, that farmer who turned out to be a complete miser . . . and now there was that doctor she had said something about—the one who had invited her to a medical fancy dress party and had suggested that she went dressed as Matron. Had something gone wrong with that too? A doctor sounded as if he might bring some stability, but perhaps not.

He decided to raise the subject. "That fellow," he began. "How's . . ."

Lou turned round. She shook her head. "No good, Matthew. No good."

"Oh Lou . . ."

She looked at him, and he saw her disappointment. She looked away.

"You don't have to talk about it, Lou," he said. "Not if you don't want to."

She busied herself with making his cappuccino. "No, it's all right, Matthew. I feel I can talk to you. I can't talk to Angus about it, but I can to you."

"That's fine, Lou. You can tell me. So things didn't work out?"

She pushed the cup of coffee towards him over the counter. "No, they didn't," she said. "Well, not quite as I hoped."

He took a sip of his coffee. "You said something about a party? A fancy dress party?"

"Aye, it was in Fairmilehead. Somebody's hoose there. Another doctor at the Infirmary."

Matthew tried to imagine it. He had not been to a fancy dress party for years—not since his first year at university, in fact, when he had gone to one in Tollcross dressed as Harlequin. It had been rather a flat occasion, as he remembered it, with too many people dressed as policemen or ballerinas.

"I haven't been to one of those for years," he said. "It's always struck me as being a bit . . . well, it's not really my scene, Lou. *Chacun à son goût*, as they say."

"Oh, it was all right," said Lou. "There was a lot to eat and drink and there were some nice folk there. There was a whole group that went dressed as characters from that film, you know, *Casablanca*. The one with Rick and that French policeman. There was a very good French policeman. He had the *képi* and everything."

"You went dressed as Matron, didn't you?" said Matthew.

"Yes. I found a place where you could hire outfits."

Matthew smiled. "So you ended up with one of those blue outfits with a watch pinned on upside down? And a sort of white cap?"

Big Lou nodded. "People liked it," she said. "They laughed. And he introduced me as the new matron of the Infirmary. He said, 'Things are going to change round here, now that Matron's back.'"

"Your man? He said that?"

"Yes."

Matthew took another sip of his coffee. "But . . ." he began.

"No, there was nothing wrong with that party,"

said Lou. "We had a good time. And he said he'd give me a call. He said he was on duty for the next few days—night duty—but he'd call when he was off."

Matthew sighed. So many people were waiting for telephone calls that never came. It was a common feature of the human tragedy. "And he didn't?"

"No, he did." Lou paused. "And he asked me out to dinner."

Matthew held his breath. He was not sure that he wanted to hear what happened, but Lou appeared to want to continue the conversation.

"It's the way he asked," she said quietly. "I couldnae, Matthew, I couldnae . . ." She broke off.

"Lou, look, you don't have to speak to me about this. You really don't."

She shook her head. "No, I want to, Matthew. You see, he asked me whether I'd come to dinner with him, at his place, *dressed as Matron . . .*"

Matthew gasped. "Oh, Lou, I'm so sorry . . ."

"Aye, I said no. He'd gone on and on about bringing Matron back, but I wasn't going to be involved in anything like that."

Matthew reached across the counter and took Lou's hand. He held it briefly, patting it gently, in consolation.

"Thanks, Matthew," muttered Lou. "But look, I dinnae want to talk about my troubles. What about you? How are things with the triplets now you've got that Australian lassie helping Elspeth?"

It was typical of Lou, thought Matthew. She was more concerned with how other people were getting along. She *was* strong.

He let go of her hand. "Brilliantly, Lou," he said. "Things are going brilliantly. That girl Clare is a real find."

"Tell me about her," said Lou. "What's she doing?"

"All sorts of things, Lou," said Matthew. "She's amazing—really amazing."

60

Clare Takes Over

Matthew had every reason to be pleased with Clare. When she arrived at Nine Mile Burn, Clare had found Elspeth in a state of near exhaustion, barely able to cope with the demands of the triplets, who were now at the early toddler stage and who were exploring their surroundings with all the enthusiasm and long-range ambition of tiny Marco Polos. Try as she might to confine them to her immediate purview, Fergus, Rognvald and Tobermory had other ideas; they were keen to try every avenue of escape. What they discovered within any particular room was merely a taster of what they imagined lay beyond; a door was an invitation and a challenge, a portal to unsampled delights that it was their manifest destiny to conquer. And when one of them went off in one direction, that was a signal to the others to make a beeline in the opposite direction—a technique that escapees have always used: you run that way and I'll run this way—at least one of us will get away.

Clare had been willing to move in straight away. She was tired of the Newington flat, with its dingy decoration and its half-hearted hot water system. She had been prepared to put up with discomfort on coming to Scotland, having been warned by her father that physical hardship was to be expected virtually anywhere outside Australia, but particularly in Scotland. "It's cold over there, my girl," he said. "But it's worth it for a few months. It's your heritage, you see. Put up with it for a few months. Remember: no pain, no gain!"

The house at Nine Mile Burn appealed to her. It was far better appointed, there was plenty of hot water, and the kitchen was four or five times the size of what she had to make do with in Newington.

"I'll start right away," she said to Elspeth on the day that she and Bruce came for afternoon tea. "Bruce will get my stuff—our stuff, rather. I'll just stay. You OK with that, Brucey?"

Had she been feeling less defeated, Elspeth might have taken exception to Clare's assumption that the job was hers without further discussion. She would also have thought very carefully about the prospect of taking on both Clare and Bruce, since Clare had made it very obvious that Bruce would be sharing her room for at least some of the time. But Elspeth had no desire to deliberate; all that mattered to her was that the hole left by the departure of the two Danish girls should be plugged as soon as possible, and it seemed to her that Clare would do just that.

So Elspeth said, "I'm OK with that too. In fact, I'm really grateful, Clare."

"Cool," said Clare. "So that's it."

The triplets had been having their afternoon rest when Clare and Bruce arrived; half an hour later there were the first signs of wakefulness from the nursery.

"Company!" said Clare. "Sounds like we've got company!"

"They're sometimes a bit groggy when they first wake up," said Elspeth. "And they'll usually need changing."

"No probs," said Clare, rising to her feet. "You stay here. I'll handle this." Turning to Matthew, she said, "You show me where all the gear is, Matthew. Nappies. Changing mats. Powder, etc., etc. Elspeth, you put your feet up." Then to Bruce, "You go back to the flat and get my stuff, *toot sweet.* Pack all my clothes—the lot. And don't forget my hairdryer—the Qantas one."

Elspeth closed her eyes. She was tired to the depths of her being. Her feet ached. Her scalp itched as it always did when she was sleep-deprived. She sat back in her chair and felt waves of sleep come over her. The scone she had been eating, half-finished on the plate she had been balancing on her knee, fell to the floor in crumbs. She did not notice.

She slept for three hours, waking with a start and feeling the immediate grip of panic. Where were the boys? Had she left them somewhere? Where was Matthew?

She remembered, and then she heard voices drifting in from the driveway outside. She went to the window: Clare was balancing on a bicycle, her feet down on either side, adjusting the strap of a cycle helmet. She was dressed in electric blue Lycra. Behind the bicycle, attached by a long yoke, was a small buggy, rather like a motor-cycle side-car. Seated in the buggy, their faces just visible through its Perspex panels, were the boys.

Elspeth opened the window.

"Woken up?" shouted Clare. "You needed that sleep, I think."

Elspeth rubbed at her eyes. "Are they all right?" she asked.

Clare smiled. "Look at them—they're loving it.

I'm just going to take them up that track there. See? It goes all the way up that hill."

"Will they be . . . ?"

"They'll be fine. Don't you worry. I'll only be an hour or two."

She opened her mouth to protest. The boys would need their bath. They would be dehydrated if they did not get their water-beakers. You could not simply take toddlers up a hill track in a buggy, just like that . . .

But it was too late to raise these objections. Clare had moved off and the buggy was bouncing along behind her. And now Matthew had appeared from the side of the house and was pointing at the buggy. "Did you see them?" he called out. "They're in seventh heaven."

He came inside.

"I'm not sure, Matthew," said Elspeth. "She's a bit . . . a bit extreme, isn't she?"

Matthew was cheerful. "Just go with the flow," he said. "Australians are like that. They're can-do people."

"But that track's quite steep . . ."

"She's got brakes," he said.

"And Bruce?" she said. "Where's Bruce?"

"He went back into Edinburgh," said Matthew. "He said he had things to do."

Elspeth looked at Matthew with concern. "I hope we haven't made a mistake," she said.

Matthew was quick to reassure her. "Honestly,

she's great. She fixed up that buggy in two minutes. I'd left it in the garage because I couldn't attach it. She did it with her eyes closed. Then she took them for a walk. She tied them together with a bit of string and took them down to the rhododendron bushes."

"Tied them together with string?"

"So that they couldn't wander off on their little legs. It really worked." He paused. "And then she said something about making a flying fox for them tomorrow. She spotted some old fencing wire in the garage and she said she could rig that between that pine tree over there and the side of the garage. She said she'd make a sort of harness for them so they could slide down. I remember having one of those when I was a kid. I loved it."

Elspeth frowned. "What if they fall?"

"You can't wrap them up in cotton wool," said Matthew.

"Are we doing the right thing, Matthew? Is her judgement going to be all right? After all, if she thinks Bruce is . . ."

He put a protective arm around her shoulder. "Of course we are. They'll be fine. We'll be fine. Everything will be fine."

61

In Moray Place

The committee meeting of the Association of Scottish Nudists had been called by the Chairman and Secretary in order to address what the Secretary described as "one of the greatest crises in the Association's history." The Chairman thought this was something of an exaggeration, particularly in the light of the recent challenge to the committee's authority coordinated— *fermented,* the Chairman said—by the Glasgow membership, but he agreed with the Secretary that the issue would need to be addressed just as soon as the committee members could meet.

So it was that on a Wednesday evening all six members of the committee gathered in the Association's headquarters in Moray Place, that fine example of classical Georgian architecture perched on the cliffs above the Water of Leith. The Association was fortunate in owning such handsome premises, particularly since the elegant double flat it occupied was on the side of Moray Place that looked over Lord Moray's Pleasure Gardens and, in the distance, across the cold blue waters of the Firth of Forth, to the hills of Fife.

It was a prospect to quicken the aesthetic pulse, especially in summer, when the canopies of the trees below were dark green and the sky above them was of that particular blue associated with clear, northern light.

For the committee, though, there was little time to admire the view or engage in small talk; everybody present knew of the reason for the calling of the meeting and understood what was at stake. So rather than engage in chat over the tea and biscuits served by the Social Secretary, the committee members turned immediately to the sole item on the agenda: the World Naturist Federation's conference.

The Chairman set the scene. "As you know," he said, "we put in a bid over eighteen months ago to hold the World Federation's annual conference here in Edinburgh. The competition for that event is always considerable. We heard on good authority that there were bids from three other places—from Cairo, from Reykjavik, and from Stuttgart."

"And these were serious bids," interjected the Secretary.

"Yes," said the Chairman. "The three bidders all put a lot of effort into their pitches. However, two of them were at a significant disadvantage: Cairo was too hot, Reykjavik was too cold, and Stuttgart . . ."

"Would have been just right," said one of the

members. "Rather like the porridge in the story of Goldilocks and the three *bares*."

The Chairman frowned; what was this about bears? "No, Stuttgart would have been too expensive, as it happened. And so Edinburgh was preferred."

"I must admit I was a bit surprised," said the Secretary. "The Association has a history of going for sunny places, although Cairo would have been far too sunny, I'm afraid. A large number of our members were really worried about sunburn—and quite rightly so, in my view."

"And arrests," said one of the members. "They stipulated that delegates would have to be completely covered—or face arrest. Frankly, I can't see the point of a naturist convention if you're going to arrest people who aren't entirely clothed."

"I must admit I had my doubts," said the Chairman. "But it all remained hypothetical, anyway. Their application was not favoured by the Federation—whereas we were."

"In spite of our weather?"

The Chairman nodded. "They asked for Scottish sunshine statistics and I was fortunately able to send them the figures from the island of Coll, which, as you know, gets more sun than anywhere else in Scotland. I felt quite justified in this in that they didn't ask me for Edinburgh figures, they just said Scottish figures. So I gave them Coll's."

"Well, it paid off," said the Secretary. "But then . . ." He gave the Chairman a sad look.

"And then," said the Chairman, "things started to get difficult. As you know, we had approached the Dynamic Earth people to hold the plenary sessions there, and they were perfectly agreeable to that. They said that they thought that it was highly appropriate to hold a naturist conference in a centre devoted to the natural sciences. I should have put two and two together, but, I'm sorry, I didn't."

One of the members groaned. "They misread," she said. "They thought we were talking about naturalists?"

"I'm afraid so," said the Chairman. "It's a common mistake. And when they discovered it, they said they would have to withdraw their agreement. They said that they couldn't take us as they had too many windows and members of the public who use their steps to sit and eat their lunch would be unprepared for what they might see."

"But what about curtains?" asked one of the members.

"They have none," said the Chairman. "They're all glass."

Another member had a suggestion to make. "What about the International Conference Centre?"

"We approached them," said the Chairman. "They were very helpful—they always are. But then they said that during the summer their air-conditioning was set to a particular level and could not be changed. It would have been too cold for us—or so they said."

"Nobody wants us," complained one of the members. "These days you can't discriminate against people on all sorts of grounds, but then, when it comes to us, oh yes, you can discriminate like mad."

"I can understand how you feel," said the Chairman. "It's a matter of human rights and we need to be more assertive. But that's a broader question—for the moment we are more concerned with our immediate problems—one of which is that even if we get a new venue for the plenary sessions, our major social event has run into trouble."

"You mean our Scottish country dancing event?" asked one of the members.

"Yes," said the Chairman. "That was going to be our principal entertainment—our showpiece, so to speak. We had booked the Ross Pavilion for an evening of Scottish country dancing. We were going to invite all the foreign delegates to join in. It was all set up."

"And?" asked a member.

"We had made arrangements for screens. We had paid a deposit on screens that would be deployed all the way round the Ross Pavilion and its seating so that people in Princes Street Gardens couldn't complain. Nobody would have seen us—or so we thought."

The meeting steeled itself for the worst. It had been an evening of uniformly bad news, and nothing would have surprised the members by this stage.

"The Edinburgh civic authorities had a complaint from the people up in Ramsay Garden. In fact, it was a petition that a lot of them signed. They said that they looked down directly onto the Ross Pavilion and they would see our dancing. They said they would be shocked, and they were entitled not to be shocked. And do you know what? The City Council agreed."

"We're sunk," said one of the members.

"What can we do?" asked another.

"Nothing," said the Chairman.

"People have got it in for us," said the Secretary. "Sometimes, you know, I feel defeated—utterly defeated."

62

Falling Veils of White

Stuart Pollock, statistician, husband and father, sometime community councillor, former committee member (co-opted) of the Edinburgh North Balkans Appeal and, many years ago, member of the Scottish Universities Ski Club, was now also Stuart Pollock, lover of the young woman engaged in research for a PhD in twentieth-century Scottish poetry whom he had met over pasta and salad in Henderson's in Hanover Street. This last status had crept up on him; he had not set out to become anybody's lover; he had done nothing to seek out somebody else; she had simply been sitting there, looked sympathetic when he had spilled butternut squash soup on his jacket, and that was that.

Of course, something like a high-risk love affair only happens if the ground is fertile, and in Stuart's case, although he would never have recognised this himself, the ground was more than ready for something like this. He was not by nature a fickle or disloyal man; quite the contrary, in fact. Stuart had never pursued novelty in his life; he had never questioned his role as a provider; he had never tried to evade the responsibilities of fatherhood. In many respects, he was exactly the sort of man whom the dispensers of advice in women's magazines urge their troubled readers to seek out. He was a solid, reliable man; he was the antithesis of the spiv-like Lotharios who break female hearts with such gay abandon. He was middle Scotland. He was middle management. He was middle man.

But he had been trapped. From the start, Irene had been the dominant figure in the marriage. That might have been survivable—many people accept a certain degree of dominance in their relationships—but when it becomes as extreme as it had in Stuart and Irene's marriage, when it means that all freedom to hold different, or indeed any, opinions is withheld, then the position of the trapped party may become intolerable.

He loved his sons. He would have done anything for them—and did. He wanted Bertie to have what Bertie so desperately wanted. He wanted him to live the life of a small boy, which was a business of Swiss Army penknives, of fishing in the Pentland Hills, of reading stories about other boys who go off to sea, or have dogs, or do any of the other things that small boys aspire to do. Stuart wanted that for Bertie, but Irene did not. For her, the Bertie Project was based on the notion of the malleability of masculine character. She wanted Bertie to be free of the stereotypes of gender. She wanted him to be in touch with his inner girl. She wanted him to view Swiss Army penknives as instruments of oppression. It may never be overtly stated, but Swiss Army penknives were not intended for girls. They were something by which boys could define themselves in contradistinction to girls. The possession of a Swiss Army penknife was a statement proclaiming, *I am a boy*. Irene saw all that quite clearly, and she would not allow it. It was as simple as that. *No pasarán*!

But anybody—anybody with the slightest psychological insight—could have warned Irene that what she was engaged in was a prolonged exercise in castration. It was not necessary to be an unreformed Freudian, to accept every diktat from Vienna, to realise that Irene was seeking to diminish males, and that sooner or later the male whom she was seeking to diminish in this radical way—the victim of her psychological surgery—might realise the peril in which he stood and do something about it, something symbolic, such as finding a woman who had no castration agenda—even finding her in Henderson's salad restaurant—and becoming complicit with that woman (*becoming complicit* being a demotic Edinburgh way of referring to engaging in physical intimacy).

Thus did the prospect of deliverance present itself to Stuart. And in his break for freedom, Stuart found that his monochrome world of subservience became a brightly coloured one of intense and passionate feeling. He had found somebody who liked him. He had found somebody who listened to what he had to say and who did not say that he was wrong, or reactionary, or an affront to the orthodoxy dictated somewhere down in North London or wherever it was that Irene's spiritual headquarters had its tents. Slowly, this sense of freedom began to illuminate his daily life. He began to read newspapers other than the one from which Irene obtained confirmation of most of her opinions. He listened to what people of a range of views had to say. Like a figure crouched over an interdicted radio set, fearful of disturbance, he tuned into forbidden frequencies and listened to the exchange of untrammelled messages, to the expression of scepticism and dissent. He felt more Scottish, because Irene's control, her power, seemed to come from somewhere else altogether. He would not accept it; he would *not*.

Katie, his companion on this heady voyage, read him poetry under her skylight. Officially, he was working late on a demanding office project; in reality he was in Howe Street, listening to her, saying to her things that he had said to nobody for years, confessing his weaknesses, his fears, his private reflections.

She understood. She read him the work of her twentieth-century Scottish poets; it seemed to him that much of this was written for the two of them, so perfectly did it express what he was feeling. And she wrote poems for him, too, saying apologetically, "I know I'm not much good as a poet, but I'd like you to read this one." And he would say, "But no, you're marvellous, and I love everything you write—I really do."

She composed a special poem. "It's not about us," she said. "But it's about love, about a man thinking of somebody. Anyway, here it is."

She wrote it out and gave it to him:

He thinks of her

Forgive me for telling you
That without you the day
Seems frozen, the land
Is touched with white rime,
The trees are stark against
A sky of distant blue,
Washed out by the absence
Of warmth and anything
But cold sunlight.

Forgive me for telling you
That the air outside the cabin
Of a plane in high flight
Is fifty degrees below;
Here ice crystals form
In falling veils of white,

So cold we cannot live;
I cannot live without you,
Forgive me for telling you that.

Stuart read it and smiled. He thought of how, when one looked up into the sky, one might see those curtain-like, almost transparent clouds so high up, shifting veils of white. Those were ice crystals. How lovely. How lovely.

He read the poem again, and then put it in his pocket.

63

Thoughts on the 23 Bus

The next day Irene accompanied Bertie to school as usual on the 23 bus. As the bus laboured up the first of the hills that lay between the New Town and the Steiner School, Bertie looked out of the window at the trees in the Queen Street Gardens. He felt that he knew those trees particularly well, since they—or their tops—constituted the lower frame of the view from his psychotherapist's waiting room. He had lost count of the hours he had spent in that waiting room, paging through old copies of *Scottish Field*, as his mother, closeted in the consulting room with Dr. Fairbairn and then

with his Australian successor, Dr. Sinclair, discussed . . . discussed what? Him, he supposed.

He could not understand how he could possibly
take up so much of their time, but had concluded
that the reason why they discussed him at such
length was that they had nothing else to talk
about. That, it seemed to him, was a persistent
problem faced by adults: they simply did not
have enough to do. And because there were
so many of them, and so few *real* things to do,
they had to invent roles for themselves, and
then spend a great deal of time arguing with one
another about who should occupy these roles and
then, when they were in them, what they should
do with them.

Bertie was prepared to help them, of course,
and when it came to his psychotherapy this
help took the form of making up dreams and,
indeed, anything else that he felt might interest
the psychotherapist. This did not come naturally
to him, as one of Bertie's most striking characteristics was his utter truthfulness—rare
amongst children, most of whom are prepared
to lie when it suits them. But psychotherapy, he
decided, was different, and charity, at the very
least, required him to invent colourful dreams
that would keep poor Dr. Sinclair from having
nothing to talk about and therefore having to go
back to Australia.

He had discovered that Dr. Sinclair was

particularly interested in dreams featuring buildings, spires, and columns of any sort. Bertie could not understand why this should be so, but had decided that it must have something to do with his having been abandoned as a child on a column somewhere and haunted by the thought ever since. If that were the case, then in making up these dreams he felt he was helping Dr. Sinclair in some way to get over something that must have been bothering him for a long time.

"I dreamed of the Eiffel Tower last night," Bertie had revealed only the previous week.

Dr. Sinclair made a note on his pad. "Very interesting, Bertie. Tell me about it."

"Well, there wasn't very much in the dream, Dr. Sinclair. It was just the Eiffel Tower. You know what it's like. It's this big metal tower in the middle of Paris . . ."

Dr. Sinclair smiled. "Yes, I know about the Eiffel Tower, Bertie. But what else happened? Can you remember what else happened?"

Bertie thought. If he did not come up with something else, then Dr. Sinclair would have nothing to talk to his mother about, and that meant that he would have more psychotherapy time rather than sitting in the waiting room with *Scottish Field* while Irene used up the therapeutic hour.

"Actually, there were two Eiffel Towers," Bertie said. "And one Eiffel Tower was . . ." he hesitated. "It was the other tower's father, I think. That was very funny, Dr. Sinclair. A tower can't have a father . . ."

Dr. Sinclair was scribbling frantically on his notepad, and Bertie knew that he was on the right track.

And so it went on, and so he contemplated the tops of the Queen Street trees, mute witnesses to those endless hours in the consulting room, talking at such length about imaginary dreams. Would that ever stop? Would the clouds ever part suddenly and a golden chariot reveal itself, the driver of which might say, "Come Bertie, come away with me, come to Glasgow . . ."?

His reverie was interrupted by his mother, who pointed out that they were now passing the National Gallery of Scotland. "Remind me, Bertie," she was saying, "to take you to look at the Poussins. We haven't looked at the Poussins for a long time, have we?"

"No, Mummy," said Bertie. "I'm not sure that I like the way Mr. Poussin painted."

Irene laughed. "Of course you like the way he painted, Bertie. Such nonsense. Of course you like it."

"I like the way Mr. Raeburn painted, Mummy. I like that picture of the minister skating on Duddingston Loch. I like that very much."

Irene made a dismissive gesture. "Too sentimental, Bertie. Patriarchal too. That minister may

349

look all innocent, but he was part of a church that was thoroughly repressive."

Bertie said nothing, and Irene switched the subject to the forthcoming school production of *Macbeth*. "Are rehearsals going well, Bertie?"

Bertie was silent.

"Well, Bertie?"

"Why did Mr. Shakespeare write everything in poetry?" he asked. "Did people speak in poetry in those days?"

Irene laughed. "That's a perfectly sensible question, Bertie. No, they didn't speak in poetry. That was all made up by Shakespeare."

"Daddy likes poetry," said Bertie. "He doesn't speak in poetry, but he likes to read it."

Irene was not particularly interested. "I don't think that Daddy reads much poetry, Bertie. Daddy's more interested in figures, I suppose."

"But I found a poem in the pocket of his jacket. You know the one—the brown jacket he got from that shop at the far end of Queen Street. The one he likes to wear when he wants to look smart."

Irene frowned. "A poem, Bertie? In a book?"

Bertie shook his head. "No, it was written on a piece of paper."

"By Daddy? Did Daddy write the poem on a piece of paper?"

Again Bertie shook his head. "No, it wasn't his writing."

Irene now seemed more interested. "Somebody else's writing? Not printed?"

"I don't know whose writing it was," said Bertie.

They were now passing the National Library. From where she sat in the bus, Irene looked out to see the Hew Lorimer figures, carved in stone, standing in their niches in silent reproach. These were the figures of the arts of civilisation, and one—Irene was not quite sure which one it was— represented Poetry, and another Justice . . .

"What was the poem about, Bertie?" she asked.

Bertie tried to remember. "It was about cold things," he said. "I think frost came into it, or snow maybe. I can't remember exactly which. And then it said something like *I can't live without you*." He paused. "Why can't people live without other people, Mummy? Can you tell me why?"

64

I Cannot Live Without You

Irene did not linger long at the school gate, but dispatched Bertie without ceremony and then made her way purposefully, with Ulysses asleep in his pushchair, to the nearest bus stop. This was not her normal bus stop and would entail catching a 27 bus rather than the preferable 23, but needs must. She wanted to get back to Scotland Street as soon as possible to look in the pocket of Stuart's jacket and see this curious poem that Bertie had mentioned. There was no reason why Stuart should not have a poem in the pocket of his jacket—he liked to read Burns from time to time—but as Bertie had described it, this was not Burns. National poets *never* wrote *I cannot live without you* unless, of course, they were writing about their country, in which case they were positively encouraged to reveal that they could not live without you, the you being the country, of course, or the idea of the country.

Alighting from the bus, she walked briskly along Great King Street and into Drummond Place, or Haute Drummond Place, as Irene called it, in sarcastic reference to what she saw as the denizens of the haute-bourgeoisie who lived there. Then into Scotland Street itself, and into the flat, and, having deposited Ulysses, still asleep in his pushchair, in the hall, into the bedroom and now, standing before the wardrobe, she opened the door . . .

The brown jacket, limp and innocent on its hanger, was extracted. She felt in the left pocket first—nothing—and then in the right, where she found a piece of paper. She took this out. It had been folded neatly, like a shopping list found and put away.

She opened it. Bertie had been right: it was not Stuart's writing. She read the poem. *Forgive me for telling you / That without you the day seems frozen . . .*

It was a love poem. Stuart had a love poem in his pocket. And then she thought: he loves me, my husband loves me, and has a love poem for me in his pocket . . .

But then she thought: this poem is not addressed to me. This poem is addressed to Stuart.

She read it again, this time sitting down. She closed her eyes. Then, when she opened them again, she dropped the poem to the floor. It fluttered down, a thing of lightness in every sense, and landed on the carpet, on one of the Turkish medallions that formed the rug's border. *I cannot live without you . . .* Who could not live without whom?

She reached forward to pick up the piece of paper, and she felt for a moment dizzy, as one might when the blood leaves the head. But I am going the wrong way, she thought; in reaching forward the blood should go to my head rather than leave it. What did it matter? What did it matter if she keeled over there and then and died because the blood had all gone the wrong way, and Stuart would find her and he could reflect on living without *her,* then, which would teach him . . .

She stood up. She turned round, and then sat

down again, but only for a few brief seconds. Was the poem copied from some book—some anthology of love poetry, perhaps, like that one edited by Antonia Fraser? That book of Scottish love poems with the Celtic heart in red—the Scottish heart—on the cover and those little wood-engravings inside? That book?

She suddenly thought of Angus. Angus Lordie was a poet—or fancied himself as one. She had seen one or two of his poems published in some journal somewhere, and of course he sometimes read them at occasions in Scotland Street. Perhaps Angus had written this poem and then asked Stuart to take a look at it—as a critic of some sort. But why would he ask Stuart, of all people?

She made up her mind. Ulysses could be left sleeping in his pushchair for a few minutes; she would go downstairs and show the poem to Angus, and ask him if he wrote it.

She went downstairs and rang the bell. There was barking inside the flat—that ridiculous, malodorous dog, thought Irene—and then the door opened and Angus was standing there in his stockinged feet, holding a copy of a newspaper.

"Irene! What a pleasant surprise."

She knew he did not mean it.

"May I come in?"

"Of course, of course. Would you like something . . . a glass of sherry perhaps, no, hardly appropriate; look at the time—silly me. I assure you I am not in the habit of drinking sherry at nine thirty in the morning, and nor is Domenica. I cannot speak for her on all matters, but on that one I feel . . ."

"Yes, yes, Angus. If you must make me something, then tea will do, thank you."

"No sooner said than done. The pot has recently been filled and is ready for pouring. Such serendipity . . ."

They went into the kitchen. "Sit ye doon," said Angus.

Irene overcame her irritation. *Sit ye doon indeed!* "We're not in Brigadoon, Angus."

"On the contrary," said Angus, "Brigadoon is in *us*."

"I don't have time for any of that, Angus. I wanted you to look at a poem." She handed him the piece of paper.

"You wrote this?" asked Angus.

"Don't be ridiculous," she snapped. "You know I don't write poetry."

"But people change," said Angus. "Those who once didn't now do, and that applies to so many things, not just to poetry." He paused. "We have stages in our lives, Irene. When I was a young man I did hardly any figurative painting, you know. I loved landscapes. I loved those Gillies landscapes—you know, those pictures he did of the hills down near Temple and places like that. Those gorgeous hills—so lovely before they

355

ruined them by putting great wind turbines all over them." He paused again. "They're ruining our country, you know. They're defacing Scotland with those great ugly structures. They'd never let people build tall buildings all over the hills and yet they let them erect those things. Our heartbreakingly beautiful country, our Scotland, defaced, ruined, brutalised by giant pieces of white metal. Have you ever encountered such vandalism, Irene?"

She glared at him, and he returned to the poem.

"Rime," he said. "That's a word I love. Rime, not rhyme with an h and a y, of course. Trees with rime. It outlines them so well."

She brushed this aside. "Did you write that poem, Angus?"

He shook his head. "No, I didn't."

"Do you recognise it, then? Do you know where it comes from?"

"From the heart, I'd say."

65
Clare's Proposal

Out at Nine Mile Burn, Elspeth's anxiety over the suitability of Clare as a replacement for the Danish au pairs had been largely, if not completely, assuaged. Her new helper was prepared to do anything, willingly tackling tasks that the young Danes had dismissed as "not the work of an au pair." So Clare cheerfully drove off to do the household shopping at Straiton, returning with a carful of bulk items—twenty-four cans of tinned tomatoes, thirty-eight rolls of kitchen roll, six packs of Pringle socks for Matthew, and so on. Nor was she above the cleaning out of blocked drains—a task she tackled with a vigour and efficiency that astonished Elspeth.

"I love shoving rods up drains," she said. "It reminds me of when I worked as a cabin attendant."

Elspeth could not imagine the link, but did not enquire.

And when it came to dealing with the boys, the fact that they were triplets seemed to be a bonus rather than a burden. She had worked out a technique of bathing all three at once—single-handed—and could even change two of them into their pyjamas at the same time, adjusting and buttoning with one hand while pulling and pushing with the other.

Clare's programme of outdoor activity for the boys had initially caused Elspeth some concern, but after a week or two she became quite used to it. The flying fox that Clare had constructed, running from a corner of the garage to a distant pine tree, had alarmed both Elspeth and Matthew at first, but they had been assured by Clare that the harness she had constructed out of an old car seat belt was more than strong enough and that fence wire of that sort rarely, if ever, broke. "Mind you," Clare said, "we had an incident in Fremantle not that long ago when a flying fox broke while somebody was using it. Maybe I shouldn't tell you about it."

"Maybe not," said Elspeth.

"It was very old wire," said Clare. "That came out at the inquest."

There were other physical challenges for the boys. Clare had managed to get hold of a trampoline, and the triplets, although only just able to walk, were already being taught to do somersaults.

"It's perfectly safe as long as they don't bounce right off the trampoline," said Clare. "That gets messy, I can tell you."

Apart from momentary alarm at these asides, Elspeth quickly became used to Clare's presence and even stopped resenting Bruce's tendency, when visiting her, to sit on the kitchen table and expostulate on issues of the day. And when Clare asked at the end of two weeks whether she could take two days off to go up to Skye with Bruce, Elspeth readily agreed. She had now recovered her strength, and the prospect of looking after the triplets single-handed, or with Matthew's help in the evenings, no longer filled her with dread.

The purpose of Clare's trip to Skye was to introduce Bruce to para-mountain-biking, the new extreme sport that Clare had recently take up, although she was yet to do it on mountains or hills of any size. She had her own equipment and had managed to hire a wing, bicycle, and harness for Bruce from *Extremities*, an extreme sports shop in Leith. This rental wing had a small label that read *To be returned by the renter or his/ her executor to Extremities, Salamander Street, Leith.*

Clare seated Bruce down in front of her computer and showed him several videos of para-mountain-bikers practising their sport in Switzerland and Colorado. They made it seem effortless: on their mountain bikes they cycled with complete ease, their gossamer-thin wings above them, and then, suddenly but gracefully, the land fell away beneath them: they had cycled over the edge of a precipice. Up they soared, caught in the invisible hands of a supporting updraught, suspended from the wing together with their mountain bike, to the saddle of which they were strapped, with the wheels still spinning beneath them.

"You see," said Clare. "You see, Bruce, how easy is that?"

"Quite difficult," said Bruce.

Clare leaned over and very gently licked the tip of his nose.

"You'll have no difficulty," she encouraged. "It's dead simple."

"How do I land?" asked Bruce.

"On your wheels," she said. "Bring yourself down as if you're landing a plane. Start pedalling the moment you hit the ground, and you're off. I think the next video shows you how to do that."

They travelled up in a white van that Clare had rented for the trip. This had room in the back for the mountain bikes, the folded wings, and the various other bits of equipment needed for the sport. On the drive up, Clare played Joan Baez discs and sang along with them.

"My dad liked her voice," she said. "I know she's ancient, but she had this special voice, you see, and all the songs get me here." She put the palm of her hand against her chest. "Right here."

They stopped at Tyndrum, and then again, briefly, at Fort William. Thereafter a winding Highland road took them to Mallaig and eventually to the ferry that crossed to the Sleat peninsula. It was a long drive from there to Trotternish Ridge, in the north of the island, and there was no time that evening to do their first para-mountain-biking flight.

"We'll start tomorrow," said Clare. "Oh, Brucey, we're here! I can hardly believe it—we're on Skye and we're about to para-mountain-bike!"

Bruce was silent. He looked up at the beginning

of Trotternish Ridge. He had never understood why mountains seemed to bring out in people an urge to ascend them or, in some cases, to cast oneself off them. Was life so devoid of challenges at sea level, so to speak?

In his arms that night, Clare whispered to Bruce, "I've decided."

He was sleepy. "What have you decided?"

"To marry you."

Bruce's eyes, until then half-closed in somnolence, opened wide. "Marry? Me?" The two question marks hung in the air, splitting the question into two quite separate issues.

"Yes, darling, darling boy, marry—as in get married. And you, as in Bruce."

66
Para-mountain-biking on Skye

Breakfast in the excellent Ceòl na Mara Guesthouse on Skye was exactly what the Scottish Tourist Board, now rebranded as *VisitScotland* (where *visit* may be a noun or a verb, and *Scotland* may be a proper noun or, *mirabile dictu*, an adjective) would have wanted, in its heart of hearts, the proprietors of all bed and breakfast establishments to offer: a generous, unstinting meal, sufficiently nourishing to set up the visitor for a day of tramping the hills, fishing the rivers, or simply walking about in swirling mists wondering how to get home. That morning Bruce and Clare sat down to generous bowls of real oatmeal porridge topped with cream, followed by plates of eggs, bacon, mushroom, and tomato; no continental breakfast this, but a hearty meal that might well have sprung from the pages of Marian McNeill's *Book of Breakfasts*.

Bruce had woken earlier than Clare, and had got out of bed, opened the curtains, and gazed out on the distant shape of the ridge from which they were planning to para-mountain-bike under the eye of a local instructor. It was a clear day, and at that latitude the sun had already been up for some time, covering the island landscape with a soft, diluted gold. He raised his eyes to the sky, a pale, singing blue, across which, as he looked, a tiny line of white traced its way westwards—the vapour trail of a jet heading over the islands for America or Canada. He thought of the passengers inside their fragile metal tube, looking down, perhaps, on the curved field of blue that was the sea and the ragged little chunks of earth and rock that were the Hebrides, and on the great wind turbines, visible even from that height, that covered the once-beautiful land. And he thought of freedom, and of loneliness, and of how he found himself poised between the two.

And then he thought: why should women not propose? Why should they wait to be asked, even now, when women had dealt with so much of the inequality of the past—when they no longer expected men to open doors for them or offer them seats or do any of the things that men used to do; when men could no longer condescend to women and expect to get away with it; why should so many women still imagine that they had to be asked to marry somebody, and why should men be surprised when the question was put to them rather than by them?

Nothing about that was said at breakfast until Bruce had buttered his last slice of toast and spread it with thick-cut Dundee marmalade. Then, staring at the toast, he began, "Last night, you said . . ."

She reached for the teapot. "I used to drink gallons of tea at breakfast back in Perth. In the hot weather, you know, tea seems to make you feel cooler. Why do you think that is, Bruce? You'd think that swallowing hot liquid would heat you up rather than cool you down."

Bruce shrugged. "No idea," he said. "But going back to last night, you said something about . . ." He hesitated. It was the word over which so many single men hesitated. "About marriage."

Clare poured herself a cup of tea. "Yes, I did. I said that . . . Could you pass the milk, Bruce? You know, I used to take tea without milk, but only for about six months or so. Then I went back to taking milk again."

"You said . . ."

She cut him short. "Yes, I said that I'd decided to marry you. And I had—or have, should I say. I assume you're cool with that." She looked at him now, and he lowered his eyes. "I mean, everything you've said or done made me think that we were an item. Right?"

He was quick to reply. "Of course we're an item. We've been living together, sort of, haven't we?"

"Well that settles that," said Clare. "I don't want to get married tomorrow, but maybe in a couple of months. We could go somewhere, or just do it at a register office. I don't mind. I suppose my folks will want to come over from Australia, or . . ." She broke off as if to consider a new possibility. "Actually, we could do it out there. Or in Thailand maybe—lots of Aussies get married in Thailand. You can have one of those Thai beach weddings where this guy in military uniform comes with the papers and you sign everything and that's you. I went to one once in Phuket, and it was really cool. We had the best man and his boyfriend at our table and he was this chef from Sydney, see, who was on the television a lot and . . ."

That was breakfast; now they were at the beginning of the ridge, having met the local extreme sports instructor who had transported them and their equipment to the starting point.

"You done this much before?" the instructor asked Bruce as he helped strap him onto the bike.

Bruce shook his head.

"Dead simple," said the instructor. "No worries. Keep the front wheel straight—if it goes over to the side your balance can be disturbed. Enjoy."

Clare was ready. "OK, Bruce, let's set off together. See that track? We go down there and then it gets to the edge. That's lift-off point—make sure you get your canopy full before you reach it. OK?"

She did not wait for an answer. The wind had come up, and it was in the ideal direction, floating their canopies gracefully above their heads.

"Now!" shouted Clare.

And Bruce followed her. The instructor shouted something, but Bruce didn't hear what it was. It was something about the wind, but it was the wind that swallowed the words.

He picked up speed, feeling the tugging of the canopy above him. This made the mountain bike seem light; it was almost as if it wanted to detach itself from the ground beneath him. The path was rocky, but the bike seemed to bounce over the rocks rather than jar against them. And then, far too quickly, he reached the edge and the ground suddenly disappeared. Beneath him now was no immediate earth but heather and green and expanses of distant rock.

Bruce glanced about him. There was no sign of Clare. He looked up, but became dizzy because all he saw was blue.

Why did I agree to do this? he asked himself. *Why did I let it all end like this?*

The wind seemed to catch the canopy. They were only meant to travel a few hundred yards, mere feet above the ground, Clare had said— that was the point about para-mountain-biking— it was like kite-surfing: you were meant to hop briefly and then come down to land again. But the wind now embraced Bruce, took him in its arms, and was carrying him skywards.

He closed his eyes. He thought of his mother. He thought of Crieff.

67

Freedom Come All Ye

Stuart finished early at work that day, having told Irene that he would again be late. He knew that she was going to her Melanie Klein Book Group at four in the afternoon; he knew, too, that Ulysses was going to Stuart's mother in Northumberland Street; and that Bertie was to be spending the afternoon and early evening at Ranald Braveheart

Macpherson's house in Church Hill. That meant that he would be able to drop into Scotland Street, shower and change, and then go off to meet Katie in the St. Vincent Bar. He had thought of meeting her in the Cumberland Bar, but had ruled that out on the grounds that he was known there, and his being in the company of Katie could give rise to gossip.

He unlocked the door of the flat and entered jauntily, humming Hamish Henderson's *Freedom Come All Ye*. It was a song that he had always loved, right from that electric moment when as a young man he had heard the poet himself singing it in Sandy Bell's bar in Forrest Road, and the bar had fallen silent, knowing it was witnessing something quite out of the ordinary, some fragile line of experience and feeling going back to the Spanish Civil War and to Cyrenaica.

But he got no further than a few bars into the tune, for it was then that he realised that he was not alone and that for some reason Irene was there.

He stood quite still, his rapid heartbeat sounding in his ears, the back of his neck suddenly intensely warm.

"Stuart?"

She came out of the kitchen, and he knew immediately from her expression that his world was about to end. There was no room for optimism; there was no room for evasion, for explanations. Like a truant caught lurking in his hiding place, the light of authority shone upon him quite mercilessly.

"You said you were working late," challenged Irene. "You said you'd be back after nine."

"Ah . . ." said Stuart. And then his mouth stayed resolutely closed. His jaw, it seemed to him, had frozen—locked in a muscular spasm caused by intense fear. But then, after a few moments, it loosened, and he said, "But you were going to your Melanie Klein . . ."

She cut him off. "Let's leave me out of this," she said icily. "What happened at the office?"

He shrugged. "The minister . . ."

Again he could not finish. "Don't bother to lie, Stuart."

He caught his breath. "I wasn't . . ."

"Perhaps you came back to read poetry," said Irene.

For a moment he struggled to understand; he had forgotten about the poem, but now Irene, like a prosecutor producing a piece of damning evidence at a trial, reached into the pocket of her blouse and took out the piece of paper she had found in his jacket. She waved this at him, and he saw, and recognised, the handwriting. He felt giddy. He was going to collapse. He was going to die.

"I was given that by somebody," he said. "It's just a poem. Nothing important."

He looked down as he spoke. He felt that he was denying poetry itself, that he was saying that it did not matter; it was a small treason, a small and grubby betrayal of all that really mattered, just because he was frightened of this woman to whom he was married; yes, he was frightened of her; he lived in fear, and would lie and deny and do anything rather than face the gross inequality in their relationship.

He took a deep breath. "I've had it," he muttered. "I've had it up to here."

She was staring at him, her eyes fixed on his. Her voice was low and steely. "I shall pretend that I didn't hear that, Stuart. And I shall pretend that I never found these pathetic lines of so-called poetry. And you, in turn, will forget that you ever met the pathetic girl who wrote it. You will forget her, Stuart. You will not think of her, speak to her, see her, let alone sleep with her. She's over, Stuart—she's completely over. She is erased."

From somewhere deep within him, he summoned such resistance as he could muster. It was not much, but it enabled him to issue the challenge: "And if I don't? Can you make me? I don't think you can, Irene."

She smiled. "Oh, can't I?"

"No, you can't," he retorted, but his voice lacked conviction.

"What about Bertie?" she said. "What about Ulysses?"

He closed his eyes. He could not look at her. And within him, a cold hand clutched at his heart.

"You see," said Irene, "if you choose to go off with some floozy, Stuart, then you will have to bear the consequences. And the consequence of leaving your family will be that your family will leave you."

"You can't . . ."

"Oh, I can, Stuart, the law will prefer me when it comes to custody. I'm the one who's stayed at home to bring them up. You'll never get custody of the children. And I'll go and live in Aberdeen, Stuart. I'm warning you, Stuart, I shall. And Bertie will come too. You'll see him once a month, if that."

"Aberdeen?" said Stuart, his voice becoming a bit stronger. "Why Aberdeen, might I ask? Is it by any chance to do with a certain Professor Hugo Fairbairn, Irene?" He paused, and then he said what he had wanted to say for so long but had been inhibited from doing so by fear.

"Leave him out of this, Stuart," warned Irene.

"But why? Don't you think he's relevant? Don't you think it's relevant that you had an affair with that man and that according to Bertie, at least, there's a striking resemblance between Ulysses and the good professor."

"How dare you!" shouted Irene. "You're the one. You're the one who's gone off with some ghastly little slut you met in a bar or wherever.

370

You're the one, Stuart. Hugo and I were friends, nothing more . . ." She began to choke.

"Your lies are making you choke," said Stuart.

She recovered, and moved closer to him. "It's over, Stuart. Look at me. Look me in the eye. It's over. The choice is not between me and that other woman, but between her and your son, your Bertie. You choose, Stuart. You go right ahead and choose."

He looked into her eyes, and felt his courage melt away. No, there really was no choice—not when it was put in those terms.

Irene suddenly smiled. "That was *Freedom Come All Ye* you were humming when you came in, wasn't it? Well, you're free, Stuart—free to choose. Go ahead and make your choice."

68

Walking Home

Bertie was meant to be picked up by Nicola and returned by her to Scotland Street by seven that evening. Stuart changed this plan, though, telephoning his mother to let her know that he would fetch Bertie instead. "You can put your feet up," he said.

"I'm perfectly happy to go," she said. "And besides, weren't you working late at the office today? I thought you had some big project on."

He blushed—a telephone blush, unwitnessed, but as warm and as guilty as any blush may be. To mislead one's wife was bad enough, but to compound the offence by misleading one's mother took deception to a new level. And that appalled him, because Stuart, for all his weakness, had an underlying good will. He was unselfish; he was concerned about the feelings of others; and he recognised that the borderline between good and bad was a subtle one, sometimes not immediately visible, easily transgressed.

Within minutes of his showdown with Irene, when she had retreated to the kitchen like a triumphant general allowing a defeated counterpart time to go over the terms of the unconditional surrender—no terms, of course—Stuart had realised that his duty to his sons—to Bertie in particular—outweighed any other consideration. He had found love and affection in his brief affair with Katie, but these were small things beside the obligation he owed to Bertie. He knew what Bertie thought of him; he knew that to a young boy a father was the sun, the central point of the universe, the source of all things. He just was. That was how a boy should feel about his father. That was what being Dad was all about.

To have that was an immense privilege. To have somebody, some little centre of consciousness looking to you for all these things, was a responsibility as large as any responsibility could be. To be at the heart of a young life, to be able to help it into the light, to introduce it to the world, was something before which you should do nothing but stand in complete awe. And now he did.

"Stuart," said his mother, "are you all right? You sound . . ."

Mothers could tell; even over the phone, mothers could tell.

He began to assure her that he was fine, but even as he spoke it dawned on him that this was another lie, and so he said, "I'm not really all right. No, I'm not. But I'm going to be."

"Oh, my darling, what's happened? Something at work?"

"No. I can't really speak about it now, but I will. I'll tell you everything later on."

And with that, she knew. But she knew, too, this was not the time to offer sympathy beyond a few words, which is what she did before they rang off.

Now Stuart had another telephone call to make. This he made on the landing outside the flat, so that Irene should not hear. It was to Katie, and it was to say that the proposed meeting in the St. Vincent Bar was off.

"Later?" she said. "How about later?"

The telephone wire between Scotland Street

and Howe Street is not a long one, but it seemed to Stuart that it crossed an ocean.

"I'm sorry," he said. "I can't. I just can't."

With that, his affair was brought to a close, although they talked for a few minutes more, in a strained, emotional way. By the time the call ended, they were strangers again.

Irene said nothing, but she made him a pot of tea and a cucumber sandwich. "I hope I've put enough pepper on the cucumber for your taste, Stuart," she said. "I know how much you like pepper on cucumber."

He looked at her, and felt, in a way that slightly surprised him, gratitude for her consideration.

"I'm so sorry," he muttered.

She said nothing for a moment. Then she said, "We all make mistakes—you in particular."

She left the room. "I'm going to the Melanie Klein Group," she said. "It wasn't cancelled—just put off for an hour. That's why I was here when you . . ."

She left the sentence unfinished.

"I'll go to fetch Bertie," he said. "We can leave Ulysses with my mother. I'll make Bertie his tea if you're late." The Melanie Klein Book Group frequently got bogged down in discussion of what Melanie Klein had really meant, and so Irene was often late back from it.

Irene nodded. "Make sure Bertie eats his broccoli," she said. And with that she left.

He stood up. He rubbed his eyes. He felt as if he had been crying, but he had not. The tears he wanted to shed were still in him, unreleased, and he thought: *they will never come out*. He took the shower he had planned to take and thought, as he did so, how the nature of a shower might change from the sort of shower taken in anticipation of an assignation, to a shower one has because one is broken and one hopes the shower will wash something away. Guilt. Disappointment. The unfulfilled yearnings of our lives.

He took the 23 bus to Church Hill and walked the short distance to the Macpherson house. Ranald Braveheart Macpherson and Bertie had reached the end of some long and complicated game, and Bertie was ready to go.

"I think we'll walk home," said Stuart, taking Bertie's hand. "We could pick up an ice cream at that place at Holy Corner—you know the one, Bertie?"

Bertie nodded.

"Provided, of course, you eat your broccoli later on."

Again Bertie nodded.

The ice cream cone lasted from Holy Corner to the edge of the Meadows. Stuart wiped the ice cream from his son's face, and that was the most difficult moment. That was when he almost cried.

They continued their walk. There was something happening on the Meadows—the erection of a large tent. As they drew closer to the scene of activity, a young man came up to them with a leaflet. "Please come to our circus tomorrow," he said.

Stuart read the leaflet as they walked on. *The Acceptable Circus*, it was headed. "A strange name for a circus, Bertie," he said, and tucked the leaflet into his pocket.

"I love circuses, Daddy," said Bertie. "I've never been to one, but I love them."

"I'll see what I can do, Bertie," said Stuart.

They continued their journey. At the corner of the High Street, just beyond the statue of David Hume, a young man was playing the pipes. They stopped briefly and listened to him. The piper caught Bertie's eye, and smiled, and Bertie smiled back. A man and a woman—visitors to the city—stepped forward and put a five-pound note in the cap the piper had placed before him. The piper nodded to them and continued to play.

They walked on. Now the Mound sloped down below them and there were flags fluttering on the National Gallery, the saltire against the sky.

Bertie said, "I really like our flag, Daddy. Don't you?"

When Stuart did not reply, he looked up.

"Are you all right, Daddy?" he asked.

Stuart squeezed his son's hand.

"I'm all right, Bertie. Don't worry about me."

"Sometimes I do, Daddy. Sometimes I worry."

"There's no need, Bertie—no need. I'm going to be absolutely fine."

"Promise?"

Stuart squeezed his hand again. "Promise."

69

Kitchen Talk in Scotland Street

"Too many cooks," said Domenica to her full kitchen. "Two volunteers are needed to go to the Cumberland Bar and remain there until dinner is almost ready." She looked about her, as if uncertain as to the identity of the volunteers. Then she added, "Two volunteers and a dog, I should say."

The dog, of course, had to be Cyril, who was sitting under the kitchen table, dozing fitfully, enduring a dream in which he was being taunted by squirrels in Drummond Place Gardens—the stuff of canine dreams, which are never very profound, consisting largely of energetic pursuits of various lesser creatures—cats, squirrels, rabbits, all so deserving, in dog eyes, of an ignominious end. Only occasionally does a dog have a real nightmare, and that usually consists of separation, of the disappearance of his owner, which for the dog is like the death of God.

Hearing his name mentioned, Cyril struggled back into consciousness and wagged his tail. *Cumberland Bar* was not in his vocabulary, which was limited to a few words: *walk, biscuits, sit, Turner Prize* and *good dog.* But he always recognised his name, even when it was surrounded by the strange soporific droning that human speech is in the ears of dogs.

The two volunteers knew who they were. "We can take a hint, can't we, Matthew?" said Angus Lordie.

Matthew nodded. "If broth is to be spoiled," he said, "then lay it not at our door. The Cumberland Bar will have to do."

"Good," said Domenica. "Then Elspeth, Nicola and I shall soldier on here. The guests arrive . . ." She looked at her watch. "In an hour. So don't be late."

As the two men and Cyril left the room, Domenica remarked, "What an interesting change in social behaviour. There was a time when men excluded women from the social space: now it's the opposite."

"Oh well," said Elspeth. "They'll survive. And it means we can talk."

"I feel so sorry for men," said Nicola. "Their conversation is so . . . how shall I put it? So circumscribed."

"I've never really worked out what men talk about," said Elspeth. "At least not when they're

378

by themselves. Do you think they talk about women?"

Nicola was adamant. "No, definitely not. Men do *not* talk about women."

"What then?" asked Domenica. "Work? Cars? Football? All the usual things they're meant to talk about?"

"Those subjects crop up," said Elspeth. "But I suspect the big difference is their feelings. Men don't talk about emotions—about how they feel. They just don't."

Nicola looked thoughtful. "And they can suffer so," she said. "Look at my poor son."

Domenica was tactful. "I wasn't going to ask, but since you mention it . . . how's Stuart bearing up?"

Nicola sighed. "It didn't work out in quite the way I'd hoped. I suppose I should feel ashamed of myself, but I really wanted him to leave her. He's put up with year after year of that dreadful woman's . . ."

"Oppression?" suggested Domenica.

"Yes, that's not too strong a word. He's put up with all that for his entire marriage and I thought at last he was going to show some courage and . . ." She broke off for a few moments. Then she continued, "Actually, my son showed something rather more significant than courage. He showed decency. And that's a different thing altogether—it's actually far harder."

Domenica was intrigued. "To be decent? Really?"

"Yes," said Nicola. "He's going to make an effort, he tells me. He says that he's going to look at things from Irene's point of view. He's going to try to be a better husband for her."

This was too much for Elspeth. "Oh really!" she exploded. "He's the most long-suffering man I know. He's bent over backwards."

"That may be so," admitted Nicola. "But now he says he's going to redouble his efforts. He's going to try to give her more time to pursue her interests."

"Which she's done relentlessly for years," muttered Domenica. "But still . . ."

"He's a saint," said Elspeth.

"Sometimes I feel I don't understand men," said Nicola. "I don't even understand my own son. But still, there we are." She reached for the glass of wine that Domenica had poured her. "Tell me, Elspeth, what about that young man who goes out with your Australian girl? What's his name again? The good-looking one?"

Elspeth smiled. "Bruce. Oh well, there's a bit of a story there, I'm afraid. Bruce didn't quite live up to expectations, I regret to say—at least from Clare's point of view. He's no longer on the scene."

"What happened?" asked Domenica. Bruce had always exerted a certain fascination for her: he was such a narcissist, and that hair gel of his . . .

"He failed to cut the mustard when it came to extreme sports," explained Elspeth. "She's fanatical about those things. Kite-surfing, jumping into the water from cliffs—that sort of stuff. The bar keeps getting raised—danger is a sort of drug, you know: you develop tolerance and you have to do increasingly bizarre things to get your fix, so to speak."

"It ends in tears, of course," observed Nicola.

"Everything ends in tears," Domenica mused. "Including life itself, don't you think? It ends in tears."

Elspeth shrugged. "*Man that is born of woman* . . . Isn't that the expression? Anyway, back to Clare: she took him up to Skye to do some ridiculous thing with mountain bikes and kites—I'm not sure exactly what was involved."

"I sense disaster," said Nicola.

"As well you might: Bruce apparently took off and went far too high. He landed in a clump of gorse, which broke his fall, but wrecked the equipment. He has an arm in plaster now."

"But surely she was sympathetic?" said Nicola.

"No. She felt that he'd shown her up in front of the instructor, who I gather was a very good-looking young man from Tobermory. Clare thought rather highly of him—in fact she rather ditched Bruce after she and the instructor had driven him to have his arm attended to down in

Fort William. She went off with this chap. She went camping with him in Callander. I suppose they jumped off something there. There must be things to jump off around Callander. She doesn't hang about, that girl. Bruce, as they say, is history."

Nicola shook her head. "Poor boy!"

"He'll bounce back," said Elspeth. "He always does."

"But she's still with you?" asked Domenica. "She's still looking after the triplets?"

"They love her," said Elspeth. "And it gives me time to breathe."

"We're very lucky," said Domenica.

"Why do you say that?" asked Nicola.

"We're very lucky to be breathing," said Domenica.

70

See, I Am Here

Matthew and Angus returned from the Cumberland Bar just a few minutes before the guests at Domenica's party were due to arrive. The long kitchen table, around which they would all gather, was laid for twelve, with a branched candlestick at each end. The faux Jacobite wine glasses, engraved in the nineteen-twenties with the white rose—of which Angus was inordinately proud—were at each place, giving guests no choice: only mental reservations would negate any toast made from such glass. Beside each place was a blue spode plate, a painful reminder for at least two at that table of the dreadful affair of the blue spode teacup that had threatened the already threadbare comity between Angus and Domenica and their neighbour, Antonia. Little had been heard of Antonia since then, although she had been frequently sighted at social gatherings with her long-term house guest, Sister Maria-Fiore dei Fiori di Montagna. The Italian nun's striking social success had gone to both their heads, thought Domenica, but that had not diminished it. Far from it: there was scarcely a fashionable party in Edinburgh or the Lothians at which Sister Maria-Fiore and Antonia were not present, or, if not present, were not talked about.

Now the friends all stood in the drawing room, enjoying a preliminary glass of wine before going through to the kitchen for the mushroom risotto and avocado salad Domenica had prepared for them.

Domenica's friend, Dilly Emslie, mentioned an advertisement she had seen for the *Acceptable Circus*, currently performing in a big top on the Meadows. "You wouldn't credit it," she said.

"A most peculiar name for a circus," said Judith McClure. "Roger saw it too, didn't you, Roger?"

Roger Collins nodded. "I can't remember when I last went to the circus," he said.

"You've been so busy with your research, I suppose," said Angus. "The correspondence of eighteenth-century Jacobite spies, I gather."

"Indeed," said Roger. "But tell me, why does this circus call itself the *Acceptable Circus*?"

Dilly smiled. "It reflects their programme. Which is . . ." She began to tell them, and as she did so, the expression of incredulity on the faces of most grew more marked. "They have a vegetarian lion," she said. "No, I'm not making this up. They have a special EU exemption certificate allowing them to show him. Then there are the clowns—the audience is asked not to laugh at them. The performing dogs behave naturally and do no tricks. Then there is the low-wire artist who performs at a height of six inches, on health and safety grounds. And one should not forget the weak man, who has difficulty tearing telephone directories in two but is not required to do so, anyway, as everybody's gone digital. All presided over by a ring-mistress."

"And a nominated person?" asked Matthew. "Does everybody attending the circus have a nominated person to deal with their needs?"

"Naturally," said Angus. "It would hardly be acceptable if they did not."

They all laughed, and then several conversations

384

broke out at once in groups of two or three of them. Dilly asked Domenica if Angus had fully recovered from his defenestration, and was reassured to hear that he had. "There were some psychological consequences," she said. "He went a bit peculiar for a few weeks—he started taking an interest in contemporary conceptual art. He'd never had any time before for that, of course. He found it utterly banal, and I'm afraid I agree with him. But all of a sudden he started making admiring remarks about installation art and the like and also about modernist architecture. He said that he actually liked the proposals for the St. James Centre. I was seriously worried about his sanity, you know."

"You must have been," said Dilly.

"But then suddenly he got better," said Domenica. "He found Roger Scruton's essay on modernist architecture. It's called *Building to Last* and it brought him back to his senses."

"What a relief that must have been," said Dilly.

It was time to go in for dinner. They sat down at the table and the conversations that had started before dinner continued, or went in new directions, depending on the seating, but the tenor of all of them was the city they lived in and they shared, and the friendship that brought them together. There were no false notes, no uncharitable remarks—just good humour, and warmth, and the exchange of ideas. *I hope*

Edinburgh goes on forever, thought Matthew.

And then one of the guests, James Thomson, who had been sitting opposite Angus, leaned across the table and said, "Angus, you usually write us a poem. Have you done so today?"

Angus looked down at his plate. "I don't want to inflict anything on you."

"But you must," said James. "Quiet, everybody: Angus is going to read his poem."

Angus stood up. He looked at Domenica, whom he loved. He looked at his friends, whose company and wisdom meant so much to him. His heart was full, and at first his voice faltered. But only for a moment. And then it became firmer, and every word, every word was received in appreciative silence by those in the room.

"Here's my poem," he said. And he began.

What we lose

A proper winter reminds us of the
    attractions of months
When it never gets truly dark, when
    newspapers
Might be read outside at midnight, or
    close enough,
If only the news of the day by then were
    not so stale;
A cold blast from a thoroughly northern
    quarter

Brings nostalgia for better-behaved winds
    from the south,
Winds which at the end of their journey
Still retain some memory of those regions
Where it is not quite so important
That windows should close-to with a tight
    fit.

What we do not have, we remember we
    once had;
Innocence glimpsed in others reminds us
Of the time when our own consciences
    were clear;
Birdsong heard on a still morning
Brings to mind the memory
That once the skies were filled with birds
And there were hedges and unruly places
For them to nest in; as the seas were full
    of fish
And there were fishermen with boats and
    songs
About fish and the catching of them.

What we lose, we think we lose forever,
But we are wrong about this; think of
    love—
Love is lost, we think it gone,
But it returns, often when least expected;
Forgives us our lack of attention, our
    failure of faith,

Our cold indifference; forgives us all this,
  and more;
Returns and says, "I was always there."
Love, agape, whispers: "Merely
  remember me,
Don't think I've gone away forever:
I am still here. With you. My power
  undimmed.
See. I am here."

There was silence. The late evening sun sent a beam through the window, golden, gentle, after ninety-three million miles reaching the end of its journey. Angus felt its finger upon his cheek, a warm, comforting touch, like the touch of friendship itself. He wanted that for Scotland, he wanted it more fervently than he had ever wanted anything before.

Books are produced
in the United States
using U.S.-based
materials

Books are printed
using a revolutionary
new process called
THINKtech™ that
lowers energy usage
by 70% and increases
overall quality

Books are durable
and flexible because
of smythe-sewing

Paper is sourced
using environmentally
responsible foresting
methods and the
paper is acid-free

Alexander McCall Smith

Alexander McCall Smith is the author of the No. 1 Ladies' Detective Agency series, the Isabel Dalhousie series, the 44 Scotland Street series, the Portuguese Irregular Verbs series, and the Corduroy Mansions series. He is professor emeritus of medical law at the University of Edinburgh in Scotland and has served with many national and international organizations concerned with bioethics.

www.alexandermccallsmith.com

Center Point Large Print
600 Brooks Road / PO Box 1
Thorndike, ME 04986-0001 USA

(207) 568-3717

US & Canada:
1 800 929-9108
www.centerpointlargeprint.com